Lonely Girl

Josephine Cox was born in Blackburn, one of ten children. At the age of sixteen, Josephine met and married her husband Ken, and had two sons. When the boys started school, she decided to go to college and eventually gained a place at Cambridge University. She was unable to take this up as it would have meant living away from home, but she went into teaching – and started to write her first full-length novel. She won the 'Superwoman of Great Britain' Award, for which her family had secretly entered her, at the same time as her novel was accepted for publication.

Her strong, gritty stories are taken from the tapestry of life. Josephine says, 'I could never imagine a single day without writing. It's been that way since as far back as I can remember.'

Visit www.josephinecox.com to find out more information about Josephine.

JOSEPHINE COX

Lonely Girl

HARPER

Harper
An imprint of HarperCollins*Publishers*
The News Building
1 London Bridge Street
London SE1 9GF

www.harpercollins.co.uk

This paperback edition 2015
2

First published in Great Britain by
HarperCollins 2015

A catalogue record for this book is available from the British Library

ISBN: 978-0-00-747673-2

Set in ITC New Baskerville Std by Palimpsest Book Production Limited,
Falkirk, Stirlingshire

Printed and bound in Great Britain by
Clays Ltd, St Ives plc

MIX
Paper from
responsible sources
FSC™ C007454

For my Ken – as always

Praise for

Jo is one of the world's best-loved writers and continues to captivate readers across the globe with her powerful storytelling. Here are just some of the many endorsements she has received about her writing:

'Another beautifully spun family epic'
Scottish Daily Echo

'Written from the heart'
Daily Mail

'Another hit for Josephine Cox'
Sunday Express

'The latest emotionally charged story from this mega-selling author won't disappoint her army of fans'
Bella

JOSEPHINE COX

'A born storyteller'
Bedfordshire Times

'Cox's talent as a storyteller never lets you escape the spell'
Daily Mail

'A surefire winner'
Woman's Weekly

'Readers will find it impossible to tear themselves away'
News of the World

'Another masterpiece'
Best

PART ONE

Dark Memories

**Tanner's Farm, Bucks Village,
Southern England, 1960**

PROLOGUE

CROUCHING LOW BENEATH the bedroom window, young Rosie peered through the murky darkness of a cold November evening.

Anxiously training her gaze along the pathway that ran by the big barn, she wondered if her mother might show at any moment. Rosie would not mind if her mother stayed away for ever, but she knew her father would be sad because he loved her, even though they were always arguing.

So, for his sake, Rosie hoped her mother might somehow manage to find her way home from the village pub where she worked as a barmaid. Often her shift would slip into her social life. She liked a drink and a laugh. She also liked the admiration of men, who were drawn to her dark looks and enticing smile.

Whenever her mother was late coming home, Rosie had good cause to fear the worst. Keeping her vigil at the window, she wondered what kind of mood her mother would be in if she did come home. Would she be in one of her dark rages? Would she be feeling spiteful and ready to fight with Rosie's father? Or would she be laughing and playful, or impossible to talk with and so drunk she could hardly stand?

Rosie could never decide which was worse, because whichever way it was, it always ended badly.

Neither Rosie nor her father ever knew what to expect when Molly Tanner returned from a night out. She never spoke about exactly where she had been, or who she had been with, and if John Tanner dared to pursue the truth, a fierce row would inevitably ensue, and Rosie would run upstairs in fear, to hide under her bedclothes.

Looking back, Rosie realised that nothing much had changed over the years except that they all had grown older and a little wiser. Her mother was forever complaining that she was 'coming up to her dreaded fifties'. She was still proud of her sultry looks, and rumour had it that she was still cheating on her loving and hard-working husband. Her dislike for her only child had reached the point where she could hardly bear to be near her.

Molly Tanner had never possessed the strong maternal instinct that bonds a mother with her child. She had neither the instinct nor the wish to be a mother, and made that clear to all who would listen. Consequently, she played precious little part in Rosie's life.

After a while, young Rosie had stopped caring. Her daddy had been, and still was, her whole life. If she was ever worried or hurting, it was her father's help she sought; she had learned long ago that there was no point in seeking comfort or advice from her disinterested mother. The little girl had grown and flourished without her help.

~

Growing irritable, Rosie brought her thoughts back to the present, while she continued watching out of the window.

'Don't get upset because your mother never loved you,' she told herself. 'You're not a baby any more. You're turned fifteen and very soon, you'll be leaving school.'

Rosie was greatly excited at the prospect of leaving school. At long last she would be able to get a job, although she was adamant on one point. When I do start earning a wage, I'll give it to Daddy . . . not to *her*, because she'll only spend it down the pub, or on fancy clothes and make-up to impress the men she flirts with, Rosie resolved.

Glancing at the bedside clock, she realised that she had been keeping her vigil for her wayward mother for over an hour.

I expect Daddy's worried sick, but what does she care, so long as she's having a good time? she thought.

She clambered up and closed the curtains. Then she crossed the floor to switch on the light, and for a while continued to pace back and forth, occasionally peering through the gap between the curtains and growing increasingly agitated.

The minutes ticked by and, with still no sign of her mother, Rosie went to sit at the dressing table. Absent-mindedly studying her reflection in the mirror, she was greatly relieved that she had not inherited her mother's striking looks – or her bad temper either.

Although her own hair was waist-length like her mother's, that was where the resemblance ended because Rosie's hair was the same light chestnut colour as her father's, while Molly's was dark and fell in luscious waves. Rosie's strong blue eyes were also inherited from her father's side of the family, although her father's eyes were tinged with a hint of green, which deepened when he was angry, which was not very often.

Anxiously, Rosie studied herself in the mirror, thinking of her mother and the unkind things she would say.

Molly often complained that she found it hard to believe that she had such a plain-looking daughter. 'You remind me of my sister, Kathleen,' she would tease spitefully. 'She was always the plain, shy girl at school. At playtime, she would stand in the corner while everyone else was having fun. When we were younger, the boys always came after me. They never went for her. Hmm! She would probably have been left on the shelf if it hadn't been for your Uncle Paddy. Like her, he's a plain-looking sort with not much about him. They're two of a kind,' she'd smirk. 'I always knew they would get together, but only after lover-boy had enjoyed playing the field.'

Rosie knew this was unjust. Uncle Patrick and Auntie Kathleen were funny, kind, and a devoted couple. Rosie loved them dearly, as she did Harry, Patrick's son from his first marriage.

Over the years, Rosie had often been shocked at her mother's cruel remarks about her family. There had been one particular occasion that she would never forget, when she was just five years of age.

As the memories of that awful episode crowded her mind, she forced herself to concentrate on the path alongside the big barn, but the darkness had thickened, and all was quiet, save for the occasional howl of a lonely dog.

Rosie moved closer to the window, peering into the darkness and listening for the familiar click-clack of high-heeled shoes against the concrete path.

'Where are you?' Rosie muttered angrily. 'Why do you never come home when you should? And who are you with when you're not with us?' She realised that she was mimicking the questions her father might ask of his wayward wife.

Troubled, she moved away from the window. 'All right, stay away then,' she grumbled. 'If you don't come home, we'll be happier without you.'

Close to tears, she recalled that many times over the years her mother had said to her, 'I don't love you . . . and I never will!' Her cruel words had cut Rosie to the heart, but it was the events of her fifth birthday that played through her head so strongly this evening.

Surprisingly, for the first time ever her mother had organised a wonderful party for her only child. She had also made a cake, with candles and pretty icing, and Rosie was especially thrilled when the children from neighbouring farms were invited to celebrate her birthday with her.

Normally, her mother did not like Rosie mixing with what she called 'the rabble', but that day, for whatever reason, she decided to break the habit and be nice to everyone.

John teasingly told his wife it was because Rosie was going to start school the following morning, and she would not have the child under her feet every day.

It was such a happy day for Rosie. All the children stood in a little group to sing 'Happy Birthday', before cheering five times – one cheer for each of her years. She was thrilled, and afterwards she thanked her mother for making her birthday so wonderful.

The joy of her party, however, was short-lived, because after everyone had gone home, Molly threw a tantrum. She complained about the noise and the mess, about the washing up, and about one of the children weeing on the bathroom floor, which she forced Rosie to clean up. Afterwards, she ordered Rosie to bed. Being afraid of her mother's swift and dangerous change of mood, Rosie ran up the stairs and quickly climbed into bed where, tired out from her wonderful party, she quickly fell asleep.

Some time later, she was woken by the loud noise of things being thrown about, and the angry voices of both her parents, yelling and arguing. Rosie felt very frightened, most especially that her mother might come upstairs to hurt her. Hiding deep under the bedclothes, she wondered how the woman who was screeching and throwing things could be the same kind person who had made her birthday party so very special.

The next day, however, Molly was remarkably jovial and attentive to her young daughter, leaving Rosie to wonder again whether this person and the crazy woman of last night were actually one and the same.

Nervous and excited about starting school, Rosie had just washed herself and cleaned her teeth when her mother appeared with her new school uniform.

Rosie had been sitting on the stool in front of the dressing-table mirror, brushing her long hair. When her mother ordered her to hurry up or they would be late for her first day, Rosie got into a panic and accidentally dropped the brush onto the floor.

Before she could retrieve it, her mother rushed across the room, snatched up the brush and flung it across the dressing table. 'You've wasted enough time brushing your hair,' she grumbled. 'You're a selfish, vain child! Now come on, move yourself! Your father has already brought the horse and cart round, and here you are . . . looking in the mirror . . . brushing your hair like we've got all the time in the world.'

She hurried Rosie out and down the stairs, then through the front door. John was waiting for them in the lane.

'What took you so long?' he laughed, hugging Rosie and wishing her well on her first day at school. Then he held the horse while his wife and daughter climbed onto the cart.

Molly Tanner surprised the horse with a sharp flick of the whip and he shot forward at speed.

Rosie looked back to see her father waving her off and she happily waved back.

Molly, however, was all het up. 'We'll be late now, and all because you thought it more important to spend half an hour fussing yourself in the mirror.'

Casting her mind back now, Rosie remembered the incident so vividly it seemed as though the frightening journey to school was only yesterday.

Her mother, using the whip and yelling at the top of her voice, had forced the poor old horse to career along the winding lanes.

'This is your fault,' she screamed at her daughter, 'spending precious time pampering your hair, like you were a film star or something.'

Terrified for the horse, who was soon foaming at the mouth, Rosie begged her mother to slow down. 'You're frightening the horse . . . you're hurting him, and it's not his fault. I promise I'll get up earlier tomorrow, Mummy . . . only please don't whip him.'

'Don't tell me what to do, child – not if you know what's good for you.'

By now concerned herself that the horse was beginning to panic and might well bolt, Molly drew in the reins and eventually calmed the nervous animal.

Her daughter, however, was shown no such kindness.

'Too damned right you'll get up earlier tomorrow,' Molly continued, 'because I'll make sure of it. I'll have you out of that bed as soon as the cock crows, you see if I don't!' Her dark eyes flashed in anger. 'What's more, you can go to bed an hour earlier tonight, and no arguing.'

Hanging on to the wooden rail at her side, Rosie was made to endure a harrowing chase down the lanes. Once she dared to glance up at her mother. Molly's dark eyes were angry, and her thick dark hair hung in deep waves across her shoulders, and Rosie couldn't help but wonder how her mother could be so wicked when she looked so beautiful.

Throughout the remainder of the short journey not another word passed between them.

On arriving at school, with the cart and sweating horse safely secured, Molly rushed her daughter across the playground to the school doors. All the other children must have gone in already, though there was a young woman standing as if waiting on the other side of the road.

'You'd better be on your best behaviour, my girl,' Molly warned. 'Make sure there are no bad reports from your teacher when I come to pick you up, or you'll have me to answer to, and no mistake. All right?'

Rosie nodded, but her mother's warning and the prospect of another nerve-racking journey had made her afraid. 'Please . . . I don't want to go to school.' The tears began to fall. 'I want to go home.'

'Don't be such a softy! If you let the other children see you crying, they'll just laugh at you. I'm sure you wouldn't want that, would you?'

Rosie shook her head. 'No.'

'Then you'd best do as you're told.'

Without further ado, Molly grabbed Rosie by the arm and marched her into the entrance hall. 'I mean what I say,' she hissed. 'Behave yourself.'

She then hurried Rosie into the main hall and handed her over to the headmistress. After saying her goodbyes she hurriedly departed, leaving behind a strong hint of the exotic scent she used, while the sharp tapping sound of her dainty high heels receded into the distance.

~

That afternoon, when Molly came to collect Rosie after school, the headteacher called her into the office while another teacher took Rosie to wait in the library.

'I've been rather concerned about Rosie.' The headmistress was most formal. 'She's hardly spoken a word all day, and she's made no effort to play with the other children. In fact, I found her hiding in the playground after the other children were brought inside. She was crying, but when I questioned her, she refused to confide in me. It is obvious that something or someone has upset her, but she would not be persuaded to tell me.'

Molly was angry. 'I'm not surprised. It sounds to me like you've blown this out of all proportion. Of course I understand you might want to know why she was crying, but what you really should know is that my daughter has a bit of a temper. Moreover, she does not take kindly to being questioned by strangers. I'm fully aware that she can be a little madam when she puts her mind to it. But if you don't mind me saying, it is not your place to sort her out. My daughter is my business, and I shall talk to her about this, you may depend on it.'

The headmistress remained adamant. 'I thought the two of us might discuss the situation quietly so we might get to the bottom of it. Indeed, that's why I asked our Miss Harrison to take charge of Rosie for a few minutes.'

'Really?' Molly had taken an immediate dislike to this figure of authority. 'Look, we've had our little talk, and now you can safely leave the matter of my daughter's behaviour in my hands. I am used to dealing with Rosie's tantrums.' She stood up to leave, though she was not done yet. 'I sincerely hope for your sake that my daughter has not been too upset by all this ridiculous fuss, and if I do find that to be the case, I shall have no choice but to refer you to a higher authority.'

'I'm sure that will not be necessary.' The headmistress was taken aback. 'But if you really think me to be inadequate, then of course you must do what you will.'

Having taken stock of Rosie's angry mother, however, the headmistress had her suspicions. 'Meantime, Mrs Tanner, as we have no idea what might have upset Rosie, I have a suggestion. It's just a thought, but I was wondering . . .' in the wake of Molly Tanner's hostility, she took a deep breath, '. . . is it at all possible that something, or someone, at home might have upset her *before* she came to school this morning?'

'What the devil are you implying?' Incensed by the teacher's probing questions, Molly instantly dismissed them with a sharp rebuke. 'I resent that implication, and I think you and your staff should be a little more sympathetic. My daughter is a very nervous child and, as I have explained, she can be prone to tears and tantrums. And might I remind you that this is her first day at school. Did it not occur to you that she may have been overwhelmed by everything and everyone?'

When the headmistress made an effort to reply, Molly cut her off viciously. 'If you ask me, the reason my daughter is so upset must be something to do with you and your staff. In fact, I am beginning to wonder if you're capable of doing your job responsibly.'

Surprised by Molly Tanner's verbal attack, the headmistress asked an older, responsible child to return Rosie to her mother, who then marched Rosie out of the school, and onto the cart. Again, Rosie thought she glimpsed a young woman standing a distance away, but by the time Rosie was seated, there was not a sign of anyone about.

On the way home, Molly complained incessantly. 'You cause me nothing but aggravation. I should never have had you in the first place. I never wanted kids, but it didn't matter what I wanted – oh, no! Because your father wanted to play daddy! But who is it that has to take care of you, eh? Me! That's who. From the day you were born, you've been like a real thorn in my side!'

She gave Rosie a stark warning. 'If I get called in again by your teacher, I'll take the cane to you myself, and I promise you I will not be lenient with it.'

When suddenly the horse stumbled into a shallow pothole, she angrily flicked the whip over his back, causing him to throw his head up and lose his footing momentarily.

When she prepared to raise the whip again, Rosie cried out, 'Please, Mummy, don't hurt him.'

'What have I told you, girl?' Molly glared at Rosie. 'Who are you to tell me what to do and what not to do?' She viciously flicked the whip in the air again. 'Think yourself fortunate . . . after what you did at school, you're lucky I haven't taken the whip to you!'

All the way home, the volley of abuse continued: 'I have never been so humiliated. I warn you, my girl, you'd best tell me what lies you've been spreading.'

Rosie assured her mother that she had not said anything to anyone, but as always her words fell on deaf ears.

When they arrived back at the farmhouse, Rosie was snatched off the cart and given a sound thrashing, but even as the frightened girl was sobbing, Molly Tanner showed no remorse.

∼

At eight years of age, Rosie's cousin Harry was a well-built and handsome boy. The son of her uncle Patrick, Harry loved nothing better than doing odd jobs at Tanner's Farm after school.

Now, on hearing the commotion, he went at the run across the yard, yelling, 'Uncle John!'

He found John in the far barn, chopping firewood.

'You'd best come quick.' Harry was in a panic. 'It sounds like there's trouble over by the house.'

Swinging the heavy axe into the log of wood, Rosie's father wiped the sweat from his face, and threw off his thick gloves. 'What d'you mean, boy? What kind o' trouble?'

'I'm not sure, but there was a lot of shouting and yelling. I think I heard Rosie cry out, so I thought I'd best find you, and quick.'

'You did right, Harry.' John hurried towards the house with the boy following close behind.

Turning the corner, and with the house now in his view, John was shocked at what he saw. It was painfully obvious that his wife was in one of her vicious moods, with Rosie at her mercy.

'Molly!' Surging forward, he screamed out, 'Leave the child alone!'

He quickly realised that Rosie had her arms folded across her face so as to protect herself, but she was no match for the woman who was viciously thrashing her with the belt from her coat.

John threw himself between his wife and the child. 'For God's sake, woman! What the hell is wrong with you?'

Taking her by the arms, he thrust Molly away and grabbed Rosie to him. Then, giving her into Harry's safekeeping, he shot forward to pin his wife against the cart. 'What kind of bully are you, eh? Just look at her – whatever she might have done, she did not deserve a beating like that. What kind of a mother are you, for pity's sake?'

Without a backward glance, and filling the air with

obscenities, Molly fled into the house and slammed the door behind her.

'Ssh . . . it's all right, sweetheart, you're safe now.' John went to collect Rosie from his nephew, who was still visibly shaken by what he had witnessed.

'Don't worry, son,' John assured him, 'Rosie will be all right. Just leave the stables for now – I'll finish them later – but please see to the horse. He looks badly shaken.'

The horse was foaming at the mouth and anxiously treading the ground with his front hoofs, as though at any minute he might take flight.

John stroked a tender hand over the horse's neck. 'Easy, boy,' he quietly reassured him, 'you're in safe hands now.'

Mindful of Rosie, and eager to get her inside, he said to Harry, 'I'll check him thoroughly the minute I can, but could you gently unshackle him and make him comfortable in the stable? Make sure he's got water and hay in the rack.'

Though desperate to get Rosie indoors, John swiftly examined the horse to reassure himself that this gentle animal was not badly injured, and when he saw the shadowy stripes of the whip, he had to hold back his temper. 'Rushed through the lanes, and whipped for your trouble, eh, boy?' He ran a firm but gentle hand over the horse's velvety neck and back. 'No lasting damage, though, thank goodness.'

Scooping Rosie into his arms, he then began to make his way to the house, calling to Harry as he went, 'Just run the cart into the barn and leave it. When the old fella is calm and fed, you should go home. Your mother will be watching for you.'

Harry was still shocked at the way Molly had vented her anger on the lovely Rosie, and by the look of the horse's back he also had taken a harsh punishment. Like Rosie, that quiet old horse did not have a bad bone in his body, so what could either the horse or Rosie have done to warrant such a beating?

He was deeply concerned about Rosie, and so he told John, 'I don't want to go home yet. Please may I stay with the horse until you come back out?'

John understood and was grateful for Harry's concern. 'You're a great help to me,' he told him. 'Remember, just keep the old horse calm, and I'll be out as soon as I can.'

Now, his priority had to be Rosie. The little girl was his life.

He felt Rosie clinging tighter to him the closer they got to the house.

'It's all right, sweetheart,' he promised. 'Your mother will never hurt you again . . . not if I can help it.'

Molly watched through the window as her angry husband approached, their daughter in his arms. 'That's right,' she muttered spitefully, 'fussing over the little brat as usual! Oh, but don't worry about me, and the humiliation I've endured today, and all because of your precious little innocent.'

When he came into the house, John could hardly look at her. 'Take a look at what you've done. What kind of mother would do such a thing to her own child? You should be ashamed.'

He pointed to two red marks on Rosie's arm where her mother had held her in a vicious grip. Dark bruises on her neck and face were becoming increasingly visible, and trickles of blood were running from her nose.

Molly looked away.

'Yes! You *should* look away,' John said in a low, trembling voice. 'This is your daughter, just turned five years old, and this is how you treat her.' He pointed to the swelling weals and bruises on Rosie's face and arms. 'What you've done here is assault . . . pure and simple. People get put away for less than this. If it was reported to the police, you'd be locked up for a long time, and you would damned well deserve it, too!'

'Hmm!' Taking a step closer, Molly sneered, 'Report me then, why don't you?'

John glared at his wife in disgust. 'I don't even know who you are these days . . . maybe I never did. Why would you want to hurt a helpless child like that . . . our own little daughter? It beggars belief.' Leaning forward, he whispered harshly, 'I should hurt you, just like you've hurt Rosie. That way, you might realise how it feels.'

Molly Tanner smiled nastily. She knew he would never hurt her. He was too kind. And far too weak.

Unable to look on her a moment longer, John hurried Rosie away to bathe her wounds.

As her father carried her to the kitchen, Rosie looked back to see her mother smiling.

For a moment Rosie thought her mother was trying to say she was sorry, but then she realised the smile was neither reassuring nor warm, but cold and hateful, and the little girl held on all the tighter to her father.

John carefully settled his daughter at the kitchen table while he drew a bowl of warm water and found a flannel, which he rinsed under the cold tap.

Bringing the flannel to her face, he told her, 'Put your head back a little, sweetheart. Keep this pressed to your nose, and the bleeding will soon stop.' He then treated the bruises with saltwater and camomile, constantly assuring her that by the morning the bruises would be almost gone. Privately he thought it would be a long time, if ever, before Rosie would be able to forget how badly her mother had beaten her, and for what? He was determined to get to the bottom of it all.

When she was cleaned up he carried his small daughter upstairs and put her to bed.

'I'll be up again in a while to see if there's anything you need,' he promised.

Leaving the door slightly open in case she might call out, he paused on the landing, and when it seemed the ordeal had tired Rosie out, he leaned on the banister and softly cried, asking himself over and over how Molly could be so wicked as to hurt their child like that.

Somewhere along the way, deep in his heart, he had lost a huge measure of respect for this woman whom he felt he hardly knew any more. In fact, at some time during the past six years, since they were married, he had come to realise she was not the woman he had believed her to be.

If he had known at the outset what she was really like, he might have walked away, but even now, after what she had done, he still loved and needed her, and if that made him a weak man, then so he was. Above all else, John Tanner was a good and forgiving man. In spite of what he had witnessed this sorry day, he convinced himself that the woman he had taken as his wife must surely have a measure of compassion in her soul.

One way or another, he meant to find it.

PART TWO

Badness Will Out

CHAPTER ONE

THRUSTING THE UNHAPPY memories to the back of her mind, Rosie, peeping between the curtains, concentrated on keeping her vigil at the window. She now truly believed that tonight her mother would not come home. The troubling thought was tempered with an odd sense of relief.

She was startled by a gentle knock on her bedroom door and turned to see her father peeking round.

'I didn't mean to startle you, sweetheart,' he said, coming into the room, patting the thick neck of his black Labrador, Barney, at his heels. 'Is there any sight of your mother yet?'

'No . . . not yet.' Rosie knew how concerned he was.

When the dog came to sit beside her, Rosie ruffled his coat. 'Hello, Barney. Come to see me, have you?'

She hugged him close, imploring her concerned father, 'Daddy, please don't worry about Mother. I'm sure she must be on her way home.'

John chuckled. 'Hark at you, young lady. All grown up and reassuring me. It wasn't all that long ago that it would be the other way round.'

He came over and placed his hands on her shoulders. 'I'm so proud of you, Rosie,' he told her. 'We both know your mother can be hurtful at times, but you've learned to take it all in your stride. Fifteen going on forty-five, that's what you are.' He slid a comforting arm about her. 'Hand on heart, Rosie, I do believe that she never purposely sets out to be spiteful. It's as if she just can't help herself.'

'But she *is* spiteful, Daddy, to both of us, and to Harry, also. Sometimes she flies into a temper for no reason. She's always been like that, and I don't suppose she will ever change.'

'I know, and you have every right to feel aggrieved,' John said quietly, 'although I think your mother has been more in control of her temper these past few years. You must have seen that for yourself, sweetheart.'

Rosie shrugged. 'Maybe . . . but that's probably because we all do what Harry does, and try to keep out of her way.'

Sitting on the edge of the bed, John momentarily lapsed into silence. Then, cautiously, he asked, 'Can I tell you something, Rosie?'

She thought he had something weighing on his mind. 'Of course.'

'It's just that I have good reason to believe that she was never really meant to be a mother.'

'How do you mean, Daddy?' He had Rosie's full attention. 'All I know is, she never wanted me. She's always telling me that.'

'Yes, and I'm sorry she has ever said such a terrible thing, but it only strengthens my belief that some women are truly not meant to have children. But to be honest, Rosie, I really don't think she means half of what she says.'

Rosie looked him in the eye. 'Well, I know she does, otherwise why would she say it?'

'I don't think it's altogether her fault.'

'Whose fault is it, then?'

John took a deep breath. 'Some time back, I read an article in a medical magazine in the dentist's surgery, when I had to have that back tooth out.'

Rosie was curious. 'What kind of article? And what's it got to do with Mother's spiteful ways?'

John went on quietly, 'It explained how some women, through no fault of their own, can never see themselves as mothers. They do not have a natural instinct with children, and they are unable to cope with the responsibility of raising them.'

'I don't understand.'

John admitted that he did not really understand either. 'From what I can recall, it seems that some women – from every walk of life, and for many different reasons – are born without any maternal instinct whatsoever, and they don't, and never will, possess the urge to bear a child or to love and take care of one.'

'But that's not natural . . . is it?' Rosie was nonplussed, though she knew her own mother found it hard to love her, and there had been many occasions when she would rather hurt her than care for her.

'If that article really is true, then there must be other women like Mother.' Suddenly afraid her mother might appear at the door, Rosie lowered her voice to a whisper. 'Sometimes, even when I haven't done anything wrong, she screams at me and says hurtful things to make me cry. And she never, ever cuddles me. One time, I threatened to run away but she just laughed in my face and offered to pack a bag for me.'

'You mean you actually meant to run away?' John

asked. 'Why didn't you come to me? Maybe by offering to pack your bag, your mother was trying you, thinking that if she pretended to go along with your threat you might give up the idea.'

'No, Daddy. You weren't there. She really wanted me to leave.' Rosie was adamant. 'She chased me upstairs and started packing my clothes into a bag, and she was angry . . . saying bad things. She told me that when she was just fifteen she was made to fend for herself and that it never did her any harm. She said it was time I learned to take care of myself, because I would be fifteen soon and old enough to fly the nest.'

'I see.' John was angry that his wife had spoken to Rosie in such a way. 'She never mentioned it to me,' he remarked quietly, 'and she was wrong to say such a thing. I know she left home early herself – and from what your Auntie Kathleen has told me, it seems your mother was a difficult child – but after leaving home she did largely what she wanted, and never looked back. She had various factory jobs and bar work and always had just enough money to keep her in style. Yes, she's always had tremendous style.'

Rosie was impressed despite herself. 'I don't know if I could do that. I don't think, even though I said I'd go, that I'm really ready to be sent packing, and besides, I would miss you too much . . . and the farm . . . and I expect I would even miss Mother.'

'I'm sure you would,' John smiled. 'Yes, she's a difficult woman, but we're all made different, and we have to live with what we've got. And you are nothing like your mother. You're strong, too, but in a different, calmer way.'

He was keen to reassure her. 'You've no need to worry about what your mother said to you because I promise you, hand on heart, you will never be "sent packing". This is your home for as long as you need it. It will be for you to decide when the time does eventually come for you want to fly the nest.'

'Don't you think I'm brave enough to go out in the big wide world?'

'I'm not saying that, sweetheart.' John found it difficult to choose the right words. 'You are so different from your mother. You're a strong, deep-thinking girl, with a heart full of love and compassion. So many times I've seen how you put other people's feelings before your own. Look at that time last spring when we had weeks of rain. Everything was flooded, including the big pond in the valley. When one of our new lambs escaped from the barn and slipped down the bank into the pond, you waded in after it without any thought for your own safety.' He smiled.

'You gave me one hell of a fright. In the end I had to save the pair of you.'

Rosie had not forgotten. 'I'm sorry I scared you,' she said, 'but the lamb was so frightened.'

'Ah, but not my Rosie, eh? Though running into the water was a foolhardy thing to do. I'm only thankful that I was there to retrieve you.'

He lowered his voice and spoke in a gentler tone. 'You do see what I'm trying to get at, don't you, Rosie? I could never imagine your mother going in after that lamb, but that does not make her a coward. It makes her cautious and protective of herself. But you care deeply about everything and everyone . . . even your mother. You're quieter and more thoughtful than she is. You're just altogether different. While she sees this farm and the land as a kind of prison, you've always loved it . . . much like I do. As you know, this farm was handed down to me from my father.' He smiled warmly. 'It gives me such joy to know that you share my passion for this place.'

He had long been saddened by his wife's dislike of the farm and the surrounding countryside. 'Your mother has never really settled here. She's forever saying she wants us to move, bag and baggage, into the town centre, though she knows I could never agree to it. Maybe that makes me selfish – I don't know. But you see what I'm saying, don't you? The two of you are unalike in so many ways.'

Rosie spoke her mind. 'I don't want to be like Mother.'

John understood, although what lay behind her comment saddened him. 'Do you know what would make me happy, Rosie? I would feel so much better if you could just try not to be too hard on your mother. She can't help the way she is. I know she's got many failings but don't we all have failings of some sort or another? None of us is perfect, Rosie. Let's take a look at the good things she's done, shall we? First of all, she allowed me the greatest gift I could ever have . . . and that is you, Rosie. She raised you, and here you are, a lovely, kind and gentle girl on the edge of womanhood. You've turned out to be a fine human being, so somewhere along the way your mother must have done something right. I'll admit you have good reason at times to think she doesn't love you, but I'm sure she does . . . in her own peculiar way.'

Hoping he was getting through to Rosie, he went on, 'Having said that, I have to agree that just lately she's been on a really short fuse, but over the sixteen years since I married her I have seen glimpses of tenderness in her. Not often, I'll admit, but somewhere under her hard shell there must be a softness in her character.'

Rosie instinctively glanced through the window. 'Well, if there is, I don't think I've ever seen it.'

'Maybe you didn't want to . . . not really.'

While Rosie thought about his comment, he went on, 'Auntie Kathleen told me that your mother left home after a furious row with her parents, apparently over some small issue that was never resolved, even though Molly dearly loved her mother. It would seem that she's always been strong-minded, but I like to think she doesn't mean half of what she says . . . that maybe her sharp tongue is just the nature of her.'

'You really do love her, don't you, Daddy?' Rosie asked softly.

'Yes, Rosie . . .' he gave a deep sigh, ' . . . I think I must.'

Rosie felt guilty now. 'I really don't hate her, Daddy.'

'I know you don't, sweetheart.'

'Is it my fault that she hasn't come home yet?'

'Of course not. She's probably met up with a friend.'

'I don't think she has many friends.'

'Well, there you go, Rosie. Just because we haven't seen them doesn't mean they don't exist.

But you're right. I know she's not one for making friends easily.' He confided, 'According to her, the two girls who used to work with her at the pub were – in your mother's own words – too young and silly for their own good. Also, as I'm sure you probably heard, she's already had a set-to with the new barmaid who works alongside her. On top of that, for whatever reason, she hasn't spoken to your Auntie Kathleen for ages, and why she seems to have taken against Harry, I have no idea. He's a decent young man. If I searched for a month o' Sundays, I might never find such a fine, hard-working young man.'

Rosie had also been thinking about that. 'Maybe the reason Mother doesn't like him is because Auntie Kathleen is not his real mother, so he's not part of the family.'

'Well, yes, that may well be so, though, as far as I'm concerned, Harry is now and he always will be part of this family. As you may recall, Harry's mother died after a long illness, and some months after that, his father, Paddy, met your Auntie Kathleen. According to Kathleen, both Paddy and his son were two lost souls. Harry was a bit too young to understand exactly what was happening, but like Paddy, he was very unhappy.'

'I know what happened,' Rosie remarked thought-fully, 'and I'm really glad that Auntie Kathleen and Uncle Patrick found each other.'

'So am I, Rosie. Sometimes good things happen, and they help us forget the bad times. Kathleen never had children of her own and she took young Harry to her heart as though he was her own. In her quiet, kindly way, she got the little boy and his father through the bad times, and the three of them are now a strong family. I had hoped your mother would accept that, but if she hasn't accepted Harry by now I don't believe she ever will, more's the pity.'

'I don't suppose Harry cares much for her either,' Rosie remarked angrily.

John understood. 'There's always hope. Maybe, after all, she'll see him for what he is: a fine young man who works hard and takes a pride in his many responsibilities. He's a foreman in the making. The truth is, I honestly don't know how I would manage without him.'

The thought of Harry not being around on the farm made Rosie sad. 'Harry told me that Farmer Bennett offered to take him on if he ever left you. But Harry told him he would never leave, that he was happy here learning how to be a good farmer.'

John smiled knowingly. 'I'm well aware that Harry could get a prime position at any one of the farms hereabouts. I also know he's been approached and has turned down other farmers, and I truly appreciate his loyalty.'

'Well, if you want him to stay tell Mother to stop yelling at him and blaming him for anything that goes wrong. Yesterday she threatened to sack him. I was in the kitchen and I heard her screaming and shouting because he brought the horses in from the fields.'

'I'm afraid that was my fault,' John said. 'I forgot to tell Harry that the blacksmith had to rebook as he'd been called out to an emergency. Unfortunately, it was still down on Harry's work schedule to bring in the horses for shoeing. I explained to your mother that the employees must remain my responsibility, and if ever there might be a reason to reprimand anyone, I would deal with it. The matter is now done and dusted.'

'I bet Mother didn't take any notice.'

'Oh, I think she did. I made it very clear . . .' He now recalled Molly's response to his words of caution. 'In fact, to be fair – although she did not actually say it – I got the distinct feeling your mother was sorry for blaming Harry after I explained that it was not his fault.'

He stood and moved to the window, peering into

the darkness. 'What's keeping her? Where the devil is she?' He glanced at Rosie's bedside clock. It was gone eleven o'clock. 'Your mother is usually home by now. I'd best go and meet her. I know she won't thank me for it, but it's pitch-black out there, and you never know who might be hanging about in the shadows. If that clock is right, the Magpie will have closed its doors an hour or so back,' he added under his breath.

He kissed Rosie on top of her head. 'I'm going to find her, Rosie, and I need you to stay upstairs with Barney. I'll secure the house and lock the doors on the way out. You know where the spare key is, don't you?'

'Yes, Daddy.'

'Good.' He gave Rosie a stern look. 'Whatever you hear, or whoever might knock on the door, do not go outside. I'll be as quick as I can. Close the curtains and keep them closed . . . and make sure you stay well away from the windows.'

He hurried across the room, then stopped at the door. 'Remember what I said, Rosie. Do not open the door or answer to anyone who might call, no matter who it might be. D'you understand?'

'Yes, Daddy. But can't I come with you?' she asked, following him to the door.

'No, sweetheart. I don't want you out there in the dark, and anyway I might need to go into the Magpie, and a pub is no place for a young girl.' He gave her a quick hug. 'Don't you worry. I'll be back in no time. Here, Barney. Good boy.' He called the Labrador to him and ruffled the big dog's collar. 'I want you to look after our lovely girl. Don't you leave her . . . not even for a minute.'

He gave Barney a little push and the dog went straight into Rosie's arms. Holding him tight, she laughed out loud when he began washing her face with his long pink tongue.

'I'll be back before you know it,' John promised, 'and with luck I'll have your mother in tow. Now remember, before I come into the house I'll call up to you. When you hear my voice, take a little peep through the window to make absolutely sure it's me. D'you understand?'

Feeling safe and loved, Rosie assured him that she did.

'Right then, sweetheart . . . I'm glad we managed to clear the air and I'm glad we've been honest with each other. We should have had this little chat long ago, but we'll do it again, I promise. Now I'd best be off.'

For the next few minutes, Rosie heard her father

going from room to room, securing her inside the house. Then she heard him close the front door and she waited for the click of the key in the lock. When she heard that she ran back to the window and gingerly turned up a corner of the curtain in order to catch a glimpse of him.

For a moment or so she could not pick out his tall, strong figure; then he passed under the big automatic security lights attached to the largest building in the yard.

Last winter, after a spate of thefts from farms in the area, Rosie's father had made this barn strong and secure enough to house his valuable farming equipment.

Rosie watched him, thinking he cut a fine figure in his long dark coat, his black-and-white checked cap pulled down to his brow. 'Love you, Daddy,' she whispered. She thought about her mother, out there doing whatever it was she did and not caring who might be at home worrying about her.

Within moments her father was gone, having quickly dodged through the space between two farm buildings to cut across the fields. Rosie often used that same short cut into town, but never in the dark. The very idea made her shiver with fright.

Now, with the dog nudging her, she carefully

lowered the curtain and turned to fuss him. 'Well, Barney, Daddy says we have to stay here and not open the door to anyone.' She giggled. 'Though I reckon if anyone tried to get in here, you'd have them for breakfast, wouldn't you, eh?'

Looking up with soulful eyes, the dog stretched out on the carpet to await his master's return, although Rosie knew he would leap up should he be needed.

~

'I think it's time the pair of you called it a day.' Peggy Benson, the landlady of the Magpie, was none too pleased when Molly Tanner refused to climb down from the bar stool. In truth, having been made irritable by the booze, she was actively looking for trouble.

'Come on, Molly,' Mrs Benson insisted. 'I need to lock up now. If you don't mind.'

'Hey! What's your problem, lady?' As she leaned forward, Molly was in danger of tumbling from her perch. 'Want us out, do you? OK then, but before we leave, it would be nice to have one last drink . . . on the house, perhaps, as I'm one of the staff.'

'Sorry! No more booze for you two . . . at least not in this pub,' the landlady insisted.

'Is that so?' Molly was in fighting mood. 'Right then, we're not budging from here. Not until we've had another round to finish off the evening. Go on, off you go . . . back behind the bar!' She waggled her finger towards the rows of bottles. 'My friend will have a pint of your best beer, and another G&T for yours truly – and don't skimp on the gin this time.' She laughed as she dug a handful of coins from her handbag. 'See!' She threw the coins across the bar. 'I've got money, if you're too tight to give us them on the house, so you needn't worry about that.'

'I don't want your money, Molly, I want the pair of you out of here,' said Mrs Benson, swallowing down a retort at the difficult woman's insults. 'It's way past closing time, and I am not serving you any more drinks. The bar is officially closed so the two of you might as well get off.'

'We will, but not until you pour us each a generous nightcap.'

'Sorry, did you not hear me? I just told you, there will be no more drinks served here tonight. So take your fancy man and get off home.' She added with a knowing smile, 'I'm sure your husband is wondering where you are.' Leaning forward, she lowered her voice confidentially. 'I'm thinking maybe I should call him to come and get you.'

'What! You spiteful old cow!' Agitated, Molly dashed the empty glasses off the bar. 'You'd best mind your own damned business if you know what's good for you!'

She glared at the landlady before ambling over to her companion, a small-built, wiry fellow with a shock of fair hair and a well-worn but curiously attractive face. A man well versed in chiselling a living out of anything that came his way, whether legal or otherwise.

Right now, though, he was lying prostrate on the floor. 'Come on, you . . .' Tugging at his coat sleeve, Molly tried to get him up, but the more she struggled and failed, the sulkier he got.

'Bugger off, Molly!' Eventually, pushing her aside, he staggered to his feet, taking a moment to lean on the back of a chair. 'I'll have you know . . . I am quite capable of . . . woa!' Giggling, he managed to stand up straight. 'Like I said . . . I am perfectly capable of looking after myself.'

Eager to have them gone, Mrs Benson now took charge. With one hand she gripped Molly's arm, and with the other she grabbed the man's shoulder, then marched the two of them across the room, and eased them over the threshold and into the outer foyer. 'Good night then. Mind how you go.'

Satisfying herself that they seemed just about capable of walking away, the weary landlady watched them depart, smiling when she saw how Molly took charge.

The two drunks lumbered along the wide, empty pavement, laughing and joshing and pushing each other onwards. When a lonely dog threatened to cock its leg over her, Molly gave it a swift kick in the nether regions. 'Dirty hound, bugger off!'

As she hurriedly closed the outer doors, Peggy Benson heard Molly's angry departing words.

'Go on, get back inside, you old trout! Call yourself a landlady? Well, I won't forget this night in a hurry, you see if I don't! I'll put word out that you take your customers' money then chuck 'em out into the night like some old rubbish.'

'You can tell 'em whatever you like, Molly.' Mrs Benson did not feel threatened. She was used to dealing with difficult customers and staff, especially the formidable Molly Tanner. Over the years, she had learned to take it all in her stride, knowing by now that any aggravation would be forgotten by the morning.

Molly was irritated to find that while she'd been threatening the landlady her companion had broken rank and was now lolloping along in front, seemingly with no idea of where he might be headed.

Quickening her footsteps, she caught up with him. 'Hey, you dozy sod, Tom. Where the devil d'you think you're going? That's the wrong way.' She gave him a shove to halt his progress. 'You should have turned off back there, down Edward Street. You've gone straight past it, you daft bugger!'

'Oh, Molly darlin', don't be like that.' His small bright eyes shone out of a face reddened by too much beer. 'I must have missed the turning in the dark, that's all.' Refreshed by the cold night air, he turned round, and headed back towards Edward Street. 'It's all right, though,' he grumbled sulkily, 'I get the message. You don't want me, but that's OK 'cause I can manage without you. And for your information, I can find my own way home, thank you.'

'Oh, for pity's sake, stop moaning!'

Linking her arm with his, she pulled him forward, much to his delight. 'Hey! Behave yourself, woman!' he joshed. 'Anyone would think you were after getting your wicked way with me.'

There was no doubt that Molly Tanner was still a very attractive woman, with those dark alluring eyes . . . he looked up at her now, as she walked along. Something she did with her hips reminded him of Marilyn Monroe in that film where she plays the ukulele . . .

He felt rather proud – so proud that he felt brave enough to address her with a suggestive wink and a knowing smile. 'Hey . . . Molly darlin' . . .'

'What now?'

'I'm not ready to go home just yet.'

'What d'you mean? If you're not going home, where the devil d'you think you're going?'

'I've no idea. When I'm with you, Molly, I can't even think straight.' He giggled childishly. 'I really don't have a single idea about where I'm going, except . . . well, I want to go where you're going because, like I said, I'm not ready for home just yet.'

'Why not?'

'Because you and me, we have unfinished business.'

'Oh, yes? And what kind of "business" would that be, eh?' As if she didn't know.

Tom sniggered. 'Ah, come on, Molly, you know very well what kind of "business"!' Clumsily grabbing her by the shoulders, he drew her towards him. 'My lovely, wonderful Molly Tanner! I'm not letting you go this time, at least not until we've said good night in a right and proper manner.'

'I know what you're after, you crafty devil,' Molly teased him, laughing. 'You're after a goodnight kiss from your old sweetheart, isn't that it?'

'Sort of, yes, but I want a bit more than that. We

both do, and don't you deny it, Molly . . . because drunk or sober, you want me as much as I want you. Go on! Admit it.'

'I do not want you, Tom Stevens. At least not in that way.'

'Yes, you do, and we both know it.'

'All right then . . . maybe I did, a long time back. But I'm over you now.'

'Liar! You still want me. I know it. So, come on, be honest with me, Molly darlin' . . . you an' me together, like it used to be. Tell me the truth – you do want that, don't you?'

Molly shook her head. 'I don't know, and that's the truth. Anyway, you haven't actually said what it is you really want from me. So come on, what do you have in mind?'

'Well, for now, I just want to take you in my loving arms and ravish the hell outta you. And now you know. So, what d'you reckon?'

For what seemed an age Molly gave no answer, and when she did her quiet reply pleased her companion. 'D'you know what . . .' she paused to remember how it had been between her and this likely fella, and how she had never been happy since breaking up with him, '. . . it's been a long time since I had a real man's arms wrapped about me.'

'Ah! Well, now, Molly my love, it's your lucky day – or shall I say lucky night?' Giggling boyishly, he began to leap about in a mad little jig of glee, which went on for a full minute before he lost his footing and fell against the wall. 'At last I've got the truth from you, Molly. I knew you still wanted me. I knew you would see sense eventually. All these years and I've never been really in love with anyone else, because I knew I would get you back one day.'

When Molly laughed, he lunged forward to take her by the shoulders. Planting a clumsy but passionate kiss on her mouth, he slyly drew her to the nearest dark shop doorway.

For a moment she gave no resistance, but then she began fighting him, while yelling at the top of her voice, 'Get off me!'

'For pity's sake, Molly, stop that shouting! What's wrong with you?' he pleaded.

Thinking he'd lost his only chance of getting her back, he changed tack. 'Oh, come on, my lovely, you said you were up for it, and you really got me going. And now you're acting as though you want no part of me. That's a wicked thing to do, especially to a man who loves the arse off yer!'

'Don't you dare lay a hand on me!' Molly shook him off. 'If you must know, I want it as much as you do.'

'So, what was all the shouting about then?'

'I'll tell you what it was, you dopey begger! I'm not as easy as I used to be. I have a bit more pride these days. And the time is certainly long gone when I let myself get squashed into a dirty old doorway, where wandering mongrels pee up the wall and tramps might spew out their guts. I'm worth more than that! So if you think I'm some kind of cheap little tramp, you can bugger off right now!'

'Aw, Molly, I'm sorry . . . I didn't think. But we can't go back to my lodgings. The old trout is already threatening to kick me out 'cause I'm a week behind in my rent.'

'Well, that's a shame.' Molly was genuinely disappointed. 'And we definitely can't go back to the farmhouse.'

She suddenly grabbed him by the coat collar and kissed him full on the mouth, while an idea played on her mind. 'It's all right, Tom, I know where we can go.'

'Where's that, then?'

'You'll see, and you won't be disappointed.'

As she led the way, he wrapped one arm about her shoulders. 'You're such an exciting woman, Molly. I should never have let you go all them years back.' He added fondly, 'I still love you, Molly. You're not like other women. You're not afraid to go for what you want, and to hell with the consequences, eh?'

'You make me sound ruthless.'

'Well, that's 'cause you are! But I love you too much to let you slip away from me again. I want us to find a place of our own together. You know it's right, Molly, 'cause me and you . . . we were made for each other.'

Molly laughed. 'Me and you . . . living together, eh? Well, you can get that stupid idea straight out of your head because I am not about to hitch my star to a loser like you.'

'That's not very nice, is it? I hope you're not playing games with me, Molly.'

Molly laughed in his face. 'Would I do that?'

'You might, but I hope not, because I really love you, girl . . . I've always loved you.' He gave an almighty shiver. 'Brr! It's bloody cold, Molly.'

'Walk a bit faster then.'

'Where are we going?'

'Wait and see.'

Edging him away from the main street, she led him down a side alley. 'Come on! We'll cut through here.'

'D'you love me, Molly . . . I mean, really love me?' he wheedled drunkenly.

'Stop it!' Molly gave him a warning shove. 'Just stop saying things like that. I know it's only the booze talking.'

'Aw, come on, Molly, I might be a bit tipsy but I'm telling you the truth, and now I need to know something.'

'What's that, then?'

'I need to know why you went off and married the farmer when you knew how much I wanted you. I know you loved me then . . . and you still do. So why did you refuse my offer of marriage?'

For the longest minute, Molly's thoughts went back to when she was young and vibrant. She had made choices back then, both good and bad.

'First of all, I did love you. In fact, like I said, I still have strong feelings for you, bloody fool that I am! But back then I was young and desperate to build a life for myself. I had to make a calculated choice, and when the opportunity came up I chose to marry the farmer.'

'Yes, I know all that. What I don't know is why you chose him instead of me. Was it because you loved him more than you loved me?'

'Leave it, Tom,' she warned him firmly. 'Let's not go there, eh? It's no good talking about something that happened a long time back. We've both had too much to drink tonight. Anyway, what's done is done and it can't be changed.'

'Leave him, Molly!' Tom shouted. 'Come home with me . . . please. I'll make you happy, I will!' Surging forward, he fell clumsily against the wall, where he slithered down and sobbed like a child. 'I miss you, Molly. That's why I never got married. It's why I follow you about and want to be near you. I sometimes watch you, Molly,' he confessed. 'I hide in the spinney and I watch you . . . hanging out the washing, and going about your business. I can't get enough of you, Molly. That's how bad it's got. Earlier, when I saw you heading for the pub, I followed you. I needed to see you, to talk to you.'

'What? You followed me to the pub? You crafty devil. You told me you were just passing; that you were on your way home from work and you needed a drink or two. You even acted surprised at seeing me there.'

'I'm really sorry, Molly, but I had to see you.'

'Well, I'm damned . . . you're a bloody stalker!' She laughed coldly. 'You've been watching me and I never even knew. What next, eh? D'you know, I could get you put in jail for stalking me.'

'Ah, but you wouldn't, would you?'

'I might. You never know.'

'Leave your husband, Molly . . . please?'

'Why the hell should I?'

'Because you're mine, Molly. You were always mine!'

'I'm not leaving him, so you can forget that.'

'Do you love him?'

'No.'

'So why do you want to be with him?'

'I don't need to explain my reasons to you or to anyone else.'

'But I thought you wanted to be with me.'

'I do.'

'Well, now you're confusing me. You say you don't love him and that you love me. And yet you refuse to leave him and make a life with me. Why, Molly? Explain it to me, because I don't understand.'

'You don't need to understand.'

'Oh, but I do! If you don't love him, why did you marry him when you could have had me?'

'Are you absolutely sure you need to know?'

'Just tell me.'

'Aw, bugger it!' She pushed him away. 'You're getting me all wound up. I need a fag.'

Leaning against the wall, she rummaged in her handbag and drew out a packet of Woodbines and a box of matches.

Having lit the cigarette, she took a long drag on it and blew the smoke out slowly. Then she turned back to Tom.

'It's true I really did love you, Tom, but you had nothing to give me . . . at least not by way of material things, like a home, and nice clothes, and all the trimmings. Then, when John's father died and left him the farm, I saw where my future lay, and I went for it. I thought nothing of him – I still loved you – but he came with a farm that was worth a tidy penny, while you had nothing worthwhile to offer me. Even now, I don't need to work if I don't want to because he provides everything. Working gets me away from the pair of them. I do what I like with my wages, and that suits me fine.'

'I see.' He was shaken at her cold manner. 'You really are a bad lot, aren't you, Molly?'

'I suppose . . . It all worked out so well, except I could never love him. To this day he doesn't even realise how much I hate him . . . and the girl. When the girl appeared, I was sorely tempted to leave the pair of them, but common sense got the better of me.'

'And you've stayed all these years. But you could have come to me, Molly. I had my own little place back then. I would never have turned you away.'

'I stayed because it was part of my plan,' she admitted. 'I was a good wife to him.' She paused, remembering the difficult times. 'The girl ruined everything. She was never part of the big plan, but he adored her and so I learned to pretend.'

'But why could you not genuinely love that innocent child?'

Molly gave him a long, inscrutable look. 'I never wanted children. I was determined to be careful, but in spite of that, I still got pregnant. John never knew about his son, and I never told him. Instead, when I first found out I was carrying, I went to old Ma Battersby on Acament Street. She's known for helping pregnant women who want her kind of help, and my secret was safe with her. So, as soon as I realised he'd got me up the duff, she got rid of it for me. She told me she'd made an educated guess as to its gender. I feel no guilt at having denied him a son.'

She gave a drunken, pathetic little giggle. 'If he'd known how I got rid of his son, it would have broken his heart. Then along came another baby. Ma Battersby couldn't do anything to help me with that one, and the girl gave me a bad time. She made me so wretched that on certain days I couldn't even go to work. She just made me feel terrible. Suddenly, there I was, literally left holding the baby. It was almost as though John and his brat had planned it all, and I hated them both. I still do.'

Molly fell silent, while Tom Stevens reflected on what she had told him. How could he ever have fallen for this cold-hearted woman?

'Shocked, are you?' Molly's shrill voice invaded his thoughts. 'Still want me, do you?'

'I must be a sad man,' he replied thoughtfully. 'How in God's name can I love a hard-hearted woman like you? It's as if, all those years ago, you crept into my head and my heart, and now I'm only half a man without you. So what does that say about me, eh?' He felt ashamed and guilty, and yet he still needed her so badly he could hardly breathe.

'It sounds to me as if you're utterly miserable on the farm. You don't love your husband and you don't want the girl, so why not leave it all behind? We're both working – we could rent a place somewhere. Nothing too grand, but at least it'll be ours.' When she gave no answer, he asked again, 'What d'you say, Molly?'

'Don't talk stupid!' Cursing herself for having confided in him, Molly reacted viciously. 'Do you really think I've gone through years of hell, only to move in with you, to live in a grotty bedsit down some godforsaken backstreet? Hell will freeze over before I do that. My plan is to brave it out. Then, when he pops his clogs – hopefully sooner rather than later – I intend getting everything. John Tanner might be a first-class farmer, but he's not too bright when it comes to paperwork, except when it's to do with agricultural stuff.'

She smiled knowingly, lowering her voice. 'Everything else – the more personal, official stuff – falls to me to deal with. So I am fully aware of what he's worth and, consequently, what I am also worth, if you know what I mean?'

'No, I don't know what you mean, Molly. You might need to spell it out for me. What exactly are you getting at?'

In a soft, intimate voice she explained, 'Well, let's just say you should not be at all surprised if amongst John Tanner's paperwork is a copy of his last will and testament. So I now know that, thanks to his father and grandfather before him having always had property and worked hard to keep it safe, John Tanner is not only worth a bob or two, but so am I. If I bide my time, I should end up a very wealthy woman. Think about it. There's the farmhouse itself. The many acres of prime land, and the woods beyond. The solid furniture that belonged to his parents and grandparents before them, and their every single possession – bits of family jewellery, pictures – all now worth a pretty penny. On top of that, there's all the machinery, which has cost a fortune over the years.'

She smiled. 'So you see, Tom, that's why I chose him over you. Not because I loved him, but because I saw a comfortable future, and if that makes me a bitch, then so be it. You asked for the truth, and now you've got it.'

'You're a bad lot, Molly. In truth, I'm only just beginning to see how devious you can be. But even now, I still want you in my life. In fact, I'd even be willing to take on the girl.'

'Well, I'm not! When the time comes, I have other plans for her.'

'What do you mean? What kind of plans?'

'I mean that when I'm rid of John Tanner, I have no intention whatsoever of raising his daughter.'

'I don't understand. She's your own flesh and blood. You have no choice but to raise her.'

'I don't have to do any such thing. She's ruined my life since the day I first clapped eyes on her. I have never felt an ounce of affection for her, and I never will.'

Then, to Tom's astonishment, she murmured softly, 'The one thing I have always regretted is not smothering her when she was too small to know anything about it.'

Silence fell heavily before Tom, becoming more sober by the minute, was urged to voice his thoughts. 'Shame on you, Molly. That was a shockingly wicked thing to say.'

She gave no answer, but slid her arm through his and walked him forward. 'Forget about the girl,' she advised brightly. 'I'm sure she'll be well taken care of when the time comes. But for now, my love, we need to get out of the cold.'

For her, the subject was ended, but her dark confession remained strong in her companion's mind. He realised that if he and Molly were to have a future together, he must work through his troubling thoughts and reconcile them with his conscience.

'So if and when you do get your hands on Tanner's Farm and everything, what plans do you have for the child?'

'Oh, that's easy!' Molly replied. 'I've got it all worked out. I have no motherly feelings for the girl, but my sister, Kathleen, positively dotes on her, so it should be easy enough to dump her on Kathleen, especially as she's so unbelievably trusting. Even when it comes to choosing men, she has no idea. She chose to marry a widower who is also a good eight or nine years older than her. Patrick's not the best-looking fella in the world either, but for reasons I will never understand she worships the ground he walks on. Mind you, to be fair, I must admit he looks after her very well. While he's not a wealthy man, he makes good money from his two successful tack shops, selling horsey stuff to the local hunt and the many riding schools hereabouts.'

Tom was impressed. 'Well, successful business or not, your sister obviously loves him. Good luck to them, that's what I say. He sounds like a decent sort.'

For a fleeting moment, Molly felt the teeniest twinge of jealousy. 'He's OK, I suppose. He seems to make Kathleen happy, but he's not my cup of tea. Also, he came with baggage in the shape of Harry, the teenage son who now works on the farm with John. For my money, Patrick fell on his feet when he met Kathleen.' She gave a disapproving grunt. 'She's so happy it makes me cringe! Like I said, my sister is far too easy to please. So turning the girl over to her should not be a problem.' She smiled. 'My sister is a fool to herself, but her soft nature might well work in my favour.'

Silently congratulating herself, she then remarked grandly, 'Trust me, Tom. It will all work out for the best, you see if it doesn't.' Threading her arm through his, she kissed him soundly on the cheek. 'Come on, then. Let's get in the warm, eh?'

'Lead on, my dear,' he said, thinking the child would have a good life with her doting aunt. He snuggled up to Molly. 'I forget where we're going. The booze must have addled my brain.'

'Don't be daft! You didn't forget,' she laughed. 'I just never actually told you, so you'll just have to wait and see, won't you? Relax. You'll know when we get there, and I promise we'll be safe enough . . . even from John Tanner. All right?'

Tom nodded. 'Yeah, all right . . . if you say so.'

'I do. So stop your moaning, and trust me.'

~

While Molly and her man hurried to their destination, John Tanner hurried through the backstreets towards the Magpie.

Keenly aware of how late it was, he remained vigilant, hoping to catch sound or sight of his wayward wife.

What the devil was she playing at staying out so late? When he heard the market hall clock chiming midnight his concern heightened. Where are you, Molly? he asked himself, looking about him. Surely the pub must be closed by now, so she couldn't still be there. Nevertheless, he decided to check.

Within minutes he was at the door of the Magpie. As he had guessed, the pub was closed and in darkness except for the small, flickering outside light over the door. With the flat of his hand he pushed hard on the door but it was obviously locked from within.

He tried the handle several times, with no luck. With no other ideas, and increasingly worried, he rapped his knuckles on the wooden panelling; all to no avail.

Lifting the cover of the letter box, he peered through. The inner door to the saloon was closed and there was no evidence of anyone inside: no laughter or chatter, and no rattling of glasses.

Stepping back, he looked up at the bedroom windows. Disappointingly, the curtains were drawn.

Hesitating, he wondered if he should shout up but he knew the publican wouldn't thank him for waking him and his wife if they were asleep. But he was frantic to know Molly's whereabouts, so he decided to call anyway. He was aware that the landlord might occasionally organise lock-ins, when he would invite a chosen party of friends to have a quiet drink outside of normal hours.

First he rattled the letter box again, but there was still no response from inside. Desperate, he leaned forward to call through the aperture. 'Hello,' he yelled, 'it's John Tanner. I'm sorry, but I need to know if my wife is in there with you.'

When there was still no answer, he raised his voice and shouted up for a second time: 'It's John Tanner, Molly's husband. She hasn't come home yet, and I'm worried about her. Is she in there? Hello?'

He listened for a moment but the silence thickened, so this time he pressed his face even closer to the letter box, yelling as loud as he dared: 'I'm sorry to disturb you when it's so late, but I'm really worried. Molly hasn't come home, and I don't know where she is. I was hoping you might be able to help me.'

Upstairs, Peggy Benson and her husband, Roger, woke with a start.

'What the hell's going on?' Leaning up on one elbow, Roger looked a sorry sight with his wild, ginger hair standing on end, and his eyes like two sunken holes in his features.

'Dammit! Can't a person get a decent night's sleep after a long working day?' Peggy grumbled. When her husband fell back and seemed to be nodding off again, she shook him violently. 'Roger, wake up!'

He groaned as though in agony. 'Aw, dammit!

Leave me alone. It's probably some drunk lost his way. He'll soon get fed up if we ignore him.'

'How the hell can we ignore him? We'd best get rid of him, or he'll wake the entire street.'

Roger lazily opened one eye. 'I said leave him. He'll soon get the message. Go back to sleep, woman.'

'I can't!' She shook Roger again. 'Listen! He's causing a commotion out there.' She gave a long yawn. 'Please, Roger. It's all right for you; you've been out for most of the day, while I've been stuck behind the bar. I'm bone tired. Please, Roger! Just go down and chase the bugger off, whoever he is!' Frustrated when he didn't move, she gave him a hard dig with her elbow. 'Go on then!'

'Why can't *you* "chase the bugger off"?'

''Cause I'm a woman, and you're a man . . . or you should be.'

'Like I say, ignore him. He'll get fed up when he realises we're closed.'

The shouting stopped and they lay back to catch up on their much-needed sleep. But after a few minutes the peace was broken yet again.

This time the voice was even louder. 'It's John Tanner. I'm looking for Molly . . . my wife. She hasn't come home yet. Is she in there?'

'Well, I never,' Peggy said, hearing clearly this time.

'It's Molly Tanner's husband. He's asking after Molly. He says she hasn't come home yet.'

'Damn and bugger it, woman!' Bleary-eyed, Roger sat up again. 'What makes him think she's still here? For pity's sake, get down there and tell him we need our sleep, and that his wife left ages since.' He lowered his voice. 'I didn't see her leave but she must have gone while I was fixing the light in the cellar. But do I recall you saying she left with some bloke?'

'That's right. They went off ages ago, both of 'em the worse for the drink.' Now Peggy was concerned. 'You don't think something's happened to them, do you? I mean, they were more than a bit jolly. What if they wandered into the road and got run over, or fell into a ditch or something?'

'Don't be so dramatic, woman. She's probably gone back to her friend's house for a good old time – lucky beggars! And there's us, can't even get a decent night's sleep, let alone enjoy a bit o' slap and tickle.'

'Aw, you poor thing. Well, unlike you, I've been up since five this morning, and I need my sleep more than you do. So get down them stairs and get rid of him. Oh, and you'd best not mention how Molly left with a man on her arm.'

'You needn't worry about that because I am not

getting involved. Please, sweetheart, you're much better at this kind of thing than I am.'

'But I'm so tired, Roger.' She tried a change of tack. 'I don't know where Molly is any more than you do. So please, help me out here, will you?'

He turned away, saying, 'Get down there and see him off! You can have a lie-in, and I'll get up and oversee the brewery's delivery.'

'No. What if I work the late shift again tonight instead?' She much preferred that.

'Nope.'

'Hmm. Call yourself a man?' Slinking out of bed, she gave him a parting slap across the shoulders. 'And don't think you can have your wicked way with me when I get back.'

'Spoilsport!' He turned over and gave her a cheeky little wink. 'I really hoped I might be on a promise.'

'Well, you were wrong.' She threw her dressing gown over her nakedness. 'You get back to sleep. I won't wake you because I'll be sleeping in the spare room tonight.' She thrust on her slippers and strode angrily across the room, banging the door behind her. 'Lazy git.' Her sharp cursing echoed back to him.

'Yeah, you too!' Making a face, he turned over again and went back to sleep.

John Tanner was relieved when he saw the lights

going on. A moment or so later, the door was opened by the landlady, who looked harassed and dishevelled in her hastily thrown-on dressing gown. 'What the devil d'you think you're doing, banging and shouting through the letter box? We were fast asleep in bed. Don't you know what time it is?'

'I'm sorry,' John said. 'I'm looking for my wife, Molly. She hasn't come home from work yet.'

'Well, I'm sorry, I have no idea where she might be. She ended her shift as usual, and then she had a last drink or so with her friend. As I recall, it was past closing hour when I turned them out.'

'Who was it, this friend?' John asked.

'I have no idea.' Peggy recalled that Molly and her friend had had a relationship before Molly married John Tanner, but she decided it would be best to keep her mouth shut.

'Did they go off together?'

'Well, I suppose they parted company once they were out of here . . . I don't know.' She was wishing she had not even mentioned Molly Tanner's 'friend'.

'What did this friend look like?'

'Sorry, I was run off my feet . . . too busy to take notice.'

'When they left, though, did you see which way they went?'

'Nope.' The landlady hunched her shoulders. 'Like I said, I was run off my feet. But I'm sure she'll be home when you get back. Now, I need to go to my bed. I'm up at five in the morning.'

John was feeling desperate. 'So you really can't describe this friend to me?'

Increasingly uncomfortable at being put in this position, the landlady replied with a slow shake of her head.

'Was it a man or a woman?'

Peggy cautioned herself against getting drawn into any business of Molly's. Although she had never actually met John Tanner before she was well aware of his reputation as a decent, hard-working man and a fine husband. However, jealousy could change the situation in a minute.

'I really must get back to bed,' she pleaded. 'Like I say, she's bound to be home by the time you get there.'

Peggy was not the only one who had been surprised at John Tanner's marrying Molly. It was local belief that he had settled for the wrong woman, although he appeared happy and contented.

For her part, Peggy Benson tried to distance herself from the gossip. It wasn't good for business to be known for spreading tittle-tattle, especially about her own staff. She saw Molly as a good barmaid, but possessed of a sense of her own importance.

Peggy found herself feeling for John, who was obviously not aware of his wife's devious nature.

'Please . . .' John pressed her for an answer. 'What did her friend look like?'

'Oh, he was nothing special. I didn't take too much notice. Like I said, I was run off my feet.'

'But she was with a man – that's what you said.'

'Did I?' She could have kicked herself.

'Yes. Just now, you said, "He was nothing special."'

'That's right, but I didn't get a good look at him.'

John needed more information. 'This man – can you recall anything else? For instance, what he was wearing?' He had an idea, though if he were less desperate he'd have realised he was clinging on to a very faint hope. 'Did he have a mop of fair, wavy hair, because it might well have been her sister's husband, Patrick. She may have gone with him to see her sister, although they surely would have rung us at home first.' He was babbling now.

'I can't describe the friend,' Peggy informed him. 'I saw him only from the back. I was busy all night, so I didn't get a proper look at him.'

John gently insisted, 'Try and think back. Did the man have a thick mop of fair, wavy hair?'

'I can't recall. Sorry.'

John had by now convinced himself that Molly must have bumped into the amiable Paddy, her brother-in-law. 'Thank you, and I'm truly sorry to have bothered you.' He bade Peggy good night.

'I'm sorry I couldn't be more helpful . . .' She began closing the door, regretting being so impatient with him. 'Only I've had one hell of a day. I really need to get some sleep before I'm on my feet again.' She was also wishing she had been more careful with the little information she had offered.

'So you really have no idea where they were headed?' John was not altogether content with the outcome of their little chat.

'No, I have no idea whatsoever,' she assured him. 'I'm really sorry.' She truly sympathised with his dilemma, but was most reluctant to add anything to what she had already said. Fearing he might ask more questions, she continued closing the door. 'Good night then.' Feeling mean, she quickly shut and secured the door behind him.

She then hurried up the stairs and went straight to the bedroom window, ignoring her husband's sleeping form. She peeped through the curtains to see John Tanner hurrying away down the shadowy street.

She considered him to be a well-built figure of a man, in his long dark coat and black-and-white checked flat cap. She also believed him to be a good and kindly soul although if the occasion demanded it, she sensed, he could be a man to be reckoned with.

For a few minutes more, she kept him in sight but then he turned the corner and was gone.

She now called to mind how his feckless wife had flirted shamelessly with her male companion. 'You're a downright fool, Molly!' she murmured under her breath. 'You don't deserve a fine man like John Tanner.'

~

Eager to get home, John quickened his steps. He felt somewhat relieved by the landlady's assurance that he might find Molly waiting at the farmhouse.

Hurrying from the intrusive lights of streetlamps and passing vehicles, he turned into the long lane towards home. Maybe she's right, he thought. Perhaps Molly really will be home by now, and no doubt wondering where I am.

He wondered if Rosie might tell Molly he was out searching the streets for her. He hoped not, because

Molly would be angry about that and he was in no mood for an argument.

Taking a moment to think about it, he convinced himself that Rosie wouldn't say anything. Regrettably, Rosie and Molly were never going to be best friends. He thought it understandable, especially when one of them was gentle and giving, while the other was hard-hearted and capable of wickedness.

He was painfully aware of how Rosie had not altogether forgiven Molly for spitefully whipping that poor old horse all that time ago, although, in truth, on that particular day Molly had shown a depth to her wicked temper that he had never seen before.

Even now, it was difficult for him to forgive Molly's actions, although in time he hoped he would.

Rosie, however, with her caring nature and huge love for the tired old gelding, might take longer to forgive her mother. If she ever did.

CHAPTER TWO

'COME ON, BIG BOY!' Feeling playful, Molly drew Tom towards the big hay barn at Tanner's Farm. 'Nobody ever comes in here outside of work,' she explained. 'We could stay here all night if needs be, and no one would ever know.'

'I'm not sure I'd want to stay here all night.' Tom was surprised and a little concerned that she had brought him onto the farm after all. It made him nervous. 'I bet there are mice and even rats hiding in here . . . and what if someone *does* come in and find us?' He stole a look behind him.

'Trust me, there won't be anyone here at this time of night.' Reaching into the deep crack under the window ledge, she collected the big iron key along with a bulky torch. 'Ah,' she waved the key at Tom,

'I'm glad they still hide the key there.' With a flourish she slid the big key into the lock and eased open the heavy door. 'Come on, hurry up!'

When they were both inside, she spread her hands across the big door, and pushed it shut. That done, she carefully directed the narrow torch-beam in order to locate the switch, then switched on the light.

'Hmm. There's not much more light now than there was with the torch,' Tom commented.

'No matter,' Molly retorted. 'As long as it's just enough to guide us, that's all we need.' She swept the place with a long, searching look, quickly satisfied that they were the only people there. 'See, quiet as a graveyard. We'll be all right in here.'

Greatly relieved, Tom chuckled like a naughty schoolboy. 'So it's just us two lovebirds, eh?'

'Come on, you big old softy!'

Taking him by the hand, Molly led him further into the barn. The two of them followed a well-worn path between the bales. Wide enough to get a man and barrow through, it led them to the heart of the barn.

'Wow!' Tom was amazed to find himself surrounded by mountainous walls of hay bales, neatly stacked almost to the roof.

With the overhead light being barely adequate,

Molly kept the torch trained low to the ground as she went, keeping a wary eye on Tom, who followed nervously not far behind.

'Good grief! Where the devil are we going, Molly? . . . Are you sure you closed that door tight? . . . Ooh, look at that; I've never seen so much hay all in one place. It must have taken a long time to get it all stacked and safe.'

'You don't know anything about farming, do you?' Molly teased him, rolling her eyes.

'No, I don't, and am never likely to. I work in a factory and I live in town. There ain't no fields there, an' there ain't no hay-eating animals that I know of!'

'Well, just so you won't be totally ignorant, I'll explain. The hay is cut and collected off the fields towards the end of summer, and fed to the animals over the winter months. John grows some of it for his own animals, but at least half gets sold to local beef and pork farmers who don't have enough land for growing their own fodder. That works out well for everyone: it helps the farmers to feed their herds, and it also brings in more cash for us. Once the hay is inside, it's no trouble as long as it's kept in the right conditions.'

'Hey, I'm not altogether stupid, Molly. But thanks for the information.'

Proceeding into the belly of the dimly lit barn, he glanced furtively about him, as though fearing some dark shape would leap out and swallow him up. When Molly quickened her steps, he broke into a clumsy little run behind her. He was definitely not comfortable in amongst this mountain of hay. What if the bales should fall on him? What if someone was watching them right now? And what about rats – how could he be sure they were not waiting to pounce? The thought made him shiver.

Mentally shaking himself, he concentrated on Molly. He did love her, even though, through all the years, she had never once contacted him. Tonight he had engineered a meeting in the pub, and it proved only how much he had missed her and how lonely his life had been without her. Molly was his only true love, and always would be.

Looking at her now, he smiled as she led him along the meandering corridor. Molly always had a good pair of legs, he thought. She was the best-looking girl he'd ever clapped eyes on, and when he was younger it had taken him a long time to find the courage to woo her. One thing he knew for sure, though: the few years when he had been with Molly were the best of his life.

He wondered if she would ever come back to

him – not just for a tumble in the hay, but to be with him for the rest of his days. That would be his heaven: he and Molly together for the remainder of their lives. If he could have just one wish it would be that maybe – just maybe – she might learn to love him again as deeply as he had loved her all these years past.

Right now, though, he needed to concentrate on the reason she had brought him here. When he dared to imagine she would give herself to him, his heart leaped in his chest. Molly had always been his woman and he needed her now more than ever.

Nevertheless, this adventure was making him highly nervous, even though they were nearing the far end of the great barn. 'Molly, I don't like being in here. What if somebody finds us?'

'They won't. Once the hay is stacked and safe, hardly anybody ever comes in here, except young Harry when he brings the hay bags from the stables to fill up.' She paused to kiss Tom full on the mouth. 'Besides, even if someone did come in, they would never see us back here. It's so cosy and warm you'll never want to leave.' She fell into a pile of hay from a broken bale and pulled him down beside her.

'Molly Tanner, I must be crazy getting mixed up with you again. You're a bad devil; always was, always will be.' Softly chuckling, he wrapped his arms about her. 'Nobody else but you could have persuaded me in here at this time of night and, like a fool, I let you bully me. Why is it you've always been able to wrap me round your little finger?' he groaned.

'Ah, that's because you love me . . . more than you could ever love any other woman. Isn't that the truth? And you will never stop loving me . . . will you?'

He realised that her every word was true. 'You must be a witch,' he whispered hoarsely. 'So many times over the years I've tried to build a relationship with other women, but it has never worked out because when I look at them, it's you I want. It's like you've woven some kind of a spell over me.'

Her answer was to laugh in his face. 'You'll never have me,' she said quietly. 'No man will ever have all of me . . . not even my husband.'

For a fleeting moment, he was afraid. Afraid of his own feelings. Afraid that she might hurt him in so many ways. And yet he wanted her like he had never wanted anything in his entire life.

'You're a crazy woman,' he whispered, 'and I must be crazy too, because you're right. I will always love you, Molly. I know I shouldn't. I know you're bad for me, and yet I can't stop wanting you. All these years since you left me for John Tanner, I've thought about you every day. I've tried so hard to forget you. I've had many other women after you, but they were fleeting relationships. None of them could ever hold a candle to you.'

'Really?' She was deeply flattered. 'Hmm, I never realised you still loved me that much.'

'If I had any sense I would get you out of my life for good and all, and never think of you ever again,' he mumbled, 'because, much as I love you, I know how cruel you can be, but it seems I can't help myself.'

Now that he felt safe from prying eyes, he began to relax. 'Come here, my beauty.' Playfully wrapping his arms about her, he drew her close to him and, to his great delight, she made no protest this time.

'We'll be safe enough here,' Molly again assured him. 'We can misbehave and enjoy ourselves for as long as we want, and no one will ever know.' She stroked her fingers down his face, her soft voice calming his fears. 'Trust me, we'll be warm and cosy here. So . . . do you want to have your wicked way with me . . . or would you rather I show you the way out now?'

'Molly, stop teasing me.' The widening smile on his face showed his expectations. 'It had better be worth the effort,' he laughed.

'Oh, it will be.' They snuggled into the hay.

'You were right!' Giggling like a child, Tom gathered her to him. 'It's warm as toast in here.'

'Come on then, let's not waste precious time!' Having helped him to take off his jacket, she threw it aside. Then, sliding her fingers under the buckle of his trouser belt, she teasingly undid it.

A moment or so later, she hurriedly tore off her outer clothes and was driving him to distraction with her wicked teasing.

Greedily drawing her into his arms again, Tom was happier than he had been at any time since their last such encounter.

Molly, too, was enjoying herself. This was fun, no strings attached – no jealous husband, no unwanted brat to see to. It took her back to a time before she had ever met John Tanner.

~

'They should have been home by now.' With her father gone for so long, Rosie felt the need to defy his instructions and look out the window, from where she hoped to see his familiar figure walking towards the house. So far, though, there was no sign of either of her parents.

As always, the faithful black Labrador remained by

her side, his great squashy paws planted firmly on the windowsill and his bright, watchful eyes carefully scanning the night.

With one arm wrapped around Barney's thick neck, and the other arm bent across the sill, Rosie focused on the only direct path to the farmhouse.

'Daddy said he wouldn't be long, so why isn't he here?' With no one else to confide in, she directed her reasoning to the dog. 'He must have found Mother by now . . . unless she doesn't want to be found.' She felt a surge of rebellion. 'I've a good mind to go out and look for them, but Daddy would be cross if I did. You would look after me, though, wouldn't you, Barney?'

Fondly draping her two arms about his broad neck, she ruffled his thick, shiny coat. 'I don't want to disobey Daddy by leaving the house, but he's been gone such a long time, and I'm really worried. What if something's happened to them, Barney?'

Tears were not far away as Rosie became increasingly convinced that this must be so. 'I know Mother can be horrible, but Daddy does love her. That's why I have to try and love her, too, because that would make him so happy.'

Sensing her distress, the old dog pushed his bullish head into her lap, as though to pacify her.

'Oh, Barney . . .' Wrapping her arms about him, Rosie felt ashamed that she found it so hard to love her own mother. 'I don't mean to dislike her,' she confided, 'but she doesn't love me, and I don't know what to do.'

When she wiped away a solitary tear, Barney shifted closer to her and, licking the back of her hand, he let her know that he loved her, even if her mother didn't.

For the next half-hour, the two of them kept their vigil at the window.

Suddenly Rosie leaped up with excitement. 'Look there, Barney!' Pulling the excited dog closer to the window, she pointed to the path some distance away. 'Just then . . . did you see?' She pointed to the shadowy figure who, just for a split second, had passed beneath the flickering lamp attached to the corner of the tractor store. 'I think it was Daddy, but I'm not really sure.'

She began jumping up and down with relief, causing the dog to do the same, though when he began barking she ordered him to be quiet. 'Stop that! Daddy said I was not to look out the window, and I promised I wouldn't. Don't let him see us, Barney.' She gave the dog a hefty shove aside. 'Get away, Barney.' Grabbing his collar, she forced him back. 'Quickly, get back from the window. He'll be here in a minute.'

~

Unaware that Rosie and the dog had caught sight of him, John Tanner continued on his way along the narrowing pathway.

Disturbed by a soft rushing sound, he paused in his stride. *What the devil was that?* Raising his head, he looked across the hedge and over the darkened fields, but all was quiet.

He waited a moment in silence before moving on.

He had not gone far when he heard the sound again, closer this time. Concerned to get back to Rosie as soon as possible, he again quickened his pace.

Smiling, he wondered whether, despite the season, the sounds he had heard were of young lovers in the long grass.

With warmth and great affection, he recalled how over the years, he and Molly had made love in these very fields. They were good memories, which would remain in his heart for ever.

As he pushed along the darkened path, his thoughts refocused on his beloved daughter. He hoped Rosie had done as she was told and stayed inside with the doors locked. He quickly swept past the farrier's shed and along by the outer row of stables, but a moment later the peculiar sounds brought him to a halt yet again. He stood perfectly still, concentrating on the noises. They seemed to be coming from the direction of the far yard. These were not quite the same as the previous noises; they were lower . . . like a weird, smothered kind of grunting; much like an injured animal caught in a trap. Poachers! His anger rose immediately at the idea. I'll bet those damned poachers have been setting traps again, he thought. If there was one thing he hated with a passion it was the barbaric traps that caused animals to die in excrutiating pain.

He remained still, concentrating on the strange sounds, low and broken. After a minute he wondered if the sounds were in fact nothing more than wild creatures searching in the undergrowth for food. Or maybe prowling for a mate.

He listened intently again until he thought he had finally pinpointed where the sounds were coming from. Treading carefully, he made his way towards the far yard.

He had taken just a few steps when the muffled sounds faded into the night, leaving an eerie silence.

He was not certain what to do. Should he pursue the possibility of catching the poachers in the act of grabbing what was his, or should he make his way home to his daughter and hope Molly was there with her? Or, being just a stone's throw away from the yard, should he take a few minutes to investigate these other noises?

The matter was instantly decided. If I don't check it out, and in the morning I find some poor creature having met a terrible end when I might have saved it, I would never forgive myself, he thought.

With all his senses on alert, he continued forward, listening for every slight movement in the hedgerows.

As he wound his way through the maze of farm buildings, he was alerted by a volley of what sounded like laughter, and not too far away. There it was again, clearer this time . . . and closer. Then the sound died away, and all was silent again.

John waited for a moment, and then he heard it again: broken noises, like muffled laughter. With anger rising with his suspicions, he stayed very still, listening intently.

There was no doubt in his mind that this was the same gang of thieves and vagabonds who had stolen from him before. A few weeks back, he'd chased away some young ruffians he'd found in his yard, larking about near the horses. A week or so before that, he'd been robbed of a number of good leather saddles, stolen one night from a locked barn, but if they were hoping to raid his barns tonight and snatch more valuable tack, they might find they'd bitten off more than they could chew.

Cursing quietly, he turned and went at a run back along the pathway towards the big yard, where he cautioned himself to be careful. It has to be them, he thought. They got away with it once, and now they mean to try their hand again.

Going softly into the yard, he kept close to the buildings, quietly checking as he went, determined to catch the thieves red-handed. This time, he was ready for them. Pausing to listen and look, he could neither see nor hear anything untoward, although his every instinct told him they must be there.

Next, he cut a way through to the smaller stable yard, where he quickly checked on every stable and every horse, but he found nothing to concern him. He pushed on, as silently as possible, checking one building after another, determined to catch the perpetrators of the recent theft.

Had he known that Rosie was planning to leave the house to look for him, he would instantly have abandoned his search and returned to her.

~

'I'm almost sure that was Daddy I saw just now,' Rosie confided in the patient dog, 'but what if it wasn't him? What if it was the bad men who took all the saddles during the summer?' Her father had had to spend his much-needed savings on some second-hand replacements.

Her voice broke into a sob. 'I don't want to go out there, Barney, because Daddy said not to, and it's dark . . . I don't like the dark.' She would never admit that particular fear to her father, but she could tell Barney, being safe in the knowledge that he would not betray her trust. 'Oh, Barney, where is he? I'm sure something bad must have happened.'

Having kept her tears back for so long, she wrapped her arms around her beloved friend and unashamedly cried on his shoulder.

Soon gathering herself, her courage strengthened by the presence of the large dog, she was up and running to the bedroom door. 'Come on, Barney! Let's go and find him!'

As though sensing the enormity of what she was about to do, Barney stubbornly sat on his haunches: he was going nowhere and neither was she. When Rosie ran back to pull him up he sat firm, with a look in his eye that warned her he would not be moved.

'All right then, I'll go without you.'

Hoping he would change his mind once she had her coat on, Rosie ran down to the hallway where she collected her long mac from the peg, and quickly slipped it on, but Barney had moved only as far as the top of the stairs, where he sat still with a look of contempt on his weathered old face.

'I'm going, Barney.' Rosie was determined. 'You can stay here if you want, but I have to go . . . I mean it, Barney. I'm going outside to look for him, whether you come with me or not.' Reluctant to leave him here, she collected his lead and stood by the door, teasingly dangling it in the air. When it seemed he was as determined to stay as she was to go, Rosie pretended to leave. But the minute she dropped the lead, Barney ran downstairs and sat upright before her, one paw scraping the lead towards him, while he looked up at her with a sorry face.

Rosie was greatly relieved. 'Oh, thank you, Barney.' She wrapped her arms about his warm silky back and hugged him to her. 'I knew you wouldn't let me go all on my own.'

She quickly attached the lead to the leather collar about his fat neck, then gave him another swift hug while she whispered in his ear, 'Thank you for coming with me. I pretend to be brave, but I would have been frightened all on my own. Just remember, Barney, when we get outside we must be very careful because we don't really know who's hiding out there.'

A moment or so later, they were both suitably dressed for the outdoors.

'Come on, Barney, we need a torch!' Rosie made a search for the long torch, which she recalled was kept somewhere here.

'I'm not sure where it is exactly,' she admitted to her dog, who was sniffing in every corner, 'but I know Daddy keeps a spare one, and it's in here somewhere.'

Eventually she found it tucked away in the shoe cupboard by the door. She was pleased to find a short, sturdy walking stick in the umbrella stand, too. It had a fat, knobby handle and was light to carry.

'Here, Barney, you can look after that.' She gave the stick to her accomplice for safekeeping.

Wagging his tail as though he had been given charge of something very special, he grasped it firmly between his teeth, making it look like his face was suspended in a weird kind of smile.

'Don't lose it, Barney,' Rosie urged. 'It might come in handy if we meet the bad men,' though the idea of that happening made her shiver.

With torch in hand, and ready for anything, the two of them left the house. Rosie locked the front door behind her, trying it twice to make sure it was locked. Satisfied, she then slipped the key into her coat pocket.

Nervous of the dark, and ashamed of defying her father's instructions, Rosie set out along the path and into the night, her loyal friend Barney ever close by her side, the short, stout walking stick clutched tight in his mouth and his dark, silky ears pricked to every little sound.

'Remember, Barney, don't you dare start barking at the slightest thing. If there are bad men we don't want them to know we're here. We just need to find Daddy as quickly as we can.'

Nervously, Rosie continued forward, focusing the torchlight directly onto the path before them, which she hoped would be discreet enough not to draw the attention of any intruder who might be in the vicinity.

∼

Close by, John continued to follow both the diminishing sounds and his own sharp instinct. He was being extra cautious, knowing that if he was spotted before he could learn the lie of the land he could be in deep trouble.

Earlier, it was muffled laughter that led him to the hay barn, but now the laughter had ceased. However, he had to check if anyone was still in there. The door was unlocked and the light was on so he feared they might be lying in wait to jump him. He crept forward, being extra careful as he silently tiptoed between the bales. As he reached the middle of the barn he could hear low murmurings. The thieves were clearly towards the far end. He readied himself for the confrontation. He had no way of knowing how many of them might be lurking back there. Obviously there were at least two, but there might be more, and the possibility of locking horns with a brutish gang of thieves made him question his position for a second time.

However many of them he would have to face, it was not in his character to cut and run. If he had a choice, he would rather not have a fight on his hands, but if it was a fight they wanted, then it was a fight they would get.

In truth, all he wanted was to send them packing; to let them know that he and his property were not such an easy target as they might previously have thought.

This time he was just a few steps away from confronting them, he had the element of surprise, and he had a sturdy spade, which he'd picked up by the barn door, in his fist. His anger made him strong, and right now he was ready for them.

Bracing himself, he crept forward until he was so near to their hiding place he hardly dared breathe.

Taking a deep, calming breath, he realised the very real danger to himself. And what of Rosie, alone in the house except for Barney?

John saw now that he might be putting himself into a situation that could end badly, yet he had no choice but to confront the intruders.

When, distracted by his thoughts, he suddenly missed his footing, he stood still, listening intently for a moment, to be sure they had not heard him.

Satisfied, he continued to focus on the soft, whispering voices and the occasional rustling of hay. He needed to pinpoint their whereabouts exactly so he could take the advantage of surprise.

It enraged him to think that thieves were actually here in his barn, furtively plotting to rob him of what had been earned through his own hard work over the years.

Apart from his father's generous gift of the farm, nothing had ever been handed to him on a plate.

The daily grind and worries of running a good farm demanded blood, sweat and tears, and he was not about to stand by while a bunch of thieving rogues helped themselves to what was his.

At the same time doubts ran amok in his mind. Was he foolish to think he could round up these thieves all by himself? Maybe he should have called Paddy, his brother-in-law. He was a good man and he would have helped, but John had not asked because the anger in him had taken away his common sense. So now he was alone and vulnerable, and possibly about to get the worst beating of his life.

His fear was palpable but he pressed on regardless, slowly, on tiptoe, with the spade at his side, and his heart beating so fast he feared it might leap out of his chest. He desperately hoped the element of surprise might just give him the edge.

He thought it strange that, in this moment of huge anxiety, he could remember every plank of wood that made up the floor beneath his feet. He recalled his tired limbs as, many moons ago, he had worked day and night to get the barn finished and the crops in before rain came.

So many seemingly irrelevant details tore through his troubled mind. Building this barn had been a mammoth task. Although he had help from neighbouring farmers, there was no let-up for any of them. With the summer ending, and the changeable autumn weather fast closing in, they'd had to get the roof on without delay.

He recalled the excruciating pain in his limbs as he drove the long, thick nails into every plank, post and joist. And how could he forget the crippling weariness when carrying the timbers across his shoulders, day after day, and into the night, until he could hardly stand up? But when the barn was finished the pride he felt was worth every bead of sweat, and every wrenched muscle in his body. He and his good neighbours celebrated the completion of Tanner's Barn together. The buzz of excitement at the sight of that monstrous barn standing proud was like nothing he had ever experienced . . .

Just now, his heart was filled with pride in this strong, handsome building; which was now being invaded by those who did not give a tinker's cuss if they ruined him.

Suddenly his meandering thoughts were brought back sharply to the present by the rustling of hay and whispered voices. Grim-faced and determined, he tightened his fist on the spade.

~

'Ssh, Tom.' Putting up a warning hand, Molly rolled away from her man. 'Listen.'

Bemused, Tom was about to reply when she pressed the flat of her hand over his mouth.

'Be quiet!' she hissed.

Suspecting she might be playing games, he pushed her hand away and smiled. 'Bad girl!' He was about to draw her on top of his nakedness when she clambered away to reach for her clothes.

'Get dressed,' she whispered. 'Hurry up.'

When Tom saw the scared look on her face, and the way she panicked when grabbing up her clothes, he realised she was not playing games. He, too, listened and he could hear the soft crunch of footsteps as they trod over the carpet of strewn hay.

Anxiously grabbing his trousers, he managed to wriggle into them without making too much noise, while Molly hastily pulled her dress on over her head.

With both of them at least half decent, they pressed deep into the hay, remaining silent and as still as possible while the footsteps closed in on them. They fervently hoped the intruder would pass by without ever knowing they were even there.

Moments passed in which they heard the shuffle of footsteps heading towards where they lay huddled together and holding their breath. Making no move, they kept their nerve. A moment later they were much relieved when it seemed the footsteps had changed direction and were receding.

Molly and Tom remained very still until they were satisfied that the intruder had truly gone away. Molly was glad of Tom's strong arms about her, though his voice trembled as he whispered, 'It's all right, Molly. I think they've gone.'

'Whew. Thank goodness.' Hugely relieved, and totally believing they were out of danger, Molly softly scrambled to the edge of one of the surrounding hay bales to peep over, congratulating herself that she and her lover had managed to avoid being discovered. Nothing, however, could have prepared her for the shock of finding herself staring into her husband's face, his horrified gaze shifting from her to the half-naked stranger lying at her feet.

Before John could even open his mouth, Molly went wild, screaming at the top of her voice and cursing him to hell and back, in a curious and desperate attempt to take the moral high ground. 'You beast! What right have you to follow me? What the hell d'you think you're doing sneaking up on me like a thief in the night?'

Her blind rage overwhelmed her guilt and shame as she continued to tear into him with a vicious volley of foul language and sanctimonious nonsense.

Not daring to move, Tom lay trembling with fear, desperate to avoid the fray and undecided whether it would be better to run or stay and take his punishment.

The decision was made for him when Molly began kicking and lashing out as John took her by the arms and held her against the hay bales.

'What the hell is your game, Molly? I came looking for you, because I was worried. Rosie is, too. We thought you might be in trouble, and here you are, lying in the hay . . . with some man.' His voice shook with disgust. 'What's wrong with you, Molly? I thought you were better than this. So come on, I'm listening. Who the hell is he, and how long has this been going on behind my back, eh? You had better explain yourself . . . if you can!'

He glared down on Tom, who had quickly finished dressing and was now sitting on the edge of a bale, rocking back and forth, his head buried in his hands, and softly muttering to himself.

Bold as ever, Molly now tried to brazen it out. 'My man here is Tom Stevens.' She saw the look of recognition on John's face. 'Yes, that's right, Tom Stevens, my old boyfriend.'

Lowering her voice to a whisper, she smiled up at

him in what she hoped was a winning way. 'We met up tonight, and I suddenly remembered the fun we used to have together and I just couldn't help myself . . . I never meant any harm. It was supposed to be just a bit of a laugh. What with my job and helping in the farm, I have such a rotten time – and you're always working. You never have time for me – and I sometimes wonder if you even love me at all.' She now became all tears. 'Maybe you'd like me to go. Well, maybe I should go, then you won't need to follow me around, spying on me!'

Shocked by the implication that this was somehow his fault, and still reeling from what he had seen and heard, John reached out, grabbed her by the wrists and drew her to him.

'Don't talk like that, Molly. We can get past this. I love you too much to lose you. Please, Molly! Let's go home and talk things through, like civilised human beings.'

'Don't touch me,' Molly wailed. 'You don't love me at all. You creep around spying on me and . . . and now you're hurting me. Let go of me. Let go!'

Working herself into a frenzy, she began hitting out with both fists as he desperately tried to restrain her. But then she seemed to go crazy, screaming and yelling for Tom to help her, and the more

John tried to quieten her, the louder she yelled. 'Help me, Tom! He's hurting me . . . Tom, please! Help me . . . get him off!' She knew from the past that Tom was never a fighting man. The idea of having two men coming to blows over her was truly exciting. She didn't care who got hurt, as long as it wasn't her. And besides, she thought herself to be worth fighting over.

While putting on the show of her life, she threw herself at John, and started squealing as though she was being hurt. 'Tom . . . for pity's sake . . . help me! He means to kill me! If you love me, get him off me . . . help me!'

John, however, was taken by surprise at her wild, confusing behaviour. Unable to calm her, he held her all the tighter, while assuring her that he just wanted answers, and he was willing to take her back to the farmhouse and quietly talk things through, but this only made her scream and shout all the more.

Fully convinced of Molly's terror at the hands of her angry husband, soft-hearted, simple Tom decided that unless he came to her aid he would surely lose her for ever. With no thought for his own safety, he launched himself at John and brought him down with an unexpected heavy punch to the chin.

Congratulating herself on the devious trick that
turned her kind-natured lover into a raging bull,
Molly made her escape to the far side of the space
from where she watched the two men locked together
in a brutal fight. Tom, foolishly believing Molly's
cunning lies, tore into John, who was left with no
choice but to defend himself with every ounce of
strength he had.

From her safe place, she continued to watch, her
mind racing ahead. Suddenly she realised this was
the perfect opportunity to inherit the farm and everything in it. Why wait any longer, when tonight could
be the beginning of her new life?

Quickly she glanced about before darting across
to collect the heavy-headed spade from where John
had dropped it.

As she made her way back, she was startled to see
Tom sent staggering backwards when John landed
him a crunching blow to the face. He slumped to the
ground, where he lay for a moment, unnervingly still.

Momentarily unsure what to do, Molly remained
in the shadows, greatly relieved when Tom scrambled
up, roaring, to make a beeline for John, who gave
as good as he got.

Molly crept forward, still keeping in the shadows
and waiting for her moment.

The two men, back on their feet, were fighting with everything they had. John continued to get the better of Tom, who was soon pinned against the wall, exhausted and with nowhere to go. Somehow, because of his blind love for Molly, he found new strength to take up the fight again, though he was coming off the worst for it.

Molly decided it was now or never. Clutching the spade, she made her way towards the two men, who were so heavily engaged in their bitter fight, neither of them realised what she was about to do.

~

Not too far away, young Rosie was continuing to search for her father. All around her she could hear the confusing cries and shuffling of night creatures. It made her nervous, but she had Barney, and that gave her a sense of security.

Suddenly, in amongst the chorus of foraging creatures, she heard what sounded like a human voice, high-pitched and excited. Alarmed, she stood still and listened, but there was only silence except for the occasional rustling in the long grass edging the paddock. When suddenly something darted out of the grass and across her path, her fears increased tenfold.

'D'you think we should turn back, Barney?' She felt so alone, despite the presence of the Labrador, and was constantly wary of the hidden creatures who might be watching her even now. 'What d'you think, Barney, eh?' She wrapped her arms about his thick, silky coat. 'I don't like it here. I want to go home. Maybe we'll find my parents are there by now.'

Barney looked her in the eye as though trying to convince her that he would look after her and she must not be afraid.

'Ssh! Did you hear that, Barney?' She tightened her hold on him. 'Just now . . . it sounded like a person calling out. D'you think it was Daddy? Or maybe it was *her*.' Made nervous by the noises all around her, she could not be sure of anything any more and could no longer trust her own instincts. The only thing that made her feel safe was having Barney with her.

Sniffing about on the ground, the faithful dog seemed anxious for her to move on. 'Good boy, Barney.' Going forward, she lovingly patted his neck, and with Rosie holding tight to his lead the two of them inched forward through the undergrowth around the paddock. Suddenly Rosie came to a halt. 'Be still, Barney!' She glanced about, unsure which direction they should take.

Barney was sniffing the ground again.

'Can you find their scent, Barney?' Rosie grew excited. 'Do you know which way they went?'

With his nose to the ground, Barney cautiously led the way, with Rosie tight on his heels. When suddenly he set off at a run, Rosie had to move as fast as she could to keep up. She wanted to call him back, but was afraid to speak loudly in case someone might be lurking nearby. Trusting in Barney, she kept close, while he stopped occasionally to sniff the air and listen before taking off again.

After a few minutes Barney slowed his pace as he came to the yard and sniffed the ground excitedly, which told Rosie he was alerted to something, or someone. 'Careful, boy . . . go softly now.'

Like two thieves in the night, they went swiftly across the open yard and on, towards the larger outer buildings.

'Hurry, Barney . . . quick. Down here!'

The soft glimmer of moonlight lit their way as they left the yard behind and followed the well-trodden path to the big barn, now just a few steps away.

'Wait for me, Barney,' Rosie told the Labrador in a whisper. 'Come here, boy . . . stay by me!' And the wise old fella did exactly that.

The path led to a shadowy yard by the hay barn. Fearful, Rosie paused a moment, indicating for

Barney to keep silent. Padding over to her, he stood vigilant by her side, his long snout pointing in the direction of the big barn, and the short hairs on his back bristling in anticipation.

Just then, Rosie heard a series of noises, dragging sounds as though someone or something were being shifted about. Someone was inside the hay barn.

'Ssh! Stay back, Barney.'

Instead of obeying her, the dog stretched himself to his full height with his head down and ears pinched forward. Pausing only to ensure that Rosie was safe, he inched forward, making a soft, rattling noise in the back of his throat, which Rosie recognised as a low warning growl.

'No, Barney . . .' Drawing him back, Rosie leaned down to tell him softly, 'Be still! We don't know who's in there. We don't know if they mean to hurt us. We need to be careful . . . they must not see us.'

When she put her finger to her lips in a warning gesture the dog appeared to understand and he obeyed, albeit reluctantly.

~

Inside the barn, Molly waited for her moment. When it came she tightened her grip on the spade and stole closer to her unsuspecting husband, who now had Tom, buckled in a state of exhaustion, pinned by the scruff of the neck. Molly realised with horror that her husband had the upper hand and, his other fist drawn back, he was ready to land the defining punch that would end the bloody fight.

She could not have been more wrong. In truth, the normally placid John Tanner was sickened by the brutality between himself and this ordinary man, who had not only fought valiantly, but had taken a heavy beating with a brave heart.

Now, as he pinned Tom Stevens against the wall with one strong arm, John realised that there was nothing to be gained from battering the hell out of him so, holding the other man at bay, he wearily suggested that the two of them should stop the fighting and talk about the situation in a calm and proper way.

Although she could not make out every word, Molly was horrified to see the two men talking in what appeared to be a civilised manner. She had a choice: to make her move now, or to abandon it altogether. She decided that she was too near her goal to back out. Her mind was made up. The deed was well within her grasp. The sooner she could finish it between them, the better.

She ran forward, the spade held upright, and a murderous look in her eyes.

Tom glanced up and saw with horror what she was about to do. 'No, Molly!' he yelled, but it seemed she didn't hear him, or didn't want to.

Tom darted forward with the intention of pushing John out of the way, but it was too late. Raising the spade as hard and as high as possible, she smashed the back of the spade-head down across John's head; the sickening sound of metal against flesh told its own story.

John sank to the floor, his lifeblood oozing from the huge, jagged wound at the base of his skull.

For what seemed an age, the silence was palpable – nothing moved, no one spoke – but when the blood-spattered spade fell to the floor, it was as if all hell was let loose.

'God Almighty, Molly . . . what have you done?' Tom ran forward, his shirt splattered with blood and his eyes big and round with disbelief as he stared at the man on the ground.

Molly caught her breath. 'Get away from him!' Her voice shook with fear.

'Oh, Molly . . . Molly . . . dear Lord . . . what have you done?' Clasping his hands together above his head, Tom began rocking back and forth, back and forth, making deep moans as though suffering unbearable pain. 'What have you done, Molly?' he asked her over and over. 'What have you done?' His hands shook uncontrollably as he bent on one knee to check the other man, who had made not the slightest move since taking the full brunt of that devastating blow.

With big, shocked eyes, Tom looked up at Molly, who was also trembling violently. 'I think he's dead, Molly.' His voice was almost inaudible, as though he was unable to speak because of the horror he felt at Molly's shocking deed.

Molly remained silent, staring down on John's lifeless body.

'You killed him, Molly!' Tom's voice rose in panic. His wide eyes remained fixed on the other man, lying so still and bloodied, his broken face splattered with his blood, and his eyes wide open to the ceiling. Over and over he accused her, as though he needed to say it out loud in order to believe the horror of it. 'May God forgive you, Molly. Look at your husband! Look what you've done . . .' He began to pace back and forth, faster and faster, as though demented, shaking his head from side to side and moaning, 'What shall we do, Molly . . . whatever shall we do?'

Molly was surprised at his reaction. She had truly

believed that this man who had cuckolded her husband without any sign of regret might understand why she did this, yet one minute he was on his knees moaning, the next he was pacing the floor like someone crazy, whining and accusing.

'You killed him, Molly . . . your own husband . . . How could you do such a terrible thing?'

'Stop it!' Clenching her fists, she rained punches on his chest. 'I did it for you! I saved your life and now you're blaming me,' she screamed. 'If that's all the thanks I get, I should have let him kill you . . . I should have let him tear you to pieces!' After all this time, she was seeing him for what he truly was – a wimp. A nobody, a little man without backbone.

His reaction forced her to consider the enormity of what she had done. Because of this timid man, she had committed murder, without hesitation and without conscience. She now grew fearful for herself. She had believed Tom would be on her side, but now she knew different. She also realised that the implications for her were devastating.

She had thought he would help to cover her tracks, but she was beginning to realise she might have to face the consequences of her action alone. It had become obvious that Tom would not help her. No, she was alone in this; alone to pay the harsh penalty for what had happened here tonight. The very thought of being locked away in prison made her sick to the stomach.

Deeply agitated, her mind running crazy, Molly began pacing up and down, making plans, looking for a way out. But the plain truth was staring her in the face. *She* had killed her husband. *She* was the one who had swung the spade across his head . . . to stop him . . . to try to save Tom, a weasel of a man. Yes, that was why she had done it – because of him, this man who was now willing to see her locked away.

The germ of a plan lit up her mind. Of course! Tom loved her; more than that, he was besotted with her. And now she must do whatever it took to save her own hide, and to hell with the cowardly man who had got her into this awful situation.

The more she thought about it, the more she actually began to believe herself innocent. It was his fault. Yes, his fault . . . not hers.

Suddenly she knew what she must do, and to that end she crumpled to the floor beside the good man she had killed only minutes before, sobbing as though her heart would break.

'I'm sorry, John, but I was so afraid you meant to kill Tom. But I swear, I never meant it to end like this.'

Forcing out the tears, she pleaded to her lover, 'I swear to you, Tom, I never meant for this to happen, but he was hurting you. I knew he meant to kill you, and I couldn't let that happen. I panicked. He meant to kill you, I know he did.'

She paused to wipe the tears from her face. 'How could I stand by and see him kill you? I had to stop him. I'm sure you would have done the same if he was hurting me. Oh, darling Tom, we've only just found each other again. And already I'm certain I want to spend the rest of my life with you. But I never wanted to be rid of him this way. You have to believe me, Tom. I wanted to stop him hurting you, but I never meant to kill him.'

Having done her best to convince him, she looked up at Tom with a sorry face. 'Please, Tom, don't let them lock me away in prison. I would never survive. I would have to find a way to kill myself. Please help me, Tom. Please!'

As she had anticipated, his kindly heart melted at her seemingly genuine fear of imprisonment. Reaching out, he drew her into his arms, telling her softly, 'You were only trying to help me. I do know that, and I truly believe you never meant this terrible thing to happen.'

He looked down at the other man's empty body,

his tortured mind racing with guilty thoughts. How could he allow Molly to be locked up when he was the guilty party in all of this? He had always loved Molly, with her irresistible curvy beauty, and when he saw her heading for the pub he was determined not to let her go a second time, even though she was now married to the man for whom she had left him.

With his sorry gaze fixed on the lifeless body of John Tanner, Tom blamed himself completely. This was a shocking situation, but having found Molly again, and knowing that she still loved him after all these years apart, he knew he must do all he could to keep her safe . . . to keep her free.

His mind was made up. 'I'll tell the authorities what happened,' he promised staunchly. 'I'll tell them how John was about to kill me, and that you only meant to warn him off. When I tell them how you saved my life, they're certain to be lenient on you. Just a few years away and then it will be over and we'll be together. I won't desert you, Molly, I promise.'

'No!' Molly reeled back in horror. 'If they put me away, I swear I'll kill myself! Without you by my side, my life would be over anyway. I want us to have a life together, and if I can't be with you, I don't want to live. I won't be locked away, Tom. I won't!'

'No, Molly, don't talk like that. You saved my life. I'll tell the police that this would never have happened if I hadn't deliberately seduced you this evening. In truth, what happened here is as much my fault as yours.'

Molly turned on the tears. 'Oh, Tom, after we made love and I realised how much I've missed you I decided to leave John and make a life with you. But now it can never happen. After I confess to the police, they're sure to lock me away, and I'll never see you again. I could never allow you to visit me because it would break my heart to watch you walk away and leave me there.'

Her false words had the desired effect on him. Placing his hands on her shoulders, he held her away from him and looked into her tearful eyes. 'Listen to me, Molly. Someone has to pay for what happened here tonight, but I promise you, hand on heart, I will not let you take full responsibility. Think about it, Molly! If I had not made a play for you this terrible thing would never have happened.'

Wrapping her tightly in his arms, he told her softly, 'I won't let you take the blame for this, Molly. If they locked you away and I lost you for ever, my life would be unbearably empty.'

Suddenly he had an idea. 'I'll tell the police that

it was an accident . . . a shocking accident. You saw him go for me and I could not stand up to him. He truly meant to kill me. You realised that, and you panicked. It was all because of me.'

Secretly delighted, Molly remained silent.

'If anyone is made to answer for what happened it has to be me, not you, Molly. And besides, you have responsibilities. You will need to keep the farm going. Your workers will be relying on you to sustain their livelihoods.'

'You're right, Tom. The farm is their livelihood, too, and they have families to take care of.'

'And you have a young child who will be shattered when she learns that her father is never coming home again,' Tom went on. 'Just think what it would do to her if you were put away for killing her daddy.' He shook his head. 'It doesn't bear thinking about.'

Picking up on his kind remarks, Molly set about making him feel even more responsible. 'Oh, Tom, you're so thoughtful. Young Rosie adores her daddy, and what has happened here will break her heart. She will be absolutely inconsolable. I can't even imagine how the poor child would cope if I was arrested and locked away in prison.'

'Oh, Molly, if I allowed that little girl to be even

more hurt because of me, I would never forgive myself.'

Taking a deep breath, he went on softly, 'Listen to me, Molly. We have to talk this through. We need to be sure of every small detail of our story. We should keep to the truth as far as possible . . . right up to the moment when he caught us in the hay together. That's when he went crazy and flew at me like a madman. Don't forget the pub landlady will have seen us leave together, and we were together when your husband found us, and that was what kicked off the fight.'

'But we needn't tell *everything*, surely?' Molly was not altogether convinced.

'Yes, Molly! Right up to the point where he was getting the better of me . . . and you believed he was about to kill me. But then we come to where he had me trapped against the wall. This is where we must change the details. Do you understand, Molly?'

'Yes, I think so.'

'Right, so now listen carefully. We don't have much time.' Tom went on softly: 'You were so afraid when you saw how he was using me like a punch-bag, and because I feared for my life, I somehow managed to reach out and grab the spade, which was leaning on the wall beside me. I swung it at him and caught him a heavy blow to the head. John went down and we were both shocked to find that, after I'd defended myself as best I could . . . he was lying on the ground and not moving. Do you understand what I'm telling you, Molly? It was me that hit him, not you. It was me who had the spade in my fist and it was me who used it to defend myself. Are you clear on that, Molly?'

'Yes.'

'Good. And whatever you do, you must remember that everything up to the point when he had me trapped in the corner must be told exactly as it happened. The truth of us being together must not be denied. Your husband found us half naked and lying together in the hay, shameful though it is. It's vital we convince the police that we are just two cheating people having a good time, who got caught up in something we never expected.'

He paused a moment. 'Remember, Molly, I was the one who grabbed the spade. It was me who hit him too hard and killed him, though it was never intended. Do you understand what I'm saying, Molly?'

'Yes.' Secretly thrilled, she could not have planned it better herself.

'Good, because if I am to take the responsibility off your shoulders we have to get our story absolutely straight. Can you do that, Molly? Can you stay calm and convince them that it was me who hit him with the spade, and not you?'

'Yes . . . I think so.' Smiling, she took hold of his hand. 'Thank you, Tom. I will never forget what you're doing for me.' She wanted to laugh out loud at how easily she had duped him, but she knew she had to appear sombre and vulnerable. Not once did she look down on her husband lying still and bloody on the ground: that good, hard-working man who had adored and cherished her, regardless of her many faults, some of which no other man would ever have forgiven.

'So . . . who should run to call the police – you or me?'

'I was coming to that.' Tom took a moment to think. 'We should call the ambulance first, as quickly as possible . . . tell them there's been a terrible fight. Your husband is unconscious and we can't seem to wake him.'

He was now beginning to panic. 'Hurry, Molly. Do it now! We've already lost too much time as it is.'

'What should I say?'

'I told you, just tell them there was a fight and your husband is badly hurt. Let them see that you're in shock, crying . . . hysterical, even. Can you do that, Molly?'

'I think so.' Ever the vulnerable innocent.

'Go on then . . . hurry.' Fighting his rising panic, he took a deep breath, then let it out in a rush of words. 'Tell them how we tried to wake him . . . to help him. That should explain how we lost precious time before calling them out. Go, Molly. Run as fast as you can.'

Molly was impressed. 'You're more capable than I realised,' she told him proudly. 'You seem to have thought of everything.'

Tom smiled wryly. 'To tell you the truth, I think I've surprised myself, but I honestly wish that none of this had ever happened. The only good thing is that it has brought us back together, and that's all I ever wanted.'

He held her face between his two hands and kissed her full on the mouth. 'Don't forget, my darling,' he whispered, 'it was me who killed him. It was never meant to end that way, and if this goes to court I have no option but to plead self-defence. You can back me up; tell them how violent John was . . . that he was tearing into me like a crazy man. You were shouting for him to stop. I was in fear for my life. You were sure he would kill me . . . and then somehow I found the strength to grab the spade and hit him across the head, but I never meant to kill him.'

Molly nodded. 'Don't worry, Tom. I'll tell them everything.'

'Good girl!' He held her close a moment longer. 'You go now, Molly. Call the ambulance. When the police are brought into it – as they surely will be – we must keep to the plan exactly as we've discussed.'

'Yes, Tom!' She played along. 'He had you trapped and he would have killed you, I'm sure of it!' She looked at his bruised and damaged face, and the trail of blood trickling from his nose and mouth. 'The police will only have to look at you to see how vicious he was.' Then she gave a heavy sigh. 'I don't like you taking the blame for me, though, Tom. I'm worried about what might happen to you.'

Tom drew her closer. 'Now you listen to me, Molly.' He looked her in the eye. 'Whichever way you look at it, what happened here tonight was truly my fault, and to be honest with you, I was so afraid he might finish me off that if I had been able to reach the spade when he was battering me into the ground, I would not have hesitated to grab it and knock him down.'

'But you didn't, did you?' She lowered her voice. 'I was the one who hit him with the spade, and I don't know that I should let you take the blame.'

Tom quietened her. 'This is not up for discussion, Molly. The decision is made, and we're not turning back now.'

'I really wanted us to be together tonight . . . and I had hoped it might be for ever. But if they do put you in prison, you must understand I can't visit, but I'll be there when they let you go. I'll be waiting at the gates, ready to take you home and start our new lives together, because I love you, Tom. I always have. I realise that now.'

'That's it! You tell them that he truly meant to kill me!'

'I will!' Molly pandered to his fears. 'I'll tell them that he had you at his mercy, and when you saw the spade, you had to grab your chance . . . I'll stand by you, Tom, and no matter what it costs I promise I will get you the best lawyer available.'

Turning her head, she stole a glance at her husband, so still and silent. It seemed wrong, that big, strong man lying lifeless on the cold floor, and for one fleeting moment she felt the slightest stab of regret. But then she reminded herself of how she would come out of this awful business with money in the bank, a thriving farm, and – with luck – her freedom. Of course, the girl still had be to dealt with, but she would address that problem when the time came.

'You need to call an ambulance, Molly!' Tom called out, interrupting her wicked thoughts. 'We've wasted enough time. Hurry!'

Tom was growing increasingly nervous about the enormity of the sacrifice he was making, but however difficult it may prove to be, he did not have the heart to let Molly down. Besides, it was only right that he should shoulder a measure of blame for this good man's lost life. John Tanner must have been devastated when he found his wife lying with another man, and worse, in a state of undress. But however hard it might be for Tom in prison, it would all be worth it to find Molly was waiting for him when he got out.

There was no doubt in Tom's mind that if Molly had not swung the spade at her husband, he himself would now be lying dead on the ground, instead of that unfortunate, innocent man. He thought now of how Molly had tried desperately to stop her husband's savage attack on him, but when her frantic calls fell on deaf ears, the spade was her last resort.

Molly had saved his life and there was no doubt in his own mind that he was doing the right and honourable thing in taking the blame upon himself, especially when he considered Molly's young daughter, and the many other domestic and business responsibilities that would now fall on Molly's shoulders.

Moreover, he was convinced that taking the blame was definitely the preferred alternative to being alone but free, while the woman he adored was locked away from him.

He anticipated suffering terrible loneliness without her by his side, although he realised that his difficulties were nothing compared to what Molly might suffer in prison. As a murderer she would stand out, and because of that, together with her fiery spirit, he could only imagine the conflict she might endure.

His wandering thoughts came back to reality with a rush when he realised she was still there, staring down at her husband, and appearing to smile.

'Molly! What are you doing? You need to call the ambulance now.'

'Yes, yes, I know, but it's just occurred to me, there will be my fingerprints on the spade handle. Clean them off while I'm gone, would you, love? Make a proper job of it, won't you? I mean, we can't be too careful, can we?' Knowing how besotted he was with her, she had every confidence that he would be most careful.

'Trust me, Molly. While I do my bit here, you must be quick as you can. Hurry now, love!'

'All right, all right, I'm going.'

Somewhat disgruntled at his panic, she lingered a

moment longer to stare down at the cold, motionless remains of John Tanner. And she felt nothing. In the depths of her wickedness, there was no pity. No love. Not even the slightest shred of regret. What little love she had once felt for him had long since disappeared. Uppermost in her mind was that his untimely death would actually mean a far better life for her. In all respects.

A moment later, she was on her way, stealing a backward glance at the gullible man who was laying his future on the line for her.

Molly's dark eyes glittered with a smile as she walked away, while reassuring herself: no one gets the better of Molly Tanner. She had always been able to wind men around her little finger. It gave her great pleasure to think that her weak-minded lover was at this very moment painstakingly wiping away any possible fingerprints of hers from the murder weapon.

Gleefully contemplating her own future, she felt a certain grudging gratitude to the good man who had been her devoted husband.

From boy to man, John had seen with his own eyes how hard and long his own father had toiled to improve what had been left to him by *his* dear father. With hard work, long hours and total dedication over these many years, John had built up what his father had inherited as a run-down farm and created a splendid and most valuable holding.

The once rough land was now highly productive. Covering some four hundred acres, most of it had been brought back from wilderness and was now such prime land that any commercial farmer would snap at the chance to own it.

Over the years a procession of determined neighbours had offered handsome money for the land and property, but always they were disappointed. John Tanner felt duty-bound to honour his father's wishes that the land and everything on it should be the inheritance of the next generation.

He made it known that he would never sell up, not at any price, even if the money offered meant that he would never have to work another day in his life, and eventually, all would-be buyers got the message.

Tanner's Farm had been handed down through many generations of Tanners, but only young John had had the bigger vision to make it into one of the most valuable and productive holdings in the region.

Through years of dedication and with little help, he had struggled hard to achieve his goal. He brought the rough, non-productive areas into pasture; he nurtured and culled the woodland to create sturdy new growth; and he used the felled trees to improve the layout and size of the farmhouse and buildings. He cleared the wider land of many years' wild growth.

He had dug out a channel and directed the precious natural spring with which his land was blessed into a cascade that flowed into the newly renovated lake, so fixing the irrigation of the pastures and the wide fields of corn that in summer made giant waves in the sunshine whenever gentle winds blew across the land.

John Tanner had considered that beautiful lake to be one of his greatest achievements. And, more importantly, he had regarded it as a fitting memorial to his beloved parents.

As with his father, the land and everything on it had been dearly loved by John, but his greatest love had been for the horses. He'd bred foals from his own peerless mares, and also brought in new young stock and nurtured them to maturity.

His young horses were tirelessly trained and he'd proudly rode or displayed them at the many shows and equestrian events hereabouts, where they won cups and ribbons of the highest recognition. John Tanner's reputation as a knowledgeable breeder and trainer of horses was second to none in the county.

When it was time for them to be sold on, he would deal only with buyers who wanted the animals for working the fields, for personal riding, or to breed from with the best bloodstock.

He would never sell to anyone who sought to obtain the horses for immediate resale into dangerous work, or for random and continuous breeding until a once-fine mare was worn down, eventually to be discarded.

John was also extra careful, after it had been made known to him, to avoid certain quarters in which young horses were dying in fear and agony when untrained men were castrating them rather than paying out for registered and responsible vets.

Anyone who had experience of horses and farming recognised John Tanner as a decent man with a proper respect for his animals. His naturally suspicious attitude where the animals were concerned meant that hard-nosed and unscrupulous dealers of ill repute knew to keep their distance, while those of his own kind respected and admired his straightforward sense of duty towards his stock, following his father's high standards and much-valued traditions.

~

As Molly Tanner walked away from the spent carcass that was her husband, she was made to recall just how dedicated a man he had been. She had witnessed his heavy toiling, often from first light to the setting of the sun. Day after day, winter or summer, he was out in all weathers. He worked tirelessly on the farmland, he improved the many pathways around the farm, and he would be forever tending the animals. He also maintained the farmhouse and numerous outbuildings, most of which he had inherited, with the exception of the great hay barn, which was a more recent addition.

The weight of responsibility for the farm was heavy on his shoulders, but rain, heat and wild storms never stopped him. If it was freezing, or wet, or blowing a gale, he would tackle some inside task, and when the fine weather came, he returned to outside work. He always managed to complete every job to the highest standards, and what he did not know how to do he soon learned to perfection.

Thinking on the past and the man she had married, Molly Tanner grudgingly admitted something to herself for the first time. In John Tanner she had caught a good and faithful man, whose lot in life was to toil and care for his family. He never shirked his responsibilities, which he executed with love and good heart, even when he was bowed down with work and worries.

To Molly's irritation her mind was haunted with images of that strong, determined man, who had emerged from his father's shadow to work from dawn to dusk caring and providing for his family, and tending to his many duties as best he could. And for what?

Even though she had no love for him, she had seen him as a man of stature, with opinions and dreams. Like any other human being he had laughed and cried, and unlike lesser men he had worked with a glad heart. Now that big, capable man was spent of life. A nothing. A no one . . . lying still and crumpled on the ground like an old sock thrown aside.

She was the one who had brought him to this sorry state. She alone had ended his life with a heavy blow to the back of his head, yet what she felt was not compassion or love or regret. It was nothing but contempt, and a pleasing sense of her own achievement.

In that defining moment when she had glanced down on him, without tenderness or conscience, she had found something to make her smile.

She smiled again now. John Tanner, the big, strong, capable man! It seems you're just as vulnerable as the rest of us, she thought. Whoever would have guessed that you would end up the loser, while I turned out to be the winner? And now that you've gone to your Maker I must consult the best lawyer I can find to make sure that everything of value will come me, and not to the next generation of Tanners.

Her smile crumpled into a dark frown. If you thought for one minute I would step aside and see your daughter snatch what is mine by rights, you don't know me, she thought.

She chuckled then at her good fortune. You were never smart enough for me, John Tanner! I knew what I was doing when I married you. I saw what you had, and I wanted it. And now I shall have it all . . . every last piece! Oh, yes, thanks to you and your hard work and dedication, Molly Tanner has just become a very wealthy woman.

She listed it all in her mind: the house and everything in it; the valuable farm machinery; the animals and land; money in the bank; every little item. The farmhouse itself was worth a small fortune, but that would be the last to go. She would need somewhere to live while being kept busy counting her many belongings, and keeping a check on just how rich she truly was.

Approaching the big doors, she addressed her dead

husband in her mind. As for you and your father's grand ideas of passing wealth onto the next generation, that's all finished now. Nothing and no one stands in my way – not your father's wishes, and especially not the girl. What was then yours, is now mine, John Tanner! D'you hear me?

Confident of claiming her husband's worldly goods, she felt ten feet tall. Clever girl, Molly, she told herself. You really are a far-sighted and devious woman. Moreover, with lover-boy covering your back you can't go wrong. Like putty in your hands, he is – the sad, deluded fool.

While she greedily relished her new-found wealth and well-fought freedom, not one single, warm thought entered her head with regard to the two men back there, one lying dead on the ground and the other, highly nervous and fearing for his liberty, but convinced of Molly's absolute dedication to him.

Molly was also thinking of what the two of them had agreed to say, but for all Tom Stevens' reassurances, she was slightly nervous, because while John Tanner was a man who would keep his word in any situation, she wasn't entirely sure what kind of man Tom Stevens really was.

When the time came, and he was facing a barrage

of questions, would he keep his word to her? Would he be strong enough to take the blame and the punishment for John Tanner's brutal death? Would he stay loyal to her and pay whatever penalty it might cost him? If his plea of self-defence was thrown out and he was charged with murder, the penalty would be unthinkable. Was he a man who could handle such pressure? Or would he break down and save himself at her expense?

The very thought of him buckling under the weight of the inevitable charges made her shiver. There would be dire consequences for her if, under the pressure of being questioned, he actually blurted out the shocking truth: that it was she who had deliberately killed John.

If that dreadful possibility did arise, though, she would fight him with everything she had. She would do her utmost to discredit him, to make him out to be a liar and a devious, manipulative man. She would tell the world just how bad a character he was, and how he used her to get rid of her husband. He knew she was happily married, but he was grimly determined to steal her away from that fine man John Tanner. She would plead that he was insistent and had tried every trick in the book to get her away from the man she had long loved.

If need be, she would go on to tell how he continuously pestered her, followed her until he wore her down, making her believe that she truly belonged to him. She felt trapped by his devious cunning and the awful pressure he put on her. He was like a demon! When he enticed her husband into the barn on some ruse she was afraid he meant to hurt John. She went after him, but she was too late.

Yes . . . that's how it all happened. That was what she would tell them if Tom refused to take the blame for John Tanner's terrible end.

If he did betray her, he would be the loser, because when her back was against the wall she knew how to play the game, and she would make him sorry.

She would tell of how, some years ago, she had left Tom Stevens to be with John Tanner. Because of that, Tom was jealous and angry, and over the years he had often threatened to kill John.

He was like a crazy thing: following her about at night; coaxing her . . . playing games and confusing her so much that she began to believe everything he said.

She would tell the authorities that he was not the quiet and simple man he appeared to be. Instead, he was manipulative, possessive and at times dangerous and threatening.

She vowed that if he should renege on their agreement she would try every dirty trick in the book to put him behind bars for so many years he would come out an old, old man.

But for now, she had to hope that he would keep his word and tell the story they had planned together.

CHAPTER THREE

HAVING CHECKED SOME barns and buildings without finding her father, Rosie, the faithful Barney beside her, had arrived at the doors of the big hay barn.

She was surprised to find the doors slightly open and the light on. She knew her father was careful to check the yards at the end of the day and to lock and secure all the buildings. Since the robbery he was especially conscientious about this.

Approaching the hay barn doors, Rosie went softly, keeping vigilant and hoping she was not about to come across anything untoward, especially strangers who might be there for no good purpose.

Increasingly nervous, she made no effort to go inside the barn, but positioned herself near the doors, where she might hear any noise from inside. After only a moment or two, she was alarmed to hear voices. As far as she could tell from the distant snatch of guarded conversation, there were just two of them: a man and a woman.

Afraid even to peep inside, she moved herself so that she might not be seen, but was better able to hear the voices and possibly what they were actually saying. But unfortunately, the voices were too soft and too far away from where she was, so she carefully shifted closer and listened harder.

Barney, with his stick, was by her side, ready and alert, but very still, as though waiting for Rosie's signal to go inside.

Silence fell, but after a few minutes, someone spoke and instantly, Rosie knew the voice belonged to the man.

There began a seemingly serious exchange of words, followed by a moment of silence before the woman spoke again . . . softly, almost purring, but not recognisable.

Then the voices fell silent again.

Unnerved, Rosie ushered Barney back into the relative safety of the shadows. 'Come away, boy. We don't know who they are or what they want. It might be best if we keep our distance, for now,' she whispered.

She thought she heard her father's name but she could not be certain. All she knew was that it was the same man's voice as before. The second, softer voice was altogether too quiet for her to hear anything in detail.

She wondered if the man's voice could have been her father's, but then she dismissed the idea. 'I thought for a moment that was Daddy talking just now, but it couldn't be, because why would he be saying his own name?' she whispered to Barney. 'No, I'm sure of it . . . that was not my father.' Though because the other man had mentioned her father's name, she could not altogether dismiss the idea that her father might be inside.

She crept away to the dark, shadowy side of the yard. Feeling a great deal safer in the shrubby undergrowth, she sat on the ground and drew Barney down beside her. 'D'you think it was Daddy in there?' she asked him. 'I think there were just the two of them. There was the man who said Daddy's name . . . and then there was the person with the quieter voice. I think that is a woman.'

So many wild and troubling thoughts raced through her head. What if they were the robbers that had stolen from them before? She wondered if she should go inside and try to see who those people were, but the very idea was frightening. What if she came face to face with them and they wanted to hurt her, or Barney?

Close to tears, Rosie decided that she and Barney would stay out of sight in the bushes and wait to see who might come out. Still, she was a little disturbed as to why the man would mention her father. Did the robbers know him? So many questions, and no answers.

As always, she softly consulted her loyal friend. 'Barney, why do you think that man would be talking about Daddy?'

When Barney softly licked her hand, as though consoling her, she wrapped her arms about his broad, silky neck, and whispered in his ear, 'Oh, Barney! I need my daddy. Where is he? What's happened to him?'

Tears were very close.

~

Inside the barn, Tom Stevens grew increasingly impatient. He was anxious for Molly to tell the exact same story as he did: that John Tanner found the two of them lying together in the hay. He flew into a rage and attacked Tom. But the fight got out of hand,

and it soon became obvious that John Tanner meant to kill him. Afraid for his life, Tom had grabbed the spade and lashed out wildly, catching the other man a devastating blow on the head. He never meant to kill him; he was just desperate to get away. What happened was done in self-defence, pure and simple.

It was imperative that Molly stick to every detail of this story, and because he had offered to take the blame, Tom had to put all his trust in this woman whom he had loved for so many years.

They had agreed, when reporting the incident, Molly must not say that her husband was dead. Instead, she must simply tell them about the fight, and that her husband was lying unconscious on the ground; try as they might, they could not wake him.

Now, though, he glanced up to see that Molly was still lingering, her head turned to look on the face of her dead husband.

'Molly, you need to go,' he reminded her. 'For pity's sake, hurry!'

If there was a chance they might get away with murder, they must be seen to have called the ambulance straight away. He gave Molly a nudge and she glared at him in the half-light.

'Don't push me, Tom. I'm on my way.'

Tom was increasingly worried about the passage of

time since John had been killed. 'As I recall, there's a telephone booth on the corner, just a minute or so along the path. It might be quicker to call the ambulance from there rather than go all the way up to the house through the yards and buildings.'

Molly nodded. 'You're right! It would be quicker.'

Now desperate to have it over and done with, Molly took off.

Crouching in the shrubbery, Rosie and the ever-loyal Barney were startled to hear the barn door creaking open.

'Ssh!' Rosie cautioned Barney.

Carefully shifting position, she peered through the bushes . . . and was astonished to find that the dark figure emerging from the barn was her mother. So what was she doing in the barn at this time of night? And who was the man she must have been inside with?

Terrified of being seen, Rosie grabbed Barney by the collar and softly drew back with him, while pressing a warning finger to her lips. Barney understood and, like the good friend he was, he followed her lead.

However, having also recognised Molly Tanner, he bent his head low and softly growled from the back of his throat.

'No . . . ssh!' Nervously chastising him, Rosie pulled him ever deeper into the shadows. Her mind was in turmoil. Why was her mother in the barn with some man? And where was her father?

Deeply suspicious, Rosie had half a mind to show herself to find out what was happening, although the idea of confronting her mother and the man in the barn was a daunting prospect. Yet she was desperate to know the whereabouts of her beloved father.

Confused, she took a moment to think.

Suddenly the tap-tap of heels against the concrete path signalled that her mother was drawing nearer. Taking hold of Barney's collar, Rosie held him to her, but there was no need to caution him as he settled silently beside her. Sensing something very wrong, he followed her instincts to remain hidden although she was by now increasingly fearful.

~

Unaware that anyone had seen her coming out of the barn, Molly stopped for a moment to light a cigarette. 'I'll be glad when it's all over,' she muttered sourly. 'I'm not altogether sure I can trust him. When it comes to the moment, I'm not sure Tom'll be man enough to keep his word and take the blame for me.'

Taking a long drag on the cigarette, she suddenly stopped and listened. What the devil was that?

Going softly forward in the direction from where the sounds had come, she listened earnestly and, yes . . . there it was again: a kind of scuffling sound. 'Who's there?' Reluctant to call again in case she startled Tom, she crept forward a little more, now deeply concerned that someone might have seen them inside the barn, or heard the plan she and Tom had agreed.

Standing still a moment, she called softly into the shadows: 'I know you're in there!' She threw her cigarette butt down and ground it to dust beneath the sole of her shoe.

'Who are you? What do you want?' She waited and listened. But while all was now eerily silent, she sensed the presence of someone there . . . hiding in the bushes. Watching her every move.

Peering into the darkness, she took another step forward to issue a low but harsh warning: 'If you know what's good for you, you'd better show your face . . . right now!' She stooped to pick up a small, fallen branch and threw it into the bushes, then listened.

She heard the branch crash through the under-growth, and then the tumble of loose foliage, and then nothing. No shouts of injury, or fearful cries that might tell her she was right about someone hiding in there.

Yet still she waited, and watched. 'Don't make me come in after you,' she warned softly. 'Another minute, and I'm calling the police.'

A long moment passed before she stepped forward yet again, fearlessly peering into the darkness. 'I can see you,' she lied, keeping her voice low so as not to alert Tom inside the barn. 'Come out now or I swear I'll set the dogs on you. They'll get you out all right, but you'll be sure to get badly hurt in the process!'

Now highly nervous, she imagined she saw something move. Yes, there it was again, shifting about amongst the overgrown bushes. 'Hey,' she called softly, addressing the intruders as though she could actually see them, 'whoever you are, show yourself. What the devil are you up to? Don't you realise you're trespassing on private property? What are you after? Answer me, dammit!'

Still no answer, but she was closer now. She could hear muted noises . . . whispers, and scratching sounds. Then nothing, only silence, occasionally penetrated by the familiar cry of foxes in the fields nearby.

Frustrated and angry, she reached out to bend the

bracken aside. 'If you don't want me to call the police right now you had best come out. And this is your last warning. I have a gang of men working late in the barn. I only need to raise my voice and they'll be in there after you!'

She stooped to pick up a chunk of fallen branch, which she flung deep into the bushes, causing a flurry of movement. When a small fallow deer shot out of the bushes and straight at her, she screamed so loud that Tom come running.

'Molly, what the devil's going on? I thought you'd be gone to the telephone by now.'

'I was on my way when I heard something moving about in the bushes. I thought we had intruders, but it was that damned thing. Gave me a fright, it did!' She brought his attention to the small deer, which was now running off towards the far yard.

'Look, it's pitch-black out there, and you never know who's about,' Tom said. 'Why don't you keep an eye on things here, and I'll go phone for the ambulance? I don't know about you, but I'm a bag o' nerves. The sooner we get this business over and done with, the better.'

'What?' Molly rounded on him. 'So you think I'm not capable of making a phone call, is that it?'

'No, of course I don't think that. It's just that I

was sure you'd already gone. Like I explained, it's important we call for an ambulance as soon as possible. You know that as well as I do.'

'Right! Then *you* get back inside and keep an eye on things. I won't be long.'

Before he could protest further, she was striding past him, round the corner of the building and quickly out of sight. Tom was about to call after her to apologise, but she was gone. In that moment, he felt more lonely and afraid than at any other time in his sorry life.

'Be quick, my darling,' he muttered. 'For both our sakes, be quick as you can.'

When the echo of her footsteps had faded away, he made no move to take up his vigil inside the barn. Instead, he glanced up at the stars overhead, thinking that John Tanner would never again look up at the beauty of the night skies.

Out there in the darkness Tom lingered a while, deeply thoughtful, heavy of heart, feeling so alone, and empty inside, unwilling to go back in the barn and greatly saddened at the thought of once more encountering the bloodied and empty figure of a once-fine man.

God alone knows, I'm not made for this kind of trouble, he thought. I need it to be over and done with so I know where I stand. The idea of being punished for something he did not do was beginning to weigh heavily on his mind. In that moment of hard reality he relived the terrible truth of what happened on this unforgettable night.

While Tom mentally revisited the awful events, he was unaware that the watchful eyes of John's daughter and her friend Barney were trained on him only an arm's reach away.

Seemingly alone in the dark, his thoughts wandered back to Molly.

Molly Tanner was bad, but in a captivating way. She possessed a kind of wild and curious beauty that he found hard to resist. She was like a force of nature. He had never known a woman with such inner strength. When she wanted something, she would go for it, and allow nothing to get in the way. Her passions were overwhelming, whether for love or for hate. Molly was the only woman he had ever needed. Without her these past years, he had not lived or loved, but merely survived, without joy or purpose.

Without Molly, he was nothing. He was no one.

He was haunted by the horror of the events of this night, yet, in spite of the terrible thing Molly had done, he could not find it in him to stop loving her.

It was as if she had cast a spell over him. Her energy, her passion made him feel more alive.

Whatever might happen now, and whichever way this awful train of events might end, he would keep his word to her. He would rather die than let Molly suffer the inevitable consequences of John Tanner's brutal and untimely death.

If his own sacrifice meant that she would share what life he might have at the end of it all, then he would not hesitate to suffer whatever punishment awaited him. Having her back in his life was all he ever wanted.

He recalled Molly's threat to end her life if she were locked away in prison. If that was to happen, what would his own life be then, without her? It would be sadly empty, and every bit as unbearable as it had been before he found her again.

It was a sorry truth, however, that neither he nor Molly could ever put right the wrongs of what had happened here. As for himself, he would never be able to erase the memory of it from his thoughts; not even if he lived to be a very old man.

John Tanner was the greatest loser in all of this because he would never again see another sunset . . . never love again, or hold his only child in his arms. Never see her grow into a woman, or walk her up the aisle, or be there when she carried his grand-children.

Through no fault of his own, that good man would never again have the pleasure of working his land. His only child would grow up without her beloved daddy in her life, and he would not follow her steps to adulthood.

That hard-working man, who had lived most of his life outdoors, would never again feel the warm sunshine or hear the raindrops pitter-patter on the ground. Nor would he ever again see a newborn foal stagger to its feet only minutes after its birth, or experience the satisfaction of watching as it grew into its full potential.

Deeply saddened, Tom walked slowly back inside the barn, carefully avoiding the pitiful sight that was John's body.

As he turned away, he murmured through his tears, 'I am so very sorry.' And he was.

In that quiet, poignant moment he questioned his promise to Molly to take full blame for this man's untimely and bloody end. Taking a few moments to reflect, he became deeply conscious of the callous manner in which she had both betrayed and killed her husband who, as far as Tom could see, had done no wrong. And he asked himself whether Molly deserved to pay for what she had done.

Maybe so, but it was not what he wanted for her. He still needed Molly. His hunger for that woman was like a drug of sorts – far stronger and more dangerous than anything he had ever encountered in his entire life.

So he decided that he would keep his word, and protect Molly as best he could. Any amount of punishment he was made to suffer would be a small price to pay if in the end it brought him the constant love of Molly Tanner.

Molly was the only woman he had kept safe in his heart for all these lonely years and now he must keep her safe again. And whatever it took to keep that promise, he was ready.

Resolved to face the music, he wondered why Molly was taking so long. 'Come on, woman, it's not that far to the telephone. Where are you, dammit?'

Maybe she was on her way back by now. He listened hard for the tap-tap of her high-heeled shoes, but when there was no such sound he began to panic.

~

Hidden in the bushes, huddling up to Barney, Rosie watched the stranger's every move. She studied him as he walked back and forth, deeply agitated, his attention constantly returning to the path her mother had followed. She heard him softly muttering, but try as she might, she could not make out what he was saying.

Suddenly, to her horror, he stopped and seemed to look straight through the bushes at her and Barney. With her arm curled around Barney's thick, warm body, Rosie lay very still and silent, afraid that the stranger might hear the fearful pounding of her heart.

Sensing her nervousness, Barney snuggled up tight to her, and he, too, kept his silence. The two of them watched the stranger pace up and down, increasingly agitated. Then without warning, he turned about and strode back inside the hay barn.

After a moment or so, Rosie ordered Barney to stay. 'Keep a sharp watch,' she told the faithful Labrador. 'I won't be a minute.'

Treading carefully through the tangle of bushes, she went towards the barn doors and peered inside. The stranger was walking away from her. She had no idea who he was, or why her mother had been with him here in the barn.

She was surprised by his pitiful demeanour. He seemed so very sad and weary, the way his shoulders were hunched up, and he walked in a slow manner that made him seem old.

She found herself comparing the stranger to her father, a tall, capable man with a bounce in his step and a warm smile on his stong face. Tanned by the sun and shaped by the elements, he was a man of character.

Rosie recalled that her father had gone out to look for his wife, yet now it was beginning to seem that while he was out searching for her, she had been here in the hay barn with this man.

She knew her daddy was careful, especially since the burglary, and she truly believed that while he was out looking for her mother he would have checked all the yards and barns, if only to make sure they were secure from thieves.

So why had he not found her when she was right here with the stranger?

Rosie had so many questions, but one in particular continued to weigh heavily on her mind. Where was her daddy?

Maybe he really couldn't find Mother, so he went back home, she thought. Somehow that possibility made her feel just a tiny bit easier, although Rosie wondered why her mother and her man-friend managed to stay hidden from her father.

In her heart and soul, Rosie instinctively knew that something was not right. She was absolutely certain that the reason for Daddy being unable to find her mother was because her mother had planned it that way. She had not wanted to be found.

Rosie tiptoed a short way into the barn and hid behind a stack of bales. Deeply curious about the stranger, she wondered how her mother came to know him, because she herself had never seen him before; not at the farm, and never with either of her parents. Yet in that brief exchange she had witnessed between the stranger and her mother the two of them had seemed familiar together.

To Rosie, it was all more than a little worrying.

For the moment, she continued to watch the man as he went slowly through the barn. When suddenly he turned to glance in her direction, she managed to dodge quickly out of sight.

In case she might be spotted and have to run from here, she nervously glanced back to check the big doors were still open, giving a sigh of relief to note that they were in exactly the same position as before: one door half open and the other more so.

She hoped Barney was keeping vigil and staying out of sight. She knew she only had to call him and he would come running, although calling him to her just now would not be wise.

Staying sharp, she kept hidden a moment longer,

and when everything remained silent and still, she dared to take another peek.

The stranger had not moved from a spot towards the back of the barn. Only now, he was kind of stooped over, appearing to look down at what Rosie took to be a pile of old rags lying on the ground. With the low level of lighting, she could not be absolutely certain as to whether they really were old rags or just a jumble of swept-up rubbish.

Staying out of sight in the darker shadows alongside the wall, Rosie crept nearer on tiptoe, afraid that at any moment the man might turn round and see her. She moved very slowly, mindful of where she stepped in case she might accidentally kick something and draw his attention to her.

Determined that she must be neither seen nor heard, she held her breath a moment, standing quite still before continuing forward with great caution, ready to run at any moment.

When suddenly the man again turned round to look in her direction, Rosie stopped and waited, motionless, ready to flee back to Barney, if the stranger spotted her.

The stranger looked away then, suddenly moving his head from side to side while nervously glancing about, as though afraid he was being watched.

Rosie pressed herself into the wall, all the time holding her breath for so long, she thought she must surely burst.

She was immensely grateful to be able to take a breath when the stranger shifted his concentration to the pile of jumble at his feet.

Rosie watched him as he continued to stare down, and then, after what seemed an age, he stooped to collect something from the ground. Carefully he turned the piece over and over in his hands, his head bent as he took a while to examine it in absolute silence.

Minutes passed. To Rosie's dismay the man showed no sign of moving on. Instead, he remained still as a statue, making no sound whatsoever. Then eventually, he bent his head low and, to Rosie's great astonishment, he began to cry.

At first he gave just low, broken whimpers. Suddenly the whimpers grew stronger, and holding the object he had retrieved from the ground in both hands, he reverently pressed it close to his chest, while softly sobbing, as though his heart would break.

His anguished cries touched Rosie deeply. She wanted to go to him, to help him in his distress, but she dared not move.

Then, as quickly as he had begun sobbing, the

man stopped to stare up to the rafters, as though searching for something . . . or someone. Now he was weaving backwards and forwards, moaning and crying as though in great pain.

Rosie was deeply torn. Should she go to him? Or should she creep away so he would never know she was there? Be still, Rosie, she mentally cautioned herself. You must be careful.

She watched as he carefully returned the dark object to the ground, laying it tenderly beside the pile of jumble. She tried desperately to focus on it, but the low lighting was not helpful. There was something oddly familiar about the piece, but for the life of her she could not think straight.

Now she could hear the man softly muttering, head bent and his hands folded together, almost as though in prayer.

Feeling completely out of her depth, Rosie grew afraid. Was the stranger really praying? And if so, why? And what was the dark object he had collected from the ground, and that made him seem so very sad?

Rosie had no answers.

Now, though, waiting for the moment when she might think it safe to move, Rosie's thoughts returned to her father.

She reminded herself of how she had only ever

been in this hay barn once before, and that was a long time ago. Her daddy had brought her inside to show her what he had been building over all those months.

A gentle smile lit her face as she recalled how excited and proud he was to have built such a beautiful barn as this.

Suddenly the stranger swung round, seeming to look straight at her. She froze, and as soon as he turned away again she grabbed her chance to get out of there.

She was fleeing through the big door when the distant high-pitched wail of sirens filled the air. Alarmed by the noise, Barney came bounding out of the bushes where he had been obediently waiting.

Rosie was running to him when she was brought to a sudden halt as her mother came out of nowhere and caught her in a vicious grip.

'You devil!' Shaking Rosie as though she was a rag doll, Molly screamed at her, 'What the hell are you doing here?'

Deeply shocked to find Rosie running out of the barn, Molly was fearful of what the girl might have seen and heard.

Her fear was palpable. Where the devil was Tom

now? How long had the girl been here? Could she even have witnessed the killing of her father?

Aware of the sirens coming closer, but frantic to be rid of the girl, Molly knew she must be careful how she dealt with this situation.

The dog had come to stand close by her, growling a warning at Molly, who spat out a vicious torrent of threats, which temporarily silenced him.

'Get home. Now!' she snapped at Rosie. 'And take the mutt with you. I'll talk to you when I get back. The ambulance is on its way. There's been an accident. Someone broke into the barn . . . a thief, I imagine, but when I chased him, he climbed high up to the roof, and then he fell.'

She was desperate to be rid of the girl. 'You can't stay here . . . it's too distressing. More importantly, the ambulance men will need to work without hindrance. Get away from here. Take the dog with you. I'll be home as soon as I've sorted everything. Do as you're told, girl. Be off with you! I want you and the mutt gone from here.' When Rosie made no move, she grabbed her by the arm and pushed her along the pathway. 'Do as you're told!' She gave Rosie a mighty shove that almost knocked her off her feet.

When Barney made a threatening move, Rosie

drew him back. She had a question for her mother. 'Did you know Daddy came looking for you?'

'I've already explained what's happening. Now get away from here. Go!'

Rosie was insistent. 'So where is Daddy now?'

'I don't know where he is. I never saw him, so he obviously didn't find me, did he? I expect he got fed up looking, and went back home.'

'But why did he not find you?' Rosie persisted. 'I don't think Daddy would go home without looking in all the barns first. And you were in the hay barn, weren't you?' She might have mentioned the stranger, but some deep instinct warned her not to.

By now the sirens sounded much closer and Molly was frantic to get Rosie and the dog away from there.

'Your daddy must be worried sick about you,' Molly told Rosie. 'You can't hang around here. I'll see you and your father back at the house. Tell him we had thieves in the hay barn . . . and there's been a terrible accident.'

She took Rosie in a firm hold and marched her along the path. 'By the way, I don't know what you might have imagined you saw or heard here tonight, but if I find out that you've been telling lies about me or anyone else . . .' Taking Rosie in a hard grip, she lowered her voice to the softest whisper, '. . . I promise, you will regret it. Do you understand me, girl?'

Knowing only too well how vicious her mother could be, Rosie gave a nervous nod of the head.

'Good. Because for your own sake, and for the sake of that mutt, you would do well to keep your mouth shut. I mean, wouldn't it be a terrible shame if you woke up one morning and found your doggy friend lying dead at your feet? And all because you were foolish enough to tell lies about something you imagined you saw and heard.' Her quiet smile was evil. 'You do understand what I'm saying, don't you, Rosie?'

From the fearful expression on Rosie's face, Molly was pretty certain the message had got through but she had to be sure. Holding Rosie by the shoulders, she looked her in the eye. 'So, Rosie, what would you say if someone were to ask what you saw or heard down here tonight?'

When Rosie was not quick enough to give an answer, Molly yanked her forward. 'I asked you a question, girl, and I need an answer.' Then she whispered into Rosie's ear, 'So, Rosie Tanner, did you see or hear anything other than me, in this place tonight?'

Rosie thought about the man her mother had been

talking with, the man who was inside the barn. He was crying . . . acting strangely. And she felt sad for him.

'You little bitch! Answer me.' Shaking Rosie like a rag doll again, Molly leaned down and pressed her mouth close to Rosie's ear. Her whispered warning was filled with hatred for this child whom she wished had never been born. 'Listen to me. There was never anyone else here, just you, me and the mutt. As for the mutt, I've already warned you what could happen to him. And don't think I won't be rid of him, because in this world there are only devils and angels. I think you know which one I am, don't you?'

When Rosie kept silent, Molly hissed, 'Did you hear what I just said?'

Rosie quickly nodded.

'I can't hear you. What did you say?'

'Yes, Mother.'

'Don't call me "Mother". I am not your mother. What I am is your worst nightmare. You need to listen to me. If you tell lies about anything that might or might not have happened here, it won't be you who gets hurt, will it?'

Fearful, Rosie shook her head.

'Speak up, girl!' Molly stared into Rosie's big, frightened eyes. 'I didn't catch that. So, tell me now, what did you see here tonight?'

Rosie had never been so afraid. 'I never saw anything,' she murmured, her voice trembling.

'Good girl!' Molly smiled evilly again. 'You need to remember that there are never any second chances. No one gives you anything. There is no one to watch out for you. No friends. No kindness. No one to help you.' She chuckled softly. 'There is only sorrow, and hatred, and the bad people always win. Angel and devil – that's you and me, Rosie! Forever on opposite sides of the fence.'

Her smile slipped away. 'Now go! Tell your father I'll explain when I get home.' She gave Rosie a hefty shove. 'Move yourself! Get away from here before I lock you up in a dark stable and leave you there all night with the hordes of hungry rats looking for a tasty meal.'

Shaking with fear and with tears streaming down her face, Rosie hurried away with the loyal Barney at her side. When the ambulance drew into the yard she thought it was safe to turn round, and she gathered her courage to hide behind a tree and watch as the ambulance men hurried into the barn, her mother trailing behind.

'She's up to something.' Stroking Barney's neck, Rosie kept him tight to her. 'Something's gone terribly wrong, Barney. I don't trust her. Why did she not mention the man she was talking to earlier, the man who was inside the barn just now? And why would she say that Daddy must have gone home when he couldn't find her? I don't believe that for one minute. Daddy would never have given up looking for her because he loves her too much. He just can't see what she's really like!'

On the way home, she continued to confide in her loyal, four-legged friend. 'I know she's lying about there being an injured man in the barn. She told us that the thief ran up to the rafters and fell from the top, and that's why the ambulance men were called. But I never saw any injured man in the barn. The only person I saw was the man she was talking to earlier.'

She could see him clearly in her mind. 'He was definitely not injured, although he looked so sad. He was crying, Barney, really sobbing. I wanted to comfort him, but I daren't show myself. I peeped about the best I could, but I did not see anyone injured on the ground, like she said. If there was anyone hurt, I would have seen them, wouldn't I?' She could not understand why her mother would lie like that.

'I don't understand it, Barney.' She glanced back to where the ambulance was waiting. 'If she was telling lies about there being an injured man in the barn, why is the ambulance here?'

A new thought crossed her mind. 'Maybe they've come to take the other man away, the one I saw inside the barn. He did not look injured to me, and he did not look like he would ever be able to climb up to the rafters, but he did look so sad.'

She was half tempted to go back and see who they were bringing out of the barn. Maybe there really was an injured man, but for some reason she just didn't see him. 'I daren't go back, Barney, because *she* would surely see us, and there would be hell to pay. But something is horribly wrong, Barney. I just know it.'

She wondered aloud, 'Don't you think it's odd, that she never once mentioned the stranger inside the barn? It's not like he stole into the barn and she didn't know he was there, because we heard them talking together, didn't we? And just now, when she caught me coming out of the barn, she must have known I saw him in there. But she did not ask me straight out if I'd seen anyone. Instead, she threatened to hurt us if I told anyone that I'd seen or heard anything.'

The more she thought about it, the more curious she became. 'Also, where was she that Daddy couldn't find her? And where's Daddy now? Is he really at home, like she said? Or was she just trying to get rid of us?'

As she and Barney neared the farmhouse, Rosie continued to chatter to her faithful friend. 'Do you think I should tell Daddy about the man in the barn? I don't want to make him angry or anything, but he has a right to know, don't you think?'

But the minute she said it openly, she realised she could not tell him. 'She'll only deny it, Barney, and if I tell she really will find a way to hurt you, I know it!'

Rosie had never felt so desperately torn in all her young life.

CHAPTER FOUR

ROSIE WAS DISTURBED to see the farmhouse was in darkness. 'What's going on, Barney?' Quickening her steps, she ran up the path and tried the door but it was shut fast.

Taking her front-door key from her coat pocket, she opened the door, and Barney bounced in past her, almost knocking her over, and dropped the walking stick on the floor.

'Daddy?' Rosie called. 'Daddy, are you there?' But the silence and darkness that had settled over the house told her her father had not returned.

She was about to switch on the light when she had second thoughts. 'We'd best not put the lights on in case it attracts people we don't want,' she told Barney.

She still had the torch she had left with and,

cautioning Barney to be quiet, she led him round the house by its dim light, careful to keep the beam close to the ground whenever possible, while thoroughly checking every room.

'There's no one here, Barney.' Rosie was close to tears. 'It's as if Daddy's disappeared off the face of the earth. So, what do we do now? Where do we look for him?'

When she dropped into the armchair, Barney sank down beside her. 'I don't understand, Barney,' she said softly. 'Mother said he must be here, but he isn't. Oh, Barney, I don't know what to think. I can't imagine where he might have gone.'

She felt hopelessly defeated but rallied sufficiently to go over all the possibilities.

'What if we missed each other on the way? What if he went out again while we were making our way back here? He must be worried that he couldn't find Mother the first time, so maybe he went back to have another look.'

When Barney shuffled closer to her, she reached out and cuddled him. 'Maybe he thought anything was better than staying here and worrying. We could go back and see if he's gone back to the big barn. It's worth a try, don't you think, Barney? At least we'll be doing something.'

Barney had been looking round the room and his worried brown eyes were now staring at the sideboard against the far wall. He sat up straight and began softly growling.

'Seen a mouse, have you, Barney?' Rosie smiled. 'You know they sometimes come in off the fields . . . drive Mother crazy, they do.'

Her decision was made. 'Look, let's go round and see if there are any clues that might tell us where Daddy is.'

Barney, however, was suddenly running excitedly back and forth across the room. Rosie tried to calm him.

'What is it, Barney? Did you hear something? Ssh!' She peered nervously through the windows but could see no one outside. 'It must have been that mouse again. But it won't hurt you, you big old softy!'

Her kind words made no difference as Barney padded backwards and forwards, making a strange kind of crying noise.

'Stop that!'

Rosie went off to check all the doors and windows. Then, double-checking she had her key in her pocket, she opened the front door and patiently waited for Barney, who was now frantically running round in circles in the hall. When she went to him, he shot away into the front room, barking and tearing about in a kind of frenzy.

Grabbing him tight, Rosie made an effort to soothe him. 'That mouse really frightened you, didn't it? Well, I promise you, as soon as Daddy gets back we'll throw that little rascal outside where he belongs. But now we really have to go. Come on, Barney!'

But instead of going with her, he turned about and ran back, going straight for the sideboard, where he got up on his back legs and pushed off the ornaments until they were scattered all over the carpet.

Astonished, Rosie ran to pull him away. 'Bad boy! What's got into you? Just look at what you've done. Mother will not be best pleased with this . . .'

Continuing to scold the dog, Rosie collected the ornaments, one of which was now chipped. The photograph of Molly Tanner and her sister, Kathleen, also had a crack running from corner to corner across the glass.

'Oh, Barney, look, it's ruined.' Rosie was cross, but when she saw how upset Barney was she stroked him lovingly. 'Don't worry, boy, I won't tell on you,' she assured him. 'I'll say it was me. I don't want her to put you out in the yard all night like she did when you knocked the clock off her bedside cabinet.'

Barney's peculiar behaviour now worsened, and

he began whizzing round in circles, and loudly barking.

Rosie was increasingly puzzled and a little impatient. 'Hey! You stop that! What's the matter with you?'

As she was reaching out to put the photograph back on the sideboard, Barney's barking grew louder. Then he leaped up and knocked it clean out of her hands. 'Barney, no!' Rosie gave him a hefty shove. 'Whatever's wrong with you?'

Barney looked up with sad eyes, but then he began gently pawing the photograph while making a low, whining noise, as though he might be hurt.

Rosie was puzzled. 'I know something's upset you, Barney, but I can't think what it has to do with the photo.'

But when she attempted to replace it on the sideboard again he looked straight at her, barking louder and louder.

Curious, she looked long and hard at the photograph. It was just a photo of her mother and Auntie Kathleen, and Barney had seen it many times.

'I wish Mother was as lovely as Auntie Kathleen,' Rosie murmured. 'How can two sisters be so different?'

Suddenly, as if a light had gone on inside her mind, she knew why Barney was behaving so badly.

She laughed out loud. 'You clever old thing! You

think Daddy went to Auntie Kathleen's house, don't you? Why didn't I think of that? Daddy must have searched everywhere for Mother, and when he couldn't find her he realised she must have gone to see Auntie Kathleen. She's done that before without telling anyone. Yes . . . that's it! That's where he'll be. Oh, Barney, you are brilliant.'

She gave the dog another hug, then ran to the telephone in the kitchen and dialled her aunt's number. Calm and quiet now, Barney followed and sat by the door, looking very pleased with himself.

'Patrick Riley here. Who is this?' Hearing his familiar Irish voice was a great relief to Rosie.

'It's me, Uncle Patrick!' Rosie assured him, 'I'm all right, but I was just wondering, is Daddy with you? Only he went out looking for Mother, and I think he must have missed her, 'cause she's in the barn. But now I don't know where he is, so me and Barney thought we should call you to see if he's there with you and Auntie Kathleen.'

'Just a minute, me darlin'.' Patrick sounded troubled, and then there was a pause, during which Rosie thought she could hear Kathleen's voice. Then Uncle Patrick was back on the line. 'Just hold on for a minute, will you, Rosie? Your Auntie Kathleen needs to talk with you.'

'Rosie?' Kathleen sounded anxious.

'Yes, Auntie Kathleen?'

'Listen to me, Rosie. Are you at home?'

'Yes.'

'Barney is with you, isn't he?'

'Yes, but we've been out looking for Daddy. He went out to find Mother, but he never came back. I thought he might be there with you and Uncle Patrick.'

'Rosie, I don't like you being in the house all on your own.'

'I'm not on my own. I've got Barney here.'

'All right, just hang on a minute. Don't put the phone down.'

Suddenly, everything was quiet except for the faintest of voices as her uncle and aunt softly conversed away from the telephone.

Then Patrick was back on the line. 'Listen to me now, darlin'. I want you and Barney to stay right where you are. Don't go outside the house. Are the doors locked?'

'Yes.'

'Good. So turn off the lights. I know your daddy keeps a torch under the stairs . . . when you put the receiver down, go and get it. If you can't find it, ring me back. Make sure you close all the curtains and lock all the doors.'

'I have it already.'

'Yer a good girl. Now then, I'm coming over. I'll be there quick as I can. Meantime, do not answer the door to anyone.'

'I won't, I promise. But, Uncle Patrick, you didn't tell me if my mother and father are with you.'

'Listen, darlin', I promise I'll be there in no time at all.'

He replaced the receiver, leaving Rosie somewhat confused.

As ever, she reported to Barney. 'That was a strange kind of conversation,' she said with a little smile. 'Uncle Patrick is such a funny man at times. I asked him if my parents were there, and he just said he was on his way here. So does he mean he's bringing them home, or what?' She shook her head. 'I suppose he must be.'

Either way, she was greatly relieved to have spoken with her uncle and aunt. 'And besides . . . we all know what Uncle Patrick is like even when he hasn't had a drop o' the good stuff.'

Barney looked at her in an odd kind of way, his head bent to one side and his ears pricked, almost as though he had no idea what she was talking about. But, from the sorry look in his eyes, she knew he sensed her fears and understood.

After that short, confusing conversation with Uncle Patrick, Rosie wasn't altogether sure whether her father was at Kathleen and Patrick's house or not. But then her darling uncle Patrick had always been a fascinating puzzle to her. He made her laugh, and he had the merriest of natures. His son, Harry, who worked with Daddy, was much like his father, and that was why she loved him so much.

Relieved that her beloved aunt and uncle were coming to help her and that, thanks to Barney, she would soon be reunited with her parents, she gave him a great big hug.

CHAPTER FIVE

'I'M REALLY WORRIED, Patrick.' Kathleen was frantically wringing her hands. 'What do we tell her?'

Patrick was equally worried but, being an honest and forthright man, he answered her the only way he knew how. 'We'll have to tell her the truth. She has a right to know. For now, though, we need to keep her safe. So I'll get her and Barney back here as quick as I can and, meantime, you can be thinking of how we can break the news to her gently . . . although it's bound to hit her really hard.'

While his parents talked of the best way to tell Rosie what had happened, Harry was pacing the floor at the back of the room. Eventually he made his way across to sit beside his stepmother, who was quickly getting tearful.

'Try not to get upset about it, Mum.' He slid his arm about her shoulders. 'We must try to be strong for Rosie's sake.' He was hurting desperately for Rosie.

For a long time, Harry had had deep feelings for Rosie, but only now, in this very serious moment, when he desperately wanted to hold her and take care of her, did he realise just how very much he loved her.

'Dad?'

'Yes, Son?'

'Try not to frighten her. I mean, do you need to say anything just yet? After all, we're not altogether sure what's happened, are we?'

Kathleen agreed. 'She's bound to ask where her parents are. But Harry's right to suggest we go gently with her. When she asks about her parents, just try somehow to be evasive, without telling any lies. When she gets here, and we're all together, we'll break it to her in the gentlest way possible. She will be absolutely devastated when we tell her what we know.'

'Yes, of course, you're right. But we don't really know the full story ourselves, do we?'

Kathleen nodded slowly. 'Yes, that's true. We don't know everything, but what we do know is so bad it threw us all into panic. That's why we have to be so gentle and careful in what we tell that lovely girl.' She wiped a solitary tear from her eye. 'Now, go and get the poor child, Patrick. And, please, be very careful what you say, won't you?'

'O' course I will, my lovely! And don't you worry. I'll have her back here in no time at all.'

'Dad?' Harry stood up. 'Shall I come with you?' He was desperately worried for Rosie and he knew how that lovable man could sometimes let his tongue run away with him.

Patrick smiled at his son; he knew what he was thinking. 'No, thank you, Harry. It's best if I go on my own, especially with that big dog taking up three places in the truck. Look, while I'm gone, you two can try to make some sense of what we've been told. And don't worry, I won't let my tongue run away with me.'

'No, you had better not,' Kathleen told him. 'Oh, and leave the truck. Take my car. I don't want young Rosie flung about like a sack of potatoes in that rattling old wagon of yours.'

'Ah now, there's me lovely girl! I thought you would never offer.'

A few minutes later, Harry went to the car with his father, while Kathleen watched from the doorway.

'You go back inside now, my love, in case we get

another call . . . if you know what I mean?' Patrick called to her.

Kathleen understood, and after blowing him a quick kiss, she did exactly what he told her.

Harry was anxious. 'Dad, are you sure you don't want me with you?'

'Yes, son, it's best if I go on my own while you watch over Kathleen. I don't expect to be gone more than a half-hour at most. I reckon Kathleen is holding back because she wants to stay strong for Rosie, but she's had a terrible shock – we all have. She hides it well, but I know she's really upset.'

'You can count on me, Dad,' Harry reassured him.

'Thank you, Harry. You're a good lad. Nobody knows better than me how fortunate I am to have you for a son, and to have that dear woman in our lives. Kathleen brought us through a bad time once before, and here we are again, eh?'

For Harry, the bad memories were never far away. 'That's true, Dad. Only this time it's Rosie who's about to have her heart broken.' Choking back a tear, he stepped away from the car and waved his father off.

Patrick drove up the road at some speed, leaving Harry shaking his head. 'Why does he always think he's on a race track whenever he gets into that car? Fifty-six going on sixteen, that's my dad!'

Harry gave a wry little smile. However bossy and argumentative his father could be at times, he was also deeply caring and supportive, and Harry worshipped the ground he walked on.

~

Since the brief telephone conversation, Rosie had stood at the window, patiently watching for her Uncle Patrick to arrive.

Equally anxious, Barney leaned over her shoulder, panting his hot breath into the back of her neck.

'Oh, look! He's here!' Relieved when she saw the car turning in, Rosie was on her feet and hugging Barney. 'Come on, boy, let's go meet them!' The two of them were outside and at the car before Patrick could even climb out.

'Woa!' Scrambling out of the car, he grabbed Rosie in his arms. 'Oh, me little darlin', have you been watching for me all this time? After I told ye to close the curtains and stay away from the windows!'

'I'm sorry, Uncle Patrick, but I was worried.' She peeked into the car. 'Where is he?' Her face showed her disappointment.

'Who?'

'My daddy. I thought you were bringing him home.'

'Ah, sure, I never promised no such thing, me darlin'.' He was dreading her next question. 'I'm just here to fetch you back to our house. Auntie Kathleen's waiting for ye, so she is.' He opened the rear passenger door and ushered Rosie and Barney inside. 'You stay there now while I secure the house.'

As he ambled away, Rosie confided in Barney. 'I got it wrong, Barney. It seems Daddy is waiting back there with Auntie Kathleen. But why didn't he come home with Uncle Patrick? Now he's got to drive all the way back, and then later he'll probably run us all back here again. It seems an awful lot of trouble to me.'

Rosie was beginning to think the world had turned upside down, and everything had gone awry.

She shrugged. 'I expect Mother's with him now and they needed to spend some time with Auntie Kathleen. Dad was saying only the other day how we haven't seen Auntie Kathleen in a long time. Ever since she and Mother had a falling-out over nothing at all. When he said Mother should apologise because it was her who had started the argument, Mother got angry and told him to mind his own business.'

The two of them watched Patrick going from window to window, checking everywhere. Finally, he shut the door, giving the door handle a little shake. 'There ye go!' He climbed back into the car. 'All safely locked up.' He handed the house key, which she'd left inside, in the lock, to Rosie. 'Right! Off we go. I expect Harry and your Auntie Kathleen are anxious to see us back, eh?'

As they drove, Rosie had many questions, but one in particular. 'Uncle Patrick?'

'Yes, sweetheart?'

'Me and Barney searched all over for Daddy, and we couldn't find him, so where was he?'

'I'm sure I have no idea.' Patrick had been dreading the question.

'But he's at your house now, waiting for us. Isn't he?' Rosie had that deep-down feeling again that something was very wrong.

Patrick began to panic. What should he tell her?

He followed the truth as far as he was able. 'No, sweetheart, he is not at our house, and neither is your mother. The truth is, I don't rightly know where your daddy is, but I do know your Auntie Kathleen had a phone call from your mother a little while ago. I'm sure she'll know where your daddy is. Don't you worry now, me darlin'. I'm sure Kathleen will explain everything when we get back.'

He felt totally out of his depth and not at all sure

what he should or shouldn't say in this sorry situation. He did not know the full story that Kathleen had been told so he was doubly uncomfortable trying to answer Rosie's questions in case he inadvertently lied to her. He recalled Harry and Kathleen's suggestion that Rosie should at least be gently warned of the serious situation she would need to face at some point.

With that responsibility weighing heavily on his mind, he parked the car at the side of the road, switched off the engine and took a deep breath. 'Rosie, sweetheart? There is something you should know.'

Rosie was concerned. 'Has the car broken down, Uncle Patrick?'

'No, no, sweetheart. Nothing like that.' Turning in his seat, he took hold of her hand. 'I've pulled over because I know you're worried, and the truth is I don't have the answers to your questions. But there is something I haven't told you, and I'm about to tell you now.'

Rosie was suddenly filled with dread. 'Is it my daddy? Has something happened to him?' Her voice trembled. 'Barney and me, we searched everywhere and we didn't find him. Has he gone away? Is he hurt? Is that why the—'

She stopped short, remembering how her mother had threatened to hurt Barney if she talked to anyone about what she had seen and heard. But she had to know. 'Please, Uncle Patrick,' she asked, fighting back tears, 'where's my daddy?'

'Well, like I said, I don't have all the answers, but what I do know is that your Auntie Kathleen had a very serious phone call. It was from your mother and, as far as I can tell, she's in a deal of trouble.'

'What kind of trouble?' Rosie felt some relief at this news. Wherever she went her mother was always causing trouble.

'Now, don't go panicking, sweetheart,' Patrick assured her. 'I'm sure I don't know the full story, and neither does your Auntie Kathleen.'

After that long and fruitless search for her father, Rosie now feared her mother's trouble must involve her father somehow. 'Is Daddy in trouble, too, Uncle Patrick? Please . . . has he gone away? Is he never coming back?' Her voice shook with emotion. 'Is that why we couldn't find him?'

'Hey, don't get yourself in a state, because then I'll be sorry I ever told you the little that I do know. But I honestly don't recall there being any mention of your daddy being hurt, or any such thing. So don't upset yourself. The thing is, apparently your mother is at the police station. All Auntie Kathleen said is that there was some kind of accident and an ambulance was called.'

Afraid he was getting in over his head, Patrick was keen to extricate himself. 'Look, sweetheart, I'm sorry, but your Auntie Kathleen will need to tell you the rest. Now you know as much as I do: that there was some kind of accident, and your mother reported it to the police.' This was near enough to the truth.

'So, my daddy is all right then, is he?'

'Like I said, you know as much as I do. There was a bad accident, your mother was there, and now she's at the police station, giving them any information she might have. That's what happens when there's been an accident. The police take statements from any witnesses, and then they follow up what they've been told. That's really all I know.'

'Maybe Daddy was there, too, when the accident happened.' Rosie grew hopeful. 'Maybe he had to tell them what he saw.'

'Maybe . . . and maybe not. I honestly don't know the full story.' That was as close to the truth as Patrick dared to say. 'We will probably learn more when we get back to your auntie Kathleen.'

Still on edge, still concerned for her father, Rosie was reluctant to wait until then. 'Did Auntie Katheen tell you what Mother said about the accident? Did she mention where it was?' She desperately wanted to tell Patrick about the ambulance men who had turned up at the barn, and how her mother had chased her and Barney away.

She could still hear her mother's wicked warning about what she would do to Barney if Rosie said anything about what she had seen or heard, but even so, Rosie was anxious enough that she was sorely tempted to defy her mother and tell Uncle Patrick everything she knew about her mother being in the barn with that man – the man she had seen talking to himself and sobbing as if his heart would break.

Who was that sad, pitiful stranger? Why was he crying like that? She wished now that she had gone to him. She had so wanted to help.

Her mother said there had been an accident, and then the ambulance came. From what Uncle Patrick was saying now, it seemed her mother was telling the truth. So who was hurt? And why had she not seen anything that could be described as an accident? Yet she had seen the urgent arrival of the ambulance with her own eyes. When Rosie tried to answer one question, it just threw up another. The one and only thing she could be absolutely certain of was that her mother was at the root of it all.

Right now Rosie desperately needed to tell Uncle Patrick everything she had seen, but for Barney's sake she had to keep her mouth tight shut. However, she could still ask about her father. Her mother had not threatened her and Barney if she spoke about him.

'Please, Uncle Patrick, I'm really worried about Daddy. He went out ages ago to look for Mother. When he didn't come back, Barney and I went to find him. We went everywhere we thought he might be, but there was no sign of him. And he still isn't back yet.'

'I do understand you must be worried, Rosie girl, but I can't tell you any more than I already have. The thing is, I heard only a snippet of the conversation between Auntie Kathleen and your mother. But listen, Auntie Kathleen might have heard more from your mother while I've been away. We shall just have to wait and see, won't we? It's best not to let your imagination run away with you.' He felt guilty, knowing that when they got back this dear girl was most likely in for a terrible shock.

'All right, Uncle Patrick, I understand.' Though even after her uncle's reassurances she was far from content.

The events of the night were like a jigsaw puzzle,

when some of the pieces were missing. She just hoped Uncle Patrick was right and that Auntie Kathleen really had learned more about what had happened, and who it was that had been taken to hospital.

Growing increasingly nervous with every passing minute, Rosie whispered a little prayer that her daddy would be safe.

CHAPTER SIX

'WHY DON'T YOU sit down a minute? Watching out the window won't get them here any sooner.' Harry walked across the room to lay a gentle hand on Kathleen's shoulder. 'I've made a fresh pot of tea.' He had set the small round tray on the coffee table. 'Please, try and drink it while it's hot, eh?'

Kathleen smiled up at him. 'Thank you, Harry. But I don't think I could even swallow it.' She gave a deep sigh. 'I can't stop thinking about what Molly told me. Passing the bad news on to Rosie will be the hardest thing I've ever had to do.'

'I know that.' Harry had never seen his stepmother so uncertain of herself, so nervous and afraid. 'I wish there was something I could do to make it easier for you . . . and for Rosie. We both know how very hard it will be for her to accept what's happened, but I'm grateful that it's you who will pass on the bad news. You're gentle and caring, and she loves and trusts you. All the same, it will be hard for both of you.'

'You're right, Harry, it will be hard. And it should not be this way. Rosie deserves a mother who would love and comfort her, and keep her safe through all the heartache to come.'

Harry agreed. 'It's what she deserves, but sadly it's not the case. That's why I'm relieved you're here to help her through the worst time in her life. Dad and I will be here for her too, but it's a mother she needs – a mother who truly cares – and for now it has to be you.'

'We won't let her down,' Kathleen vowed. 'Between us, we'll bring her through it, somehow. It's just unfortunate that poor Rosie's mother is a cold-hearted woman who never wanted her and would be happy if she never saw or heard from her again. I know I should not be saying these things, because Molly is my sister, but I am not proud of that, and I have never understood why she is like she is.'

She recalled how Molly had sounded when she relayed the bad news to her from the police station. 'There were no regrets in Molly's voice when she told me about what had happened. In truth, she sounded cold and distant, as if she was delivering a list of shopping. It was as though she felt nothing.' Kathleen shook her head in disbelief. 'I have never understood her, and I don't suppose I ever will.'

'Why was she calling from the police station?' Harry asked. 'Why did she not wait until she could tell Rosie and us face to face? That would have been kinder, don't you think?'

'That's exactly what I thought, but I imagine she wanted us to know as quickly as possible, and maybe with the police questioning her she couldn't be certain of what time she might get home. When someone is involved in a fatal accident, the police need all the details and she'd be asked to give a statement for their records.'

'Did she tell you exactly what happened . . . I mean, about the accident?'

'No . . . nothing.' Kathleen had wondered about that herself. 'All she said was that there had been an accident . . . and that John had been . . .' She stopped, unable to say it out loud.

Harry persevered, thinking it might help her get her thoughts straight if she talked about it before Rosie got there. 'Was she or anyone else hurt in the accident?'

'She didn't say, but she sounded all right, so I assume she was not involved.' She began to feel easier now. Talking to Harry was, in a strange way, helping her to relax before Rosie arrived. Rosie would no doubt have her own questions.

'Did she tell you what kind of accident it was?' Harry asked.

'No.'

'Hmm.' Harry was surprised. 'That's odd.'

'Yes . . . it is, isn't it?' At the time, she had been far too shocked at the news concerning John to ask.

'Did she say where the accident actually happened?'

'No. In fact now that I think of it, she didn't really give me any details. When I asked questions she simply acted as though she didn't hear. Mind you, it might have been because she was still in a state of shock.'

'It could be, yes . . . I suppose.'

'The thing is, you can never tell with Molly, but I know her . . . and I know it takes a lot to shock her. She's always been like that: cold and hard as nails.'

Kathleen cast her mind back to when they were children. 'I could tell you tales about when we were kids, and how she liked to taunt and hurt me when no one was looking.' She gave a wry little smile. 'In the end, I simply learned to stay out of her way.'

Harry was not in the least surprised. 'She hasn't changed over the years then, has she?'

'Obviously not. But I will never understand how she can hate her own daughter, that lovely girl. What is it that makes my sister so cruel?'

'It seems to me that some people are born wicked, while others have a goodness about them from the start. That's just the way it is.'

Kathleen smiled at his unexpectedly wise comment. 'Harry Riley, you're a young man with an old head on your shoulders.'

Harry smiled. 'How could anyone not love Rosie? She never has a bad word to say about anyone. She's thoughtful and kind. A genuinely good person, who deserves to be loved.'

Blushing, Harry self-consciously turned away. 'They should have been here by now. I'll just go outside and see if they're anywhere in sight.'

As he began to walk away, Kathleen called out, 'Harry? You don't have to worry. I won't tell.' She had a little smile on her face.

Harry stopped in his tracks. 'What do you mean?'

Kathleen felt just the tiniest bit embarrassed now. 'I'm sorry . . . only I am well aware of your feelings for Rosie. I've known for a while now. You love Rosie, don't you?'

Harry looked awkward.

'It's all right, Harry,' Kathleen assured him. 'I'm not about to tell anyone.'

Embarrassed to have been caught out, Harry managed a little shrug. 'Well, of course I love her! We all do.'

Kathleen nodded. 'You're right, of course. And, yes, we do love her. But we both know that the rest of us don't love her in the same way you do.' Her coy little smile was almost on cheeky. 'Admit it, Harry, you are head over heels in love with Rosie. Am I right?'

Harry's embarrassment was complete. 'I'd best go,' he muttered. 'Sorry, but I've got things to do.' He turned away.

'Wait just a minute, Harry, please?' Kathleen called, and he turned about. 'Harry, it's all right, trust me. There is no shame in loving Rosie for the generous, delightful girl she is. She's probably still too young to know her own feelings, so don't rush into anything.' She wagged a finger teasingly. 'Lesser men than you have had their hearts broken.'

When he made no comment, she asked him outright: 'Does Rosie know how you feel about her? Have you told her?'

Harry was so embarrassed he could not look at Kathleen. 'No, I haven't said anything to her. And I don't intend to.'

'Why not?'

'Because I don't want to frighten her away.'

'But what if she feels the same way about you? Have you thought about that?'

'Not really.'

'Why not?'

'Because . . .' He shrugged again. 'Besides, I'm not altogether sure if it's right for us to be thinking like that. To her, I'm just Cousin Harry. So I'm happy enough just to be a good mate.'

'Oh, I see.' Kathleen cursed herself. How could she be so thoughtless? 'Yes, of course. And there's nothing wrong in being a good mate. Lord knows, with a mother like that, she needs one.'

Not for the first time over these past years, she felt guilty and deeply ashamed to be related to someone as selfish as Molly, as though Molly's behaviour somehow reflected on her.

In a soft voice, she suggested to Harry, 'I think you're right, Harry. Rosie will need a friend, and the two of you have always understood each other, so you're wise to be cautious. It's definitely for the best. At least, for now.'

'Rosie has far too much to deal with now, so I won't mention any of this to her.'

Kathleen was greatly relieved. 'Rosie will need you over these next few months like never before,' she told Harry. 'Rosie trusts you, Harry. She sees you as a valued friend who understands her.'

'That's kind of you to say, and I promise, hand on heart, that I won't let her down,' Harry said.

'I know you won't. She listens to you, Harry. You, more than any of us, can help her find the strength to deal with losing her beloved father. In time she will surely come to terms with that loss; as we will all have to. With you helping her, Rosie will get through this because she is a brave and strong-hearted girl, and though she might not confide her deeper feelings to anyone else, she will always confide in you.'

Harry understood. 'Whatever happens, I will always be there for Rosie.' Just speaking her name gladdened his heart.

Kathleen smiled. 'Trust me, Rosie will need you more than ever. It's a sorry fact that her mother won't help her through this. I will never understand how a sister of mine has turned out to be the mother from hell! Our father was a good man and, as you know, our mother is loved by all around her. Neither your grandfather or your nanna ever had a bad bone in their bodies.'

Kathleen had neither love nor respect for her older sister. 'It's what you said a moment ago, Harry. Some people are born with kind and generous hearts, while other people are purely wicked.'

'Yes, that sounds like Aunt Molly all right!'

'Rosie's life has not been easy under her mother's iron rule. As far as I'm aware, Molly has never praised or encouraged Rosie in any way. Not when she managed to tie her own shoe-laces at the tender age of three. And not when she won a school prize two years later for her first attempt at writing a letter. What Molly said to her then was deeply hurtful to Rosie.'

Harry was curious. 'What happened?'

'As far as I can recall, it was Rosie's second term at school. Every child in the class got a little certificate for writing a short note to tell what they liked about school. Rosie was so proud of bringing her award home to show her parents. She was devastated, though, when her mother said she had not done anything special and that she had no right to be proud; that pride was wicked and sinful. Then she took pleasure in watching Rosie cry as she tore the certificate into a hundred pieces, in front of her.'

Kathleen shook her head in disgust. 'According to John, when Rosie came running out to him in the yard she was inconsolable.'

Harry was shocked. 'How can a mother not love someone as lovely as Rosie? It's not like Rosie is a difficult and nasty person.'

'I can't answer that one either.' Kathleen herself had always wondered how Molly could be so hateful and wicked to Rosie. 'Maybe something bad happened in Molly's own childhood and she has never told anyone about it, even me.'

'Even if there was, that is still no excuse to treat Rosie the way she does.'

Kathleen nodded. 'You're absolutely right. Let's just hope that somehow, sometime or another, Molly will realise how fortunate she is to have Rosie.'

Harry felt sad for Rosie. 'Well, at least her father loved her. They had such a special bond, although I've noticed Aunt Molly standing in the doorway sometimes, looking daggers when she sees Uncle John and Rosie laughing together at Barney's comical antics.' He gave a deep sigh. 'I'm so afraid for her. I don't dare to think how she's going to manage without her father there.'

'You're right, Son. When Molly told me the shocking news, I wasn't sure how to deal with it myself.

I'm certainly not looking forward to telling Rosie that her daddy won't be coming home ever again.'

'Did Aunt Molly tell you what happened exactly?'

'No. Molly did not go into any detail as such. So I can't really let Rosie know how her father was killed. All Molly said was that there had been some kind of accident, and that she called an ambulance, but it was too late. Then the police were involved, and that's why she was giving a statement at the police station.'

'But, if she was there – and it sounds like she was, seeing that it was her who called the ambulance – don't you think it strange that she didn't tell you everything? I mean, where exactly was this accident? And who else, if anyone, was involved? And who was it that called the police? It seems to me that she kept back more than she told you.'

'Well, obviously she must have been in a state of shock. Or maybe she was just nervous, calling me from the police station.' In truth, Kathleen had wondered herself why Molly had been so brief and straight to the point. And she never once seemed heartbroken, or conveyed even the slightest regret.

Instead, it was almost as though Molly was making a cold, brief statement . . . like Harry implied.

'Although she didn't ask outright, I understood that Molly wanted me to tell Rosie.'

'Did she ask after Rosie . . . where she was, or if she was safe? Did she even ask that Dad might go and bring Rosie back here?'

Harry thought that might have been Molly's first question on contact. But then, why would Molly care about her daughter now, when she had never cared before?

'She hardly mentioned Rosie,' Kathleen admitted, 'except to say that her father would not be coming home . . . ever again!'

'What?' Harry was shocked. 'You mean she actually said it like that . . . in those words?'

'Yes and, like you, I thought that was most insensitive. I told her I could not tell Rosie in that way. I simply promised Molly that I would make sure Rosie was told about her father, but I would try my very best to be as gentle as possible in the circumstances. And that we would keep her here with us for as long as necessary.'

Something was weighing on her conscience. 'Harry, do you think I should have asked Patrick to tell her about her father straight away? Did I do wrong to keep it from her even for this long? Only, I thought it might be easier, particularly for Rosie, if there was just the two of us together when she learned the tragic news.'

She took a deep, deep breath. From the minute Molly told her about John she had tortured herself as to how she might break the news to that darling girl, whose world was about to crumble around her.

'You did what was right,' Harry assured her. 'I think you'll be doing the right and proper thing in telling Rosie with just the two of you there. That way, it will be easier . . . for both of you.'

Kathleen was greatly relieved. 'Thank you, Harry, you've made me feel a little better. After all, it won't really change anything in the end, will it? And what can she do about what's happened? Nothing! But she will be absolutely devastated. Much like the rest of us.'

Closing her eyes, she murmured under her breath, 'How do I tell a young girl, about to grow into adulthood, that the father she adores has been taken from her? He will never advise her on her first love, or walk her down the aisle with her arm in his, while she looks up at him with shining eyes.'

The tears flowed, and she could not speak. Harry took his stepmother in his arms and held her until she was quiet again. 'I love you,' he told her softly, '. . . always. I bless the day Dad found you.' For a long moment, they sat together, comforting each other, their grief heavy because a good, strong and honest man was gone for ever. And his daughter was on her way to learn that she would never again experience the joy and comfort of being held in her father's protective, loving arms.

~

For a time, Harry and his stepmother stayed sitting together, quietly talking and drawing strength from each other, though deeply apprehensive about Rosie's imminent arrival.

'I won't be able to explain the manner of how he died,' Kathleen fretted. 'And she's bound to ask.'

'So how will you put it to Rosie?' Harry was nervous.

'Well, of course I shall be as gentle as possible, but I need to make sure she knows the truth of it, and I must be especially careful not to leave her with any false hopes . . .' Her voice broke. 'That will be the hardest part of all,' she whispered. 'No hope! Oh, Harry, that will break her heart . . . and mine.'

Angry with herself, she wiped away the falling tears. 'Come on, Kathleen . . . you can do this!' she told herself. Her resolve must be strong. For Rosie's sake.

'The awful thing is, I cannot give her any information as to how it happened. All I know is that there was an accident in the hay barn, and John was killed.

That's what Molly said . . . and then she hung up.'

Harry was intrigued. 'But what was he doing in the hay barn anyway? As far as I know, everything was put away at the end of the day. Uncle John had finished his work as I was leaving. He would have locked the barn and gone home.'

'So why would he have gone out again, and why would he open the barn?' Kathleen asked. 'Do you think he heard noises or something? You know how alert he's been after those thieves robbed him blind.'

'Yes, and I also know that there's a key hidden outside in case of fire. The thing is, only three people know about that key. That's Uncle John and me, and Aunt Molly. So either Uncle John returned to the barn because he suspected thieves were trying to get in, or the barn was opened by Aunt Molly. But why would she go into the barn after we had all finished and gone home, especially when she hates coming anywhere near the yards, even in the daytime? She thinks the yards and stables are dirty and smelly.' He shook his head. 'No, I can't imagine she would ever have gone in there at night. And why would she, anyway?'

Kathleen shrugged. 'She told me she didn't have time to go into any detail. She just said that the police were asking all manner of questions, and that she would be there for some time yet. We just need to look after Rosie. She has to be our priority now.'

Thinking of Rosie, she choked back her tears. 'Lord only knows what will happen with her. I'm wondering if we might persuade Molly to let Rosie come and stay with us – for a time, at least. But then once Rosie is away from her mother, we could maybe somehow make it more permanent . . .'

Harry was relieved to think of Rosie away from the farm and all its sad associations for her now, and also away from her mother. 'Oh, really? Do you honestly think her mother would allow it, though?'

'Well, I suppose it's possible that with John not there, maybe she would rather keep Rosie with her than be alone. You never know, she might even grow to love her. Like a mother should.'

'I doubt that!' Harry said bluntly. 'But she might keep her there so she can bully her and work her into the ground, and humiliate her whenever possible. She would – she absolutely would – because Uncle John won't be there to protect her. And if that happens, who would help Rosie then, eh?' Harry was so afraid.

'You do have a point, Harry,' Kathleen said thoughtfully. 'She might insist on keeping Rosie at the farm for such reasons. And another thing: what if she's already planning to sell the farm, lock, stock and barrel? Once she's got the money, she'll be away to distant parts, and we'll probably never hear from her again . . . which would not bother me or you, I'm sure, but what about Rosie?'

'Oh, don't worry, there'll be no danger of her taking Rosie away from us. I bet all she wants is the money from the sale of the house and farmland, and everything on it.'

'You're absolutely right. And I don't suppose Rosie will ever see a single penny of her inheritance if her mother swans off, roaming the world with money in the bank to pay for it. And once she's gone we won't see her again. Whatever happens, we must make sure that Rosie stays here with us until she's of an age to make her own choices.'

Harry was already looking forward to that particular day.

'I'm sure you're right about Aunt Molly's plans,' he told Kathleen. 'She will sell everything down to the last hay bale, and then be away before Rosie even realises.'

He had seen a great deal while working on his Uncle John's farm. 'I know she's never liked the farm,' he confided. 'I heard her tell Uncle John that she hated the sight and smell of the place. She wanted it sold so they could move to somewhere in town. She said if he didn't like that idea she was prepared to settle for a big, fancy house at the seaside, where they could take it easy and enjoy life . . . have holidays abroad, and see the world. She said it was time they enjoyed a better standard of living, like other people with money to spend.'

Kathleen smiled knowingly. 'Did she now? And I can imagine what John had to say about that.'

'Well, first of all, he was shocked, but he didn't shout or anything like that, because that was not his way. He told her it was his inheritance, and his responsibility to respect his father's wishes, and his grandfather's before him, in passing the entire holding and everything on it to the next generation. He told Molly that he had been entrusted with that duty, that he was just a part of the Tanner dynasty, which he had always considered to be an honour and a joy.'

'Oh, and I bet she took umbrage at that, didn't she?' Kathleen tutted. 'She's always wanted everything for herself. She was never sharing as a child. She certainly wouldn't be pleased for the Tanner inheritance to pass her by and go to Rosie. She'd have got angry at that.'

'She did, yes. Even after Uncle John promised her that if he died before her she need not worry because he had made generous provision for both Molly and Rosie.'

'Good for him!' Kathleen was not surprised at John's strong sense of duty, to both his immediate family, and the Tanners who had gone before. 'And how did she take that? Not too well, I can imagine.'

'Well, she went a bit crazy, and started a big argument. Then she stormed off, cursing him to hell and back.'

Harry recalled the occasion vividly. 'She never knew, but I was cleaning out the stables nearby, and I heard them arguing. After she'd gone, Uncle John called me out and apologised. "I'm sorry about the disturbance," he said. But I knew he was embarrassed, so I told a fib. I said I was so busy doing my work that I was not aware of any disturbance.'

'You're a very thoughtful young man.' Kathleen was not surprised he'd witnessed her sister's foul temper and big ambitions. 'Molly has always been a greedy, spiteful person, even when we were children.'

She fell silent a moment, remembering her childhood, when her older sister had often made her cry, for whatever selfish, cruel reason.

'Do you really think Aunt Molly will sell the farm?' Harry asked, jolting her thoughts back to the present.

'I would not be surprised. I'm pretty certain she would not want Rosie to share any of the money she would surely make from the sale of everything – yards, barns, stables, livestock, pastures and, of course, the machinery, the house and everything in it. Molly would have more money than she might ever need, but you can bet Rosie would not see a penny, either now or when she comes of age.'

Of one thing Kathleen was certain. 'I've no doubt she would ask me to have Rosie while she clears off and enjoys the grand life without the inconvenience of a child tagging along, and I shall be delighted to have her. Trust me, Molly will simply grab what she can and forget that John meant for it all to be held in trust for Rosie. His wishes won't matter one jot to her.'

She cast her mind back to a conversation she had had with her sister a long time back. 'From what she told me on the odd occasion when she talked about her ambitions, it would seem that John was somewhat naïve about matters official, and he never really trusted solicitors. So, if that's true she's bound to come up smiling, even if she has to pay a smart and devious lawyer to work for her. I mean, what with John being an only child, and the older Tanners long gone now, who's to stop her?'

'Could she really cheat Rosie out of her inheritance?' Harry was shocked. 'Surely Uncle John will have put his wishes in writing . . . or something official?'

'Oh, I'm sure he did, but remember, though he had the land and business, he was cash poor and never earned the kind of money that would allow him to hire a really top solicitor. His riches were in the land he worked, and the joy of what he did, as his father, grandfather and great-grandfather did before him. He might even have just lodged a simple letter of intent with an ordinary solicitor, while believing that if anything happened to him, Molly would respect his wishes.

'If my sister has her way – and I'm sure she has it all in hand – Rosie will be left a pauper, while Molly will come out of it a very wealthy woman. When the formalities are all done with, Molly Tanner will be off, money burning a hole in her pocket, to whichever grand bolthole takes her fancy.'

Kathleen's harsh and bitter words were borne out of knowing Molly Tanner like no one but a sister could.

CHAPTER SEVEN

KATHLEEN GUIDED THE conversation to an end. 'Whatever happens, Harry, you can rest assured that your father and I will do everything possible to help Rosie come through this dreadful ordeal.'

In spite of reassuring Harry, Kathleen herself was deeply concerned about Rosie's future. 'With regard to what might happen next, we'll just have to wait and see, but to be honest, I can never imagine Molly wanting Rosie on her coat-tails, especially if she's intent on moving up and moving on in the world. And especially when we all know she has not one ounce of motherly love or kindness for that lovely girl.'

Harry knew that, but it only made him more nervous for Rosie's future.

His quiet moment of contemplation was broken

by Kathleen softly warning him, 'Quick, Harry, I just heard the car door slam shut.'

Harry scrambled out of his seat, Kathleen was ahead, and the two of them ran into the passageway and towards the front door.

Patrick was standing back, waiting for Rosie to enter the house.

'I'm sorry it took so long to get home,' he said to Kathleen. 'We had to make sure the house was all locked.'

Just then Barney bounded through the door and down the passageway.

Kathleen seized the moment to reassure Harry. 'Please try not to worry,' she whispered. 'We'll keep her safe, I promise.'

Harry gave a discreet nod. 'I know.'

He also made the same vow himself. Whatever it took, come rain or shine, he would always be there for Rosie because, for him, darling Rosie was the one.

Over these past weeks, not being able to tell her how he truly felt had seemed like torture, but she was so young and he needed to be responsible and not frighten her. And now, following tonight's heart-breaking news, he could definitely not tell her. Maybe he never would.

Patrick gave Kathleen a brief peck on the cheek. 'Sorry, darlin', but we got here as fast as we could.'

Kathleen nodded. 'No matter . . . you're here now.'

Concerned that Rosie had so far uttered not one word, Kathleen folded her in a warm embrace. 'Come inside, sweetheart.'

Turning to Patrick, she discreetly raised her eyebrows and gave him a certain look that asked if he had revealed the worst truth to Rosie.

When he pursed his lips in that particular way and discreetly shook his head, she knew he had kept his word.

Kathleen was now desperate to get the bad news over with. She saw the tearstains on Rosie's face, and she noticed the fear in her soft blue eyes, and it was clear that Rosie suspected something very bad had taken place.

'What's happened, Aunt Kathleen? I know something isn't right. Last night, Daddy went out to find Mother and he never came back. Nobody seems to know where he is. Please . . . has something happened? He never stays away like that . . . never! So why didn't he come home?'

Her voice trembled and now she was in tears, holding onto Kathleen as though her life depended on it. 'Tell me what's happened, Auntie Kathleen, please? Where is he? Something is wrong, I know it.'

Welling up with emotion, Kathleen wrapped her arms about Rosie's slim shoulders. 'I'll tell you everything your mother told me.'

Rosie made no reply, but a deep worry gnawed in the pit of her stomach.

All the way here, Uncle Patrick had chatted almost non-stop, as though to prevent her asking questions. He had talked about all manner of things, except the possible whereabouts of her father. When she nervously ventured to ask if he had any idea where her father might be, Uncle Patrick had cleverly shifted onto other subjects.

In short, he had not been the jolly, fun-loving man he normally was. Instead, he had seemed unusually agitated. Rosie had sensed that he was panicking to get back to Kathleen.

She suspected that he knew where her father was, but try as she might, Rosie could not get him to discuss the subject. It really concerned her that he was so reluctant to talk about her father's whereabouts.

In the end, on seeing how harassed he was, Rosie had decided to take his advice and wait to see what Auntie Kathleen had to say. 'That's the girl!' His relief had been evident. 'Your Auntie Kathleen will tell you exactly what your mother told her. To be honest, I'm not altogether sure what was said between the two of them.'

A number of possibilities had then played through Rosie's thoughts. Was it possible that her parents had broken up? Had her father gone away? Where was he? Would he ever come back? She could not imagine he would ever leave her.

And what about his farm, and the life he loved? No, he would never leave Tanner's Farm. To him, that would be the worst kind of betrayal.

That solid belief in her father's good character made her feel somewhat easier. No, he would never leave her, and he would never leave his beloved farm . . . not in a million years.

Now she needed someone to be honest with her because she desperately needed to know what was going on. She even wondered if Auntie Kathleen had a surprise waiting for her, and the minute she walked through the door her daddy would be there to greet her. The thought had made her heart skip.

'Rosie? Are you all right?' Having greeted her and given Barney a loving cuddle, Kathleen brought Rosie back to the present. 'I've been talking to you, sweetheart. You seemed miles away. Did you not hear me?'

'Oh, I'm sorry. But, Auntie Kathleen, will you please tell me something?'

Kathleen anticipated her question. 'Well, of course, if I know the answer. First, though, I think the men should go into the kitchen and make a pot of tea, and search out the biscuits. What do you think, Rosie, is that a good idea?'

When Rosie merely nodded, Kathleen gave Patrick a knowing look. 'Off you go then, you two,' she said meaningfully. 'Rosie and I are off to the sun-room.' She gave them a certain glance that warned them not to disturb her and Rosie.

'Right, come on then, Son.' Patrick understood her little ploy.

As Kathleen walked Rosie along the hallway, Harry watched them go. Suddenly Rosie turned round and looked straight at him, her eyes huge. With a sad heart, he nodded in reassurance and blew her a gentle kiss. Then she was gone from sight as they turned the corner.

'Come on, Harry,' Patrick took his arm, 'we'd best make ourselves scarce.' He had seen that poignant exchange between the two young ones.

Harry walked on ahead to the kitchen, while all the time thinking of Rosie and how her heart was about to be broken.

He had loved Rosie ever since he was eleven years old. It was Rosie's eighth birthday and Kathleen had put on a party in this very house. Rosie's smile and lovely nature captivated him, so he could not take his eyes off her. Over the following years he realised there could never be any other girl for him but Rosie. As he grew into his teens, his love for her had only grown stronger. By then he could talk with her, laugh with her, and be the very best of friends. Now, having turned eighteen, Harry knew his love for Rosie was for ever. In his deepest heart, he knew there could never be anyone else for him.

~

Kathleen had caught sight of Harry blowing a kiss, and she knew her instincts were right. He did love Rosie. Now, more than ever, she was glad of that, because Rosie would need all the love of this little family.

Even as they walked on, Barney at their heels, the questions began, just as Kathleen had anticipated.

'Auntie Kathleen, have my parents broken up? Is that why Daddy hasn't come home? Are they getting a divorce? I know Mother can be difficult, and they always seem to be rowing lately. Is it me . . . something I've done? I know they argue about me – I've heard them – but I don't know what I've done wrong.'

Kathleen stopped and reached out for Rosie's hand. 'Oh, Rosie . . . I'm sure you've done nothing wrong. You must not think like that. Unfortunately my sister has a quick temper, and it never takes much to set her off. I expect sometimes your father gets angry, too, and then inevitably a row will follow. But that's the way of it, I'm afraid, and it is not your fault.'

Rosie recalled the worst row her parents had ever had. 'It was my fault when Mother got bad-tempered when I was late home from school because I'd been to play with a friend and forgot to tell her. Daddy was worried and told me off and I said I was sorry but then Mother thrashed me really hard and Daddy had to stop her, and there was a terrible upset, and Mother said it was all my fault.'

'Believe me, Rosie, the rows between your parents were never your fault. Your mother could cause trouble in a room with no one in it but her miserable self! I've been caught up in her nasty temper many a time. When I was even younger than you, she just loved to make trouble and blame it on me – more times than I care to remember.'

'Really?' This made Rosie feel better.

'Yes, believe me, Rosie, she has always been that way: selfish, quick-tempered and ready to blame anyone but herself. My sister does not need an excuse to fly into a rage, so don't go blaming yourself. That's what she does – she twists everything round so other people feel as though it's their fault. She hurts people, Rosie, and she doesn't care one jot.'

Kathleen reached out to hug Rosie close. 'Please, Rosie, promise me that whatever happens – whenever bad things might occur – you will not blame yourself.' She was dreading telling the awful news to Rosie. 'None of it is your fault. Promise me you will remember that and believe it.'

'Yes, Auntie Kathleen, I promise.' Rosie was not altogether sure what she had just promised, but one way or another she would try her hardest to keep her word.

'Good!' Kathleen took Rosie by the hand. 'Now then, while the men are in the kitchen, you and I need to talk.'

Rosie was relieved she'd learn what was happening at last. 'All I need to know is why my father never came home. Do you know where he is now?'

'Look, Rosie, hand on heart, I do not know exactly where he is, although I must tell you what your mother told me word for word.' She took a moment to suppress the rising emotion. 'Come on, we'll be more comfortable sitting down, I think.'

Rosie merely nodded. She trusted Kathleen, although at the back of her mind she could not rid herself of the deep-down feeling that something was very wrong.

Everyone had been too kind, too quiet and she knew that Barney had also sensed it because of the way he remained at her side, head down, his brown droopy eyes looking up at her in that certain way . . . like when she found a baby rabbit dead in a snare, and Barney saw her crying because she thought it was too sad.

Just then, Barney reached up to touch Rosie's leg gently with his big, hairy paw.

'All right, boy?' She stooped to hug him. He knew something, she thought worriedly, but then she cautioned herself to stop imagining things. Barney was probably just picking up on her nervousness. How could he not when she was filled with fear? Afraid as to why her father had not come home. Afraid for that man in the barn, who was crying. Afraid of her mother's warning that if she told anyone what she might have seen or heard, Barney would be hurt, or worse! She made herself shut out the frightening images.

Kathleen pushed open the big white doors into the sun-room. 'Sit yourself down, sweetheart.' Gesturing to the blue-cushioned sofa by the window, she watched as Rosie and Barney made their way there, then she closed the doors, before going to sit right next to Rosie and taking hold of her hand. 'Rosie . . .' Her heart was in her throat as she knew she must prepare Rosie for the worst. '. . . I did not tell you before because I wanted the two of us to be on our own, but when your mother called me from the police station, she did briefly speak about your daddy, though she didn't go into details.'

Seeing how Rosie had turned pale and was looking straight at her with frightened eyes, Kathleen felt the need to take a deep breath before going on. 'I'm sorry, sweetheart, but the news is very serious.' Having controlled her sorrow for so long, she could no longer stop the tears from falling.

When Rosie made to speak, her eyes big with fear, Kathleen took hold of her hand. 'Look, sweetheart, let me just tell you what your mother told me.'

She squeezed Rosie's small hand in hers. Never in all her life had she ever needed to tell someone that a loved one had died. And Rosie was just a child, a sweet, lovable girl whose heart was overflowing with love for her daddy.

Rosie was quietly sobbing, the tears running freely down her face and her small hand trembling in Kathleen's. She had seen how anxious her aunt was.

She had heard her voice break with emotion, and now she could think only of what Kathleen had just told her. 'Serious' . . . the news was 'serious'. So were her parents really splitting up? Was the farm about to be sold? Was her daddy in hospital? Had he been hurt and Molly was part of it? How bad was this news?

She did not care if her parents were splitting up. She did not care if her mother was leaving, or if she was staying. Or even if the whole family was selling up and moving to another part of the country. She cared about nothing except that her daddy was safe, and that he would soon be home.

Sensing the serious mood and being anxious for Rosie, Barney had been sitting bolt upright, but now he pushed up on his back legs and nudged his head into Rosie's lap, his big, soulful eyes looking up at her as though he knew she needed him.

'All right, Rosie?' Kathleen asked gently.

Rosie looked up, and gave the slightest nod. She heard the fear in her aunt's voice, and she was ready.

And so Kathleen told her what she knew from what Molly had said: that she happened to be in the barn when Rosie's father came in.

'. . . It seemed there was an accident of sorts, a bad accident, which involved your daddy.' She went quickly on before Rosie could start asking questions she was not able to answer. 'Your mother said she called an ambulance straight away and he was rushed to hospital.' She took a slow breath before going on in a softer voice, 'She said he had been badly hurt. So badly hurt . . . that . . . it seems he would not pull through . . . and . . . in the end, I'm so very sorry, Rosie, but there was nothing they could do for him. Oh, my darling girl . . . I am so very, very sorry.' Without breaking down, she could say no more.

When Rosie stared at her in disbelief, Kathleen reached out and held her close. Rosie then sobbed in her arms, all the while calling for her father, screaming one minute, silent the next, and then sobbing as if she would never stop.

Kathleen herself could not hold back the tears, because of her pain for Rosie and because of the loss of that good man, her brother-in-law. But her priority now was to comfort this lovely, innocent girl, who had lost someone immensely precious and totally irreplaceable in her young life.

For what seemed an age, Kathleen rocked the heartbroken girl in her arms. 'Oh, Rosie . . . I'm so sorry, sweetheart. I am so very sorry.' It was all she could say.

Seeing her distress, Barney never once took his gaze off Rosie. He watched her with stricken eyes, while making a soft, oddly musical sound from the back of his throat, much like the low, subdued sound of an injured animal.

Suddenly, without warning, Rosie wrenched herself away from Kathleen and ran to the outer doors. Before Kathleen could get to her, she ran outside, fleeing across the garden as though the devil himself was after her, Barney right behind and Kathleen running after them both, frantically calling for Rosie to come back.

Rosie came to a halt beside the now dormant flowerbeds. There was a pond, and in the early morning light she watched the goldfish swimming round and round, while the water moved in slow, curious circles around them. Rosie remembered her daddy had once made her a little pond when he got her a fat goldfish, but within days birds had swooped down and eaten it. Her daddy then offered to buy her another goldfish, and a mate to go with it, but Rosie said no, in case the birds came back and ate them, too. The thought of that happening was too sad.

But what Rosie saw now was something else. In that winter garden of neatly turned soil, the holly trees bearing berries, she saw her father as he was then, back home in the vegetable patch. The sun was shining and the flowers were in bloom. He was collecting the ripe tomatoes and plump carrots, which he'd planted some time back. He was so proud . . . and look now! There he was, smiling at her. Then suddenly he was gone and Rosie was in Kathleen's warm embrace. 'It's all right, sweetheart . . . it will get easier, I promise you.' Kathleen's gentle voice shook with emotion.

'Daddy's here,' Rosie told her tearfully.

'I'm sure he is,' Kathleen whispered. 'He always will be.'

'No! Don't tell me lies!' Rosie cried out. 'My daddy is never coming back!' Her cutting grief turned to anger. 'He's not, is he, Auntie Kathleen?' She could hardly see for the tears rolling down her face. 'Daddy's gone and I will never see him again . . . Not ever, as long as I live!'

She clung to Kathleen, her heart breaking.

Then suddenly she was pushing Kathleen away and fleeing across the garden. She fled over the long bare flowerbeds, then out to the far side of the garden with Barney tight on her heels.

She did not know where she was headed. She did not care. All she could hear was her daddy's voice calling her name . . . her daddy laughing with her when she was a small girl, squealing with excitement when he pushed her high into the air on her new swing. In her heart and soul, in every fibre of her being, she could hear his gentle voice full of his love and his great pride in her.

Kathleen was following her, shouting and pleading, 'Come back, Rosie . . . Please, stop!' But Rosie ran on. She had to get far away. She had to escape from the truth of what she had been told. Her father was dead! Those short words ran round and round in her frantic mind. Her daddy was gone for ever . . . gone for ever . . . gone for ever!

Behind her she could hear Kathleen yelling for her to stop so they could talk about it. But she was not about to stop, not about to talk. Not about to ever go home again because it could never be home from now on. Not without her daddy there.

She ran blindly on, tripping and sliding in a desperate effort to run away from the awful truth. Running faster and faster, just to get away. To get away and never come back!

Katheen could hear Barney barking. He sounded a long way away, yet she continued after them, calling to Rosie, 'Come back!' She could see Rosie with Barney at her heels, but they were far ahead. They had crested a little hill and were now gaining speed as they went. They entered the spinney and the last she saw of them was when they ran in amongst the trees, before being lost to sight.

Kathleen, determined to catch up, scrambled up the slope after them. She paused briefly to catch her breath, then ran on into the spinney, dodging amongst the trees, then on to some rough hilly ground with boulders amongst the clumps of grass. The path sloped steeply up and she was almost at the top when she stumbled on the uneven surface and slipped down, rolling out of control. Moments later, bruised and torn, she was brought to a shuddering halt when she caught her foot in a dead tree stump. The fall was bad, and in the desperate struggle to free herself, her shoe was torn off and sent tumbling further down the rough slope. She tried to stand, reaching for the shoe, and completely lost her balance, crashing all the way to the bottom of the path, where she lay breathless and in great pain.

She could see the deep grazes where the skin had been scraped off her legs as she fell.

She began yelling, 'Rosie! I'm hurt, Rosie!' When she realised that both Rosie and Barney were long gone, she decided the best thing to do now was to go back and get help.

And to that end, she began the painful journey home, going slowly so as not to lose her footing again. But every inch was agony.

After a while she stopped to rest and to assess the damage. The grazes to her legs were now covered in dirt and bracken, and when she attempted to wipe the worst off, the pain was excrutiating, so she abandoned that task, and gathered all her remaining strength to get home, though every inch she limped felt like a mile, and every step like a punishment.

After what seemed an age, she was greatly relieved to be on more even ground. 'Come on, Kathleen, girl, just a little further. You can make it.' Her spirits were stronger, but as she hobbled on, the effort and the continuing pain became too much to bear. She was too exhausted even to cry out. Too battered to care. Too weary to press on.

But with Rosie uppermost in her mind, she knew she had to. She told herself that however much pain she herself was suffering now, and however desperate and abandoned she felt, it was as nothing compared to what Rosie must be going through, alone and frightened, unable to come to terms with her grief. Her future looked bleak, and even those who loved her dearly could never fill John Tanner's big, capable shoes.

Kathleen shed a few sorry tears. 'Help her, Lord,' she prayed. 'Bring her away from the woman who despises her own daughter. Bring her home to the ones who love her, and with your help we might even fill a part of the gap that John Tanner has left behind.'

Thinking of Rosie, a deeply sad and lonely child out there somewhere, alone and broken, gave Kathleen a burst of strength, making her press on with fierce determination.

She called out, but it seemed no one heard her cries. With the pain worsening at every step, she found it difficult to go any further and she had to take a rest and catch her breath.

After a few minutes, she hesitantly pressed on, holding onto whatever she could find to help her along, while continuing to call out, 'Patrick! Harry!' But help was not forthcoming.

She was now in sight of the house but, too exhausted to go on, she fell to the ground. Yet she continued to call as best she could, though her cries grew weaker and weaker.

It seemed there was no one in that quiet backwater to hear her.

And then she was silent.

CHAPTER EIGHT

IN THE KITCHEN, Harry remarked on the length of time that Rosie and Kathleen had been in the sun-room. 'I want to go down there and check that they're all right, but I'm not really sure whether it's right to disturb them just yet.'

'Hmm.' Patrick was thinking the very same. 'I agree, they do seem to have been in there for some time.'

Glancing up at the clock on the wall, he was surprised at just how long Kathleen and Rosie had been talking together. 'Give them another five minutes or so, then we'll take a sneaky look, just to check they're all right.' He made a sorry face. 'Young Rosie must be in pieces. Mind you, Harry boy, if anyone can help her through it, your mother will, although whatever anyone says or does to help her through this crisis, it won't change the outcome, will it? Life for Rosie will never be the same. I know what she must be feeling, because it took me years to get over the loss of my father . . . your granddad Jack. You were just a small boy, but you were a great help to me just being there when I needed to hold you, and oh, but could you chatter.'

Harry listened while Patrick talked emotionally about the loss of his own father. 'Later, when you asked after your granddad, I simply told you he'd gone away to Heaven, where all the good angels go. And you were happy enough with that. Then, sometime after that day – you may or may not remember – I helped you to write a little note telling your granddad not to worry because some day we'd go to Heaven and give him a cuddle, and we would all be together again.'

Having delved into the treasured memories, he discreetly wiped away a tear. 'So there you are, Son. You and your mother got me through that terrible time, just as Kathleen is doing her best to help young Rosie deal with the loss of her daddy.'

Harry could not forget her lonely glance as she went away with his stepmother.

'Dad?'

'Yes, Harry?'

'Do you honestly think Rosie will be able to deal with it?'

'I think so, given time, and with the family behind her. After all, Son, what alternative does she have anyway? But Rosie is made of strong stuff – just like her daddy. She'll come through it, don't fret, although it may take her many months, if not years, to actually come to terms with it.'

The loss of his own father, and then his first wife, had knocked him sideways and he still felt the pain of bereavement, mostly at night before he closed his eyes to sleep.

'I feel for that girl,' Patrick murmured. 'I know only too well what she'll be going through right now. And, like I say, she's only young!'

'So, what can we do, Dad?' Harry was out of his depth. 'Like you say, she's not grown up or experienced enough to deal with this kind of grief. How can we help her to get through it?'

Patrick smiled. 'Well, we can be there for her. We can watch over her, and if she needs to talk, we can listen – it always helps to talk – that's what will help her. Right now I expect that's exactly what Kathleen is doing: allowing her to talk and helping to guide her through the pain. I'm afraid, in these circumstances, that's all anyone can do.'

He took a deep breath, then blew it out in a rush of words. 'At some time or another, Son, we all get cruel knocks from Lady Fate. But life marches on and somehow we manage to deal with its trials and keep going forward. It's a wicked world, Son,' he tutted angrily.

Harry simply nodded.

'Dad?' he asked anxiously then.

'Yes, Son?'

'I really need to know if Rosie and Mother are all right.'

'So do I, Son, so do I.'

'Would it hurt if I went and took a little peek at them now? I promise I'll be careful not to be seen.'

Patrick took a moment to mull over the suggestion. 'No, I think, on reflection, it's not the right thing to do. We shall just have to be patient. Your mother will know we're anxious. She'll be calling us any minute. So let's wait here a while longer. They know where we are.'

Reluctantly, Harry had to agree. 'All right, but they seem to have been in there for ages. If someone doesn't come soon, I'm sorry, Dad, but I think one of us ought to check on them.'

Patick nodded. 'All right, Son, let's give it another ten minutes or so. Then we'll see. Meantime, I'll make another pot of tea. What do you say?'

Harry nodded. 'If you like . . . thanks, Dad.' He

was not a tea-drinker, but pottering about would keep his dad's mind off what was happening on the other side of the house.

As his father went to put the kettle on, Harry thought he heard a scratching sound. 'What was that?' He looked across to his father. 'Did you hear that?'

'No . . . I didn't hear anything.' He took a second or two to listen, before shaking his head. 'I expect you're on edge, Son . . . but that's understandable.'

Having made the tea, Patrick stirred sugar in and handed one of the mugs to Harry. 'There you go, Son. Get that down you. It'll calm your nerves. Your grandma swears by— What was that?' He looked towards the back door. 'Hey, you're right, Son. I could swear I just heard something. A kind of scratching.'

The noise started again, more pronounced now, and they recognised Barney's unmistakable excited bark. Then he was whimpering . . . scratching madly at the back door.

'Jeeze! What the hell's going on?' said Patrick.

He made for the door, but Harry was there first. He threw open the door and Barney bounded in, running between their legs, then back outside and then in again, and Harry was amazed to see the state of him.

'He's soaking wet! And look, there are bits of mud and stuff between his toes.'

Patrick was puzzled. 'But he was in the sun-room with the girls,' he said. 'He was, wasn't he?' Now he was not so sure.

Harry was also puzzled. 'He was, yes, and I don't think he would have left Rosie's side . . . never in a million years.'

'Well, maybe he needed to spend a penny. It happens to the best of us. Look, Harry, you hang back here a minute. Keep Barney with you, and I'll sneak along the garden to check on the girls. I can peek through the side window and they won't even know I'm there. I can't imagine why I didn't think of it before.' Grabbing Barney by the collar, he gave him over to Harry. 'Keep a tight hold on him, Son.'

Barney, however, had other ideas, because as Patrick went out, the dog broke away from Harry and went bounding out the door again. Then he stood facing them, barking madly, legs astride, and poised to run again.

'What's wrong with him?' Harry asked. 'I've never seen him like this before.'

Just then, Barney ran off to the edge of the garden, where he turned round and ran back again, barking and continuing to run in circles. Patrick and Harry were totally confused as to what was wrong with him, although Harry suggested to his father, 'Maybe he saw Rosie upset and he misbehaved, like now, so Mum put him outside.'

Before Patrick could comment, Barney turned tail and ran a little way across the garden. Then he ran back again, stabbing at Harry's foot with his paw, and then he was off again, running back across the garden until he stopped and stood still, facing the two of them, while making a whining sound from the back of his throat.

'Why is he behaving like that?' Harry shook his head in disbelief.

Before Patrick could reply, Harry took off to the sun-room. 'Something's wrong, Dad, I know it,' he said over his shoulder.

A moment or so later, he was yelling for his father. 'Quick, Dad! You'd best come and see. They've gone . . . Rosie and Mum . . . they're not here.'

While Patrick made his way to see, Harry was trying to calm Barney, who was growing more excited by the minute.

'Look, Dad!' Harry gestured to the empty sun-room, and the partly open door, which was flapping in the light breeze. 'The door is left open and they've both gone.' He was panic-stricken.

Barney was continuing to bark loudly, while clawing at Harry's leg with his big, fleshy paw.

'Where are they, boy?' Harry held him still. 'Come on, Barney . . . show us! Take us to where they are!' Barney shot off at the run, with both Patrick and Harry right behind. Across the garden they went, over the pathway and out where the ground became rougher at the edge of the spinney.

Patrick saw his wife first, lying crumpled on the ground. 'Aw, dear God, it's Katheen. Kathleen!' Both Harry and Patrick ran as though their lives depended on it, Barney bounding along in front, still barking, but in a much saner manner, knowing that help was at hand.

By the time Patrick and Harry got to her, Barney was licking Kathleen's face as though trying to wake her. Pain and sheer exhaustion had got the better of her, and she felt nothing; she heard nothing.

'Kathleen, love, talk to me!' Folding to his knees, Patrick took her into his arms. 'It's me – Patrick. Talk to me, Kathleen. Talk to me.' He gently patted her face. 'Kathleen, look at me!'

When she slowly opened her eyes, Patrick took a huge breath in relief. 'Thank God! Where are you hurt, my darling? What happened?' His questions rang out one after the other, but most importantly, he had her in his arms. He could see she was exhausted and in a poorly state, muddied and with streaks of blood over her legs where her skin had been torn.

But she was safe, thank God. 'I've got you now, love. We'll get you home, don't worry.' Patrick murmured a prayer of thanks.

Taking off his jacket, he wrapped it about her, and when she reached up to him, he gently and slowly helped her to her feet, while sliding his arm about her waist and taking as much weight off her as possible. 'Are you all right? Have you broken anything?' He needed urgent answers. 'And what about Rosie? Where is she?'

'I'm all right, really. But she's gone, Patrick,' Kathleen told him tearfully. 'She ran off and I couldn't keep up. Find her, Patrick, please. Find Rosie!'

While Harry and Barney ran off towards the spinney, looking for Rosie and calling her name, Kathleen assured Patrick over and over, 'I'm fine. I'm just exhausted, and I cut my legs when I fell, but I'm fairly sure there's nothing broken. I'll be all right, I promise.'

Then she was crying; broken from her ordeal, and fretting for Rosie to be brought back safely. Now

Patrick was with her, she knew she was safe but she feared for Rosie.

'She was brokenhearted, Patrick. I'm so afraid for her. She just ran and ran, and she wouldn't come back. She's gone, Patrick.' Her voice broke and, putting her hands over her face, she told him, 'It was my fault. I should have been more gentle. I told her as lovingly as I could, but she was shocked, Patrick . . . that lovely girl was shocked to her roots and she ran out . . . ran away. She's gone, Patrick. I couldn't find her . . . I couldn't keep up . . . she was too fast. She didn't want to be found.'

Patrick was afraid for his wife. 'Ssh, you'll make yourself ill. And just look at the state of you. We'll find Rosie, don't you worry about that. For now, though, I have to get you home.'

'But I can't go home.' Kathleen was adamant. 'Not without Rosie. She's traumatised, Patrick. Who knows what she might do? We have to find her. You go after her, my darling. I got this far, and I'm sure I can make my own way home. Please, leave me. Just go now!'

'Harry's already gone ahead to search for Rosie,' Patrick assured her. 'Look, sweetheart, I'll get you home and safe, then I'll come back and help Harry in the search. Surely she can't be too far away. She might be watching us even now.'

'No! If she knew I was hurt, she would have come back to help me. Where is she, Patrick? Dear Lord, where is she?'

'I'm sure she's all right,' Patrick soothed her. 'Rosie is a strong young girl.'

But Kathleen was still desperately concerned. 'You didn't see how she was after I told her,' she said softly. 'Oh, Patrick, do you really think she's safe?'

'I do, yes.' In truth, he was every bit as concerned as Kathleen, but he was not about to fuel her fears. 'Shall I tell you what I really think?' he asked her.

'Yes.'

'I think she's hiding from us. I believe she needs to be alone for a while. And I also know that I need to get you home . . . right now.'

Just then, Harry returned. 'Dad's right, Mum. I've been through the spinney and halfway to the top and there is still no sign of Rosie. Let Dad take you home while I go back and carry on looking for Rosie. Dad can come and help me to find her once he's settled you.' He gave her a swift kiss on the cheek. 'You're hurt. Please, Mum! Just do as Dad says, eh?'

Kathleen was afraid that she was slowing the search down, and she instructed the men, 'Go after her, the both of you . . . go now! Apart from a few bruises and scratches, I'm all right. I've had a little rest, and now I'm quite capable of getting myself home.'

Neither Harry nor Patrick was having any of it. Patrick would get Kathleen home safely, and Harry would carry on with the search. 'And no arguments!' Patrick laid the law down, and being in some considerable discomfort, and also being increasingly anxious for Rosie, Kathleen gave little argument this time round.

As the two men helped her up, she leaned on Patrick's strong arm, still blaming herself for Rosie having fled. 'I don't know how else I could have told her,' she said tearfully. 'I broke the news about her daddy as gently as I could, and I cuddled her, but she went to pieces. She just scrambled out of the chair and ran! I went after her, but I couldn't catch her.' The tears ran down her face. 'I'm sorry . . . I am so sorry. She was distraught, and now she's gone and I'm desperately worried. We must find her! We have to find her!'

'And we will,' Patrick promised.

'I went as far as I could just now,' Harry assured his concerned parents, 'but I'm not giving up. I know she's hiding up there somewhere, and we will find her, Mum, I promise. Trust us, eh?'

Patrick nodded. 'Like you, I'm sure she's hiding away from us, trying to deal with the terrible news.'

He helped Kathleen onto flatter ground. 'Come on then, sweetheart. Whenever you need to rest just tell me.'

'First, I'll help you get down to the path, Mum, then I'll be away after Rosie,' said Harry.

'No.' Kathleen was adamant. 'No, Son. Leave me. Your dad will get me home all right, and then he'll be back to help find Rosie. You just mind how you go. All right, Son?'

Harry turned to Patrick. 'Dad, are you sure you can manage on your own with Mum?'

'We'll be fine, thanks all the same. You just get off and look for that darling girl . . . go on!' Patrick was proud of his only son. It showed in his voice and his face. 'When I've seen to your mother and I know that she's all right, I'll be back to help you find Rosie.'

'I can run faster on my own, and I can squeeze into places you can't. Thanks for the offer, Dad, but I'll manage,' Harry told him firmly.

Harry quickly checked on his stepmother. 'Are you hurt badly? Have you broken anything, d'you think?'

Hoisting herself into a sitting position, Kathleen assured them both. 'No, I don't think so. I'll be fine.

All I need now is a hot bath, a change of clothing, and young Rosie back with us.'

Harry agreed. 'Come on, Dad . . . I'll help you get Mum home and then I'll go and find Rosie.'

'No, Son!' Patrick was adamant. 'I'll get your mother home all right. 'You get after Rosie. She could be hurt. Be careful!' he warned. 'Don't take any silly risks. If she hears you calling, I'm sure she'll come out of hiding. She trusts you, Son, she always has.'

'I won't come back without her,' Harry assured them both. 'If she's out there, I'll find her.'

'Thank you, Son.' Kathleen choked back a sob. 'I'm sorry, I couldn't stop her. She just ran off. Oh, Harry . . . she must be feeling so alone, and frightened.'

Looking up, Kathleen saw that Barney was panting and ready for the off again. 'Barney will help you. Hurry, Son. Go! And be careful.'

Planting a swift kiss on Kathleen's cheek, Harry went off at the run, with Barney racing in front, his ears pricked up and his tail wagging with excitement.

'Take me to Rosie!' Harry urged him. 'Come on, Barney! She needs us. Find her, boy. Find Rosie!'

Patrick watched anxiously as the two of them disappeared into the trees.

Harry briefly paused to look back. When he saw that his father was still watching, he conveyed his assurance by a quick wave of the hand. It was enough. Then he strode quickly on, with Barney running ahead, then running back and barking excitedly. 'Good boy! Picked up her scent, have you? Come on then, let's find her.' And Barney did not need telling twice.

Trusting in Harry, Patrick quickly returned his attention to Kathleen. 'If I help you, do you think you could walk, my darling?'

Kathleen nodded. Her body was hurting, but her determination was strong. 'I'm not crippled, Patrick, I'm just done in. I always thought I was a fit person, but I have to admit I was really struggling. It was hard going, trying to keep up with Rosie. I can't even begin to tell you how badly my legs were hurting. I feel so weary, but I'll be all right. Just get me home, Patrick, and let's pray that Harry finds that darling girl.'

Her voice broke with emotion. 'Oh, Patrick, she took it really badly, as we knew she would. I swear, I did my best to tell her gently . . .'

When it seemed her emotions would get the better of her, Patrick made her stop. 'Here, let's take a minute, eh?' He helped her to a grassy bank and eased her down onto a well-padded grass clump. 'That should be a firm enough landing until you get your breath back.'

Kathleen was more comfortable sitting there than she had been for a while. Taking a deep, invigorating breath, she thanked him. 'You're a good man, Patrick Riley, and I don't know what I would do without you.'

'Ha! Just let's hope you won't ever be without me then, eh?'

Kathleen hoped for the very same. Feeling somewhat weary of heart and body, she brushed her hands over her face, as though to shut out Rosie's stricken expression when she had learned the truth. 'It was awful, Patrick, and strangely, even before I started to explain, it was as though she already knew.'

'How do you mean?'

Thinking about it now, Kathleen wondered if Patrick had let the bad news slip out while they were in the car. 'You didn't mention anything to her, did you, Patrick? I mean, did you accidentally let it slip when you went to fetch her? It was a lot to keep back, I know.'

He lapsed into deep thought.

'Patrick, please be honest with me. When the two of you were in the car, did you let it slip about her father? Really, I won't blame you if you did, because

I know how persistent Rosie can be when she puts her mind to it.'

'No, Kathleen, hand on heart, I said nothing. Yes, she had a question or two, but please trust me, I did not tell her. As far as I know, the first she heard about John's untimely death was when she heard it from you.'

'I'm sorry, Patrick.' Kathleen said, 'it's just that . . . oh, I honestly don't know! It must have been my imagination, but there was something that told me she had a heavy weight on her mind. It was kind of odd. I really thought she had learned of her father's death, but then I knew in my heart that you would not have told her . . . at least not without me being there. And yet I got the feeling that there was something she wanted to tell me, but then didn't.'

'All I know, my love, is that I was extra careful not to mention anything that could make her curious,' Patrick assured her. He added cautiously, 'Are you sure you didn't imagine she was hiding something? Only you've been that worried about having to tell her the shocking news, and what with the responsibility falling on your shoulders, your mind must have been all over the place.'

'No, I swear to you, Patrick, I'm absolutely certain that she had something on her mind . . . something that was troubling her even before I told her the bad news regarding John.'

'So, if you're right, what could it have been?'

'I have no idea, but I did feel it was something that she was obviously wary of talking about.' She choked back the tears. 'Oh, Patrick, I tried to be gentle, because I knew she would be devastated but even then I sadly underestimated what her response would be.'

'Don't blame yourself, sweetheart.' Patrick could see how distressed Kathleen was. 'We'll find her, don't worry.'

'Oh, Patrick! She was in a terrible state. Before I could stop her, she was out of the chair, and away across the garden. She stopped at the fish pond, sobbing as though her heart would break, and then she was away again. I could hear her crying but I could not get to her. Oh, Patrick, I ran after her as hard as I could. I called for you, but there was so little time. I just needed to go after her and get her back again.'

Kathleen's heart was heavy with guilt. 'I'm sorry, Patrick, I did my best . . . but in the end the bad news was so overwhelming it was never going to be enough.'

She buried her head in her hands and sobbed like

a child . . . deep, racking sobs that brought pain to Patrick's heart.

He understood, and for a long time he held her tight. 'I've got you, my darling. Trust me, I'm sure young Rosie won't have gone too far. In the circumstances, it's understandable that she needed to be on her own for a while. It's a huge thing for a young girl to take in – that her beloved father is gone.'

His mind was now cast back over many years. 'Believe me, I know how it feels. It must be ten times worse when you're just a young and vulnerable girl like Rosie, with limited experience of life, and no experience of death at all. She won't get over it in a hurry. We need to allow her to cope with it the best way she can, and if that means running off to think it through on her own, then so be it. Whatever it takes. As long as she stays safe.'

They moved slowly homeward then before Kathleen voiced another concern. 'Patrick, I want to keep Rosie here, with us,' she confided tearfully.

'In what way?' He did not fully understand.

'I want her to stay here with us, for as long as she needs to,' Kathleen explained. 'The thing is, Molly said she was asked to give an account of the accident, so we have no idea how long she might be kept at the police station. Meantime, what about Rosie?

There is no one else close enough to keep an eye on her except us. And should she even be going home just yet anyway, with her father not being there and her mother giving not an ounce of love or support?'

Her fears for Rosie were now multiplying tenfold. 'Rosie needs us, Patrick. You must see that. You do, don't you?'

'Yes, of course I do, my love, and you're right. It would be far too much of an ordeal to take Rosie home just yet. I only hope Molly can see it that way. You know what she's like. If she wants Rosie there, it will be the devil of a thing for us to change her mind.'

'That's true!' Growing ever more anxious, Kathleen paused to take a breath. 'I'm sorry, Patrick,' she shook her head, 'I just need a minute to think it through.'

'Of course. But don't try to deal with this on your own. First of all, you know what Molly's like. She will try anything to stop us from looking after Rosie, just to be awkward. And, besides, you've been through a bit of an ordeal yourself. I don't want you tiring yourself out. Be quiet now, eh? There will be time to talk when you're properly rested. We're only minutes away from home.'

They walked on slowly, but Kathleen had so much

to discuss with him that would not wait. 'With regards to Rosie, Molly has never once felt a single ounce of love for the girl. She never wanted her and, as we both know, she never will. But if she thought it would be good for Rosie to stay with us for a few weeks, she would go out on a limb to stop it from happening, just to be spiteful. So, how will we manage to persuade her about keeping Rosie with us for a while? At least until after the funeral.'

'Well, I reckon there might be one way of persuading her.'

'Oh, and how's that, then?'

'Much as I never thought to say this, Kathleen, just this once maybe we could ask Molly to stay over as well.' He had not meant to get drawn into further conversation just now, but because his dear wife was so persistent he felt he had no choice but to answer.

Kathleen, though, was not convinced about his solution. 'The thing is, Patrick, why would she want to be here with you and me? She doesn't even like us, for whatever reason. And, as we all know, she cares nothing for Rosie.'

'There might be another reason why she wouldn't want us to have Rosie with us on her own.'

'Oh?'

'Just think about it, Kathleen. If Rosie agrees to

come and stay with us for a time, Molly would be constantly wondering if she might be telling us things that Molly doesn't want us to know.'

'Such as what? I think we already know enough of Molly's dark antics.'

Patrick hunched his shoulders. 'That may or may not be the case, I don't know. But I bet you young Rosie has seen and heard many things – bad things – that we don't know about, and that she would normally never divulge to us or anyone else. Especially to anyone else! We know young Rosie is not one to gossip, but Molly may not trust her. Now do you see what I'm getting at?'

Kathleen was beginning to understand. 'Yes, you could be right. Molly might be afraid to leave her here with us in case she lets a few nasty tales out of the bag. Lord knows what Rosie must have heard and seen over the years. Probably enough to fuel the local gossips for months.'

'That's it. And even if Rosie had not seen or heard anything untoward, Molly could not be certain about that. Molly has a lot to answer for where Rosie is concerned. If ever any tales got out, who's to say what mischief could be stirred up? Rosie may well see and hear far worse things than we know about. Then again, she may not, but I wouldn't care to bet on that.'

Patrick shook his head. 'I would not like to think too deeply about the shameful things Molly might have got up to behind John's back.'

'Like what, for instance?'

'Well, we both know she likes the men. We've seen her flirting with anything in trousers. So, who's to say she hasn't had more than one shameful fling over the years, particularly when John's been busy with the harvest for days on end, or down at the cattle market?'

'You're absolutely right! And there have been many times when John's been away overnight, when he's travelled miles to collect a new brood mare, or when he's stayed out all night watching for poachers. Other times, he's been away shifting cattle to faraway markets.'

Kathleen stopped for a rest. 'Phew! I feel worn out,' she gasped. 'It's all this talk of having Molly under our roof. It doesn't bear thinking about.'

'It's not the talking,' Patrick informed her sternly, 'it's the effort of walking all this way and talking at the same time. Now take it easy.'

As they came into the garden, Kathleen paused to lean on the ornamental stone wall. 'Yes, you're right,' she muttered. 'I'm not as fit as I would like to be, but it's not the climbing and sliding over rough ground that's proving a bit heavy, it's too many biscuits and home-made fruitcakes.'

'Come on, you.' Patrick helped her up to the patio. 'You're tired out, what with this business about Molly and whether or not she might try and stop us from having Rosie here with us.'

'Do you know what, Patrick? I've been thinking about it, and yes, Molly could well have grabbed the opportunity to take a number of lovers to her bed. It's possible that Rosie saw some of that. I mean, we can't deny that my sister is a good-looking woman, so what man would ever refuse her advances? Even in her adolescence Molly had boys making fools of themselves over her, and she just loved the attention. Sometimes she'd be stringing two or three along at the same time!'

Patrick was not surprised to hear this. 'Well, there you have it, my darling. If we want Rosie to come and stay with us, it seems to me that we will need to invite the dreaded Molly as well in order to stop her causing any aggravation. So, what do you think?'

'I believe she could be a burden, although she might accept our offer – if only to keep a wary eye on Rosie. Then again, she could refuse for us to have Rosie, and there is not a thing we could do about it. But would she abuse Rosie if we were not allowed to have her – if she stayed with her mother at the farm?'

'Ah, Molly is likely to take the opportunity to indulge herself with any foolish man who yearns to spend a night or so with her. She just might allow Rosie to come and stay with us, if only so the child knows nothing of what dirty little games Molly is up to.'

'Sadly, what you say is very true.'

Taking her on into the house, Patrick led Kathleen down to the parlour, where he sat her in the chair before going to put the kettle on. 'Shout if you need me,' he told her as he went, 'but don't move from there. Just call out my name, and I'll come running.' He smiled at a special memory. 'Hey, cast your mind back . . . wasn't there a song title something like that?'

'Yes, and I recall that at one time you never stopped singing it. Drove me mad, it did, especially when you've got a voice like sandpaper on metal.'

'Aw, that's cruel.'

Kathleen had more important matters on her mind, although she realised Patrick was trying to cheer her up and take her mind off the present crisis. 'Look, Patrick,' she called, raising her voice as he pottered into the kitchen, 'let's get back to the question in hand.'

'Of course. Sorry, sweetheart, but I reckon we've both come to the same decision: to ask Molly if we can have Rosie for a time and invite Molly, too. As you point out, Molly will probably refuse in favour of having the run of the farm – just herself and some fancy man.'

'Absolutely! But if in the end we land up with Molly as well as Rosie, then, what is it they say: keep your friends close and your enemies closer, or something of that sort? All the same, Patrick, I can't imagine Molly under our roof. God help us all!'

'But if it's the only way . . .' he called back.

He returned with a small tray laid with a plate of biscuits and two cups of tea. 'There we are! Get that down you, and I'll run you a bath. Ease your bones, it will.'

'Thanks, love, but I'm not useless, I can run my own bath, thank you. And, anyway, Harry will be waiting for you.'

'I don't think so, and don't argue. Like he says, he can run faster than I can, and he's more able to squeeze into spaces I might get stuck in. I'll see to you first, my darling, then I'm off to do my best for Harry and Rosie.'

'All right, but be quick, won't you? Harry might need your help more than I do.' In truth, Kathleen very much doubted whether she still had the strength even to walk up the stairs, never mind to run a bath.

Ten minutes later, Patrick made his way back downstairs. 'All done. I've only half-filled the bath, and it's lukewarm, the way you like it.' He took Kathleen by the arm and escorted her upstairs to the bathroom.

'I'm not sure I can laze in a bath when they're still out there.' She was growing more anxious by the minute.

'Just let me help you then, and I'll be away all the faster.'

He helped her into the bath, and then helped her to wash.

Sooner than he would have liked, she was asking, 'Help me out now, Patrick.' Though she ached from every pore, she wanted to be downstairs and waiting, while Patrick went to find the youngsters.

'All right then, out you come . . . if you're sure?'

'I am, and stop chatting. You're wasting time!'

'And you stop your nagging, Mrs Riley, if you don't mind!' He wrapped a large, soft towel about her.

A few minutes later, donned in dressing gown and safe, flat slippers, Kathleen insisted on going downstairs, while Patrick prepared to go after Rosie and Harry.

'I won't rest until you're back, all three of you, and Barney, too,' Kathleen told him. 'Oh, and remember to fill that little flask with water – you might need it.' When he started to argue, she would not hear of it. 'If you don't take it, I shall just have to come with you, hurting or not!'

'You're a bossy boots, aren't you, eh? I'm not going to the Antarctic; I'm just going to be climbing a few hills.'

'Stop moaning, and take it with you!' Kathleen insisted.

'All right. But are you sure you wouldn't like a lie-down on the bed? You look worn out.' Patrick was worried about her.

'I'm fine, Patrick. I'll just stay here and watch for you and the young ones to come home.'

'I need to think where it might be best to search. I'm hoping Harry will have found Rosie by now, and they could even be on their way back. I know Harry won't have given up, so try not to worry too much.' He went to collect his jacket from the hallway.

'Patrick?' While he struggled into his jacket, Kathleen was reflecting on something that, apart from John and Molly, only she and Patrick knew. 'I never did tell you that I'm truly grateful you trusted me and let me in on Molly's secret with regard to Rosie and how that lovely girl came about.'

'Why Molly confided in me I will never know. Maybe it was because I found her crying in the barn, and she had to tell someone, and I was the only one there at the time.'

'Maybe. But I believe she confided in you because she knew you to be a good man. For whatever reason, she trusted you with the secret you have kept for all these years. It's obvious she never confides in me because I have no sympathy for her. She's proven herself to be a mean and spiteful woman, who has never grown out of the resentment she felt when I was born and she was no longer the sole centre of attention, and there are times when I'm ashamed that she's my sister.'

In the deepest realms of her heart, however, Kathleen actually felt a small inkling of sympathy for Molly, especially since Patrick had shared with his wife the secret with regard to young Rosie.

While he pulled his boots on, Patrick cast his mind back. 'From what I understand, she had two good reasons to be afraid for her future. First, she was absolutely paranoid about the truth getting out, with people whispering and gossiping, pointing her out in the street and such.'

'Yes, and they would have. A child created out of wedlock was always going to draw the gossips,' Kathleen assured him.

'And, of course, she was most anxious about not losing John and the farm, and all of that. She said John and the farm were her future, and she had nowhere else to go.'

'That doesn't surprise me at all. It's probably why she married him in the first place.'

'Well, I would not argue with that, but when I found her she was genuinely distressed and angry. She really was in a terrible state . . . almost suicidal. She was sobbing uncontrollably, so I put my arm about her and tried to soothe her, and then she blurted it out about the affair and everything. Then afterwards she begged me to keep her secret. And that's what I did. Telling you was not really breaking that promise; you and I have always shared every-thing.'

'So, in the end, she managed to keep her place at the farm, knowing that one day it might well be hers, lock, stock and barrel.'

'That's Molly for you!' Patrick mentally assessed the current situation, with John gone for ever, and Molly counting her gains. 'Now, unfortunately, with John gone to his Maker it looks like she's got the lot.' A quick glance at the clock and he began to panic. 'Look, sweetheart, I'd best get off.'

'Isn't that what I've been telling you?' She opened her arms to him. 'Do I get a kiss before you go then?'

'You certainly do!' He swiftly delivered one to her, along with an instruction, 'Don't you be doing too much while I'm gone.'

As he went to the door, she followed, albeit slowly because of her bruised and aching bones. 'As you say, Patrick, Molly has at long last managed to get her claws into everything John worked hard for, and you can bet your life she'll make absolutely certain that young Rosie sees nothing of her due inheritance. Although I know Rosie would rather have her daddy back than all the riches in the world.' Her voice broke in a little sob. 'God works in mysterious ways, and that's a fact.'

'You're right, as always. While I'm gone you can think of a way to persuade Molly to come and stay here so we can keep Rosie safe.'

'Don't worry, one way or another, we shall have Rosie here with us, you mark my words. If Molly does refuse to let us have Rosie here for a time I might have to quietly remind her that we've kept her secret all this time, but I might just feel obliged to accidentally on purpose let it out of the bag.'

'I'm sorry, sweetheart, but I can't let you threaten Molly with that.'

'Oh, and why not?'

'Because she has no idea that I told you, and I would rather she didn't know that I broke my promise to her.'

'Oh, of course! I'm sorry . . . I wasn't thinking. It's just that now John is not here to protect Rosie, I'm honestly afraid to leave her in Molly's charge. I have no doubt that she would harm her.'

'Are you absolutely certain about that?'

'Patrick, I'm surprised you need to even ask. Just think about it. All these years, Molly has had to keep her temper in check when John's around. He was always there to protect Rosie, knowing that Molly had no love or motherly feelings for the child. Now there is no one who can keep a wary eye on Rosie except for you, me and Harry. So, whatever it takes to keep her safe, that's what we'll do.'

'But if we have to use threats, then it has to be me who talks to her, and not you, do you agree?' said Patrick.

'Of course.' Kathleen was content enough with that.

'If we have no choice then so be it.' Being a man of peace, Patrick now felt much easier.

'Oh, Patrick . . . dear Lord above.' Growing tearful, Kathleen slowly shook her head from side to side. 'I still can't believe it. Such a fine man . . . and far too young to die. It just beggars belief!'

Patrick felt the same, and said so. 'And if it's like some kind of nightmare for us, what is it doing to Rosie, eh? She must be in pieces. And that is why we have to keep her safe . . . whatever it takes!'

He gave a peculiar little snort. 'Hmm, anyway, we all know what Molly wants to do! Here we are talking about her temporarily shutting up the house and coming here when we both know that the minute that good man is in the ground, she'll be rubbing her hands and counting her good fortune.'

'You could well be right. I worry for Rosie if that happens. Unless, of course, Molly lets us keep her. Oh, Patrick, that would be so wonderful – Rosie living with us . . . growing up here!'

Becoming emotional, she had to stop before the tears flowed.

Patrick was eager to be off. 'I won't be long. You can lock up the house behind me and have a little lie-down. I'll take my own key.'

'Patrick, do you actually think I can sleep, knowing that those two young people are out there some-where, and with Rosie so upset? If I didn't feel so damned weak, I'd clip your ear!'

Patrick laughed. 'I reckon you would, but just now,

269

you're not able to walk fast enough to catch me. So for once, just relax and do as you're told.'

'Seriously, though, Patrick, be careful. You're not as young and fit as you once were. It's heavy and bone-tiring work climbing those slopes. I mean, look what happened to me.'

'Aye well, I'm a man and you're a woman.'

'What's that supposed to mean?'

'Nothing. Now stop nagging and let me get on.' He gave her a little wink. 'You did your bit and I'm proud of you. But for now, just leave it to me, and say a little prayer that the two young 'uns are safe.'

'I will. And promise you'll be careful.'

And to appease her yet again Patrick duly set her mind at rest. Increasingly anxious to be away, he bent to hug her. 'Love you, sweetheart, even though you can be a right nag sometimes!' Before she could give him the length of her tongue he was swiftly away, out the back door.

Smiling to herself, Kathleen hobbled to the window and watched as he strode quickly down the path, through the garden and on, towards the grassy slope that led to the steeper ground, which was far more difficult to cope with.

Patrick turned to wave, then he was gone from her sight.

Kathleen lingered a moment to think on that good man of hers. She had never loved anyone else, and never could. 'Oh, Patrick! I do love you so,' she murmured with a wistful tear in her voice. 'Lord only knows what I would do without you.'

Just then she felt like the loneliest person in the whole world.

She hobbled back to her armchair, where she made herself comfortable. Fancy thinking I could ever lie down, with those three out there somewhere! I'll not rest one single minute until they're back, she thought, gazing longingly towards the window.

Within a matter of minutes she had nodded off, gently snoring, with her sore, blistered feet up on the stool.

Her man, meanwhile, was hurriedly trudging through rough terrain, calling out to Harry and Rosie, but so far there had been no response.

Undeterred, and ever hopeful, he climbed higher, over rocks and deep grooves where the soft ground sucked at his feet, impeding his progress, while the higher, hard and unyielding ground sent him tripping and tumbling in every direction.

Good grief, Kathleen girl! I'm surprised you didn't come out of this more damaged than you actually were, he thought, smiling, but then you always were

271

a tough little beggar. He recalled the time just four weeks after they'd met, when he confidently challenged her to a four-mile bike ride and, to his shame, she beat him like a good 'un.

After that humiliation, he never challenged her again, although every evening, after work, he would go on a long bike ride alone, just to strengthen his legs in case she ever felt like throwing down the gauntlet and allowing him a return match. But she never did, and he was glad of it.

Eventually, he sold the bike and bought a little Morris Minor, which took them all over the country.

Feeling nostalgic as he trudged along, he reflected that though he had been blessed with Harry, a fine young fellow any father would be proud to have as a son, it would have been another blessing to have a girl as well – a lovely, darling girl much like young Rosie . . .

He would never understand why Molly could not find it in her to love Rosie. After all, the child had done no harm to her and it wasn't her fault that she was conceived out of wedlock. Molly should realise that.

He paused to take a breath and sipped gratefully from the bottle of water Kathleen had insisted he take. You were right as always, Katheen, love, he admitted. A drop of cold water and I'm ready to set off again.

Some way on, he began calling out for Harry, but there was no response. Disappointed, he trudged on, hoping he was following in his son's footsteps.

Soon, coming to more even ground, he went forward at a quicker pace, continuing to call, 'Harry! Rosie! Where are you?'

When there was no answer, Patrick stood still a moment and listened, but there was no sound from Harry or Rosie – nothing but the gentle breeze whistling through the trees.

Determined, he persevered. Taking a deep breath, he cupped his hands about his mouth and yelled out as loud as he could, 'Harry, it's me . . . your dad! If you can hear me, shout out so I can tell where you are!'

Yet again, there was nothing to raise his hopes, or help him choose which direction to follow.

Some time later, exhausted and worried, he straddled his legs across a fallen tree stump, allowing himself a short rest. He was somewhat surprised that he felt so weary, especially as he was fairly fit. It's like the damned jungle round here, and there was I thinking all I had to do was climb up for some short distance, over a few high bumps and crevices, he thought.

Fixing his gaze onto the ground, his eyes followed the activity of the small creatures within the dips and hollows of the fallen tree. But when a small army of ants began to make their way towards his feet, he quickly jumped up, and hurried on. I can't be doing with them little devils going up my trouser leg, he thought, shivering. That was enough to spur him on more quickly.

When he again yelled for Harry and Rosie, the echo went bouncing away over the hilltops. He felt hopeful that if his voice could carry like that, it would be only a matter of time before Harry and Rosie heard his frantic cries. The thought gave him impetus to carry on to a break in the woodland.

Which way should he go now? He looked at the alternatives. One way would take him higher . . . over the hills. The other way would go through the woods, over the softer, uneven ground. What to do? Dropping his troubled gaze to the ground, he looked for any sign of footprints in the well-trodden soil, but he could see only animal tracks and clumps of dead grasses.

He took a short breather, trying to make up his mind before he set off again.

The sweat was running down his face and neck. Letting his chin drop to his chest, he closed his eyes, wrapped his two arms about his knees, and took a long, invigorating breath. Another little drink of water, and he was almost ready to move on. Patrick Riley, admit it: you're not set up for this kind of trekking, he told himself. Come on! There's no time for wasting. You need to find Rosie and your son, so get up off yer backside, and shift yourself!

Leaning forward, he opened the palms of his hands and slowly wiped the sticky sweat from his face. He hung his head and, closing his eyes for a swift moment, he whispered to Kathleen, 'Oh, wife of mine, I'll admit it, because you can't hear me. You're a stronger woman than I took you for.'

He was absolutely done in and still had no idea where Harry and Rosie could be, or which direction he should take.

Again he contemplated the two paths, one leading through the woods and the other along the hilltops. So . . . which way to go?

Suddenly, in a renewed burst of strength, he was on his feet and shouting his son's name at the top of his voice, so high and intrusive to the elements that the echoes bounced back from the hills all around.

'Harry! It's me . . . your dad! Where the devil are you?'

After waiting a minute or so and getting no response, he was growing increasingly worried. Surely they couldn't have wandered so far that they'd got themselves lost. The thought of their actually being missing was an extra worry to him.

Although when he thought about it, even he was not altogether familiar with the landscape hereabouts. Once he got over the hills he knew there were pathways leading in every direction. According to the old folks in the village, there were no maps of those meandering trails.

One or two of the very elderly folk in the village claimed to know who had laid these trails and why, but each one told a slightly different story. One would tell how loggers used to thin out the trees, and so created the pathways in order to haul the fallen trees back to the village. Others claimed that long ago a group of travellers took over the woods. They excavated deep caves in the hillsides and lived there with their families for many years before moving on. There were other legends, too, but none of these old stories was ever proven. Currently the villagers made good use of the woods and hills in walking their dogs and picking the wild flowers. Young folk took to camping out in the woods, and local teachers took classes of children up here to study nature at its best.

Looking about him, Patrick could see a fairly clean opening to the left of where he was standing, winding up the hill. 'I wonder . . . that looks to be a likely option . . .' He was thinking of Rosie running up to here, and going for the widest trail before her. He decided to go for that. If it turned out to be hard going, he could come back and try the other way.

A decision made, he went on with sore feet but a lighter heart. Also, because he sensed he was almost at the top of the trail, his hopes were higher as he took a moment to rest again.

Then, after a sip of water from the bottle, he was up on his feet once more, marching on and again calling out through cupped hands. Over and over he called out for Harry, so loudly and so fiercely that he was sure his lungs would burst.

Eventually he reached a place by the path where a rock made a natural seat. Before going on, he desperately needed a few minutes to sit and rest, and catch his breath. It had taken all his strength to reach this high spot, and he was done in. Every bone in his body was hurting. The back of his throat felt like sandpaper, and his feet were that sore, they felt as though he'd been locked in the stocks, with every woman in the village whipping a stick across his bare toes.

Grumbling and sighing, he peeled off his socks and tenderly rubbed the life back into his feet. He wiggled his toes for a minute or so, and when he felt more comfortable, he simply left his feet bare, while tenderly running his hands about his ankles and legs to keep the circulation going.

After a while, and being well rested, he was anxious to get on. So he shook himself down and prepared for the next leg of the climb, although now the land appeared to be levelling out a little. He put on his socks and boots, took just the tiniest sip of water to lubricate his throat, and in another moment he was off.

He cautioned himself to ration what remained of the water. No doubt the young 'uns would be glad of a drop of that when he caught up with them . . . and he *would* catch up with them, he vowed.

Hardened in his purpose, he set off with stout determination and a heart full of hope.

CHAPTER NINE

BARNEY HEARD IT first, and he began running round in circles.

'What's wrong with you, boy?' Harry said. 'Stop your mad antics, and come back here.'

Barney did as he was told, although when he laid down beside Rosie in the shelter, he still made that whining sound in his throat, as though warning them of something. Both Harry and Rosie were made a little nervous by this, especially as the light was fading even though it was only mid-afternoon.

Rosie patted her dog. 'You're ready to go home now, aren't you, eh?' She rubbed his ear; he liked that. It seemed to calm him.

Suddenly he was up on his feet again and outside,

going crazy, running round and round, and barking for all he was worth.

Harry went to him outside the shelter. 'What is it, boy? Is there someone out there?' He decided to go to look beyond the ridge. 'Go back to Rosie!' he ordered Barney, pointing. 'Stay with Rosie.' And as always, Barney set about his duty.

While Barney went back inside Harry went to the edge of the ridge. Staring down, he could see little through the swathes of wild growth and trees.

'I don't know what Barney was getting excited about,' he went to tell Rosie. 'I can't see anyone or anything moving down there.'

Increasingly anxious, Rosie went out to look, too, but Harry inched her back from the edge. 'It could crumble away beneath our weight and take us both with it.' He could see other places where exactly that had happened. 'Go back inside the shelter, Rosie. I'll keep a watch out.'

'Do you think we should try and make our way down?' Rosie asked.

'I reckon we might have to – when you're rested, though, Rosie. It won't be as straightforward going down as it is climbing up, but if Dad's on his way there'll be two of us to help you down. He did say he would come looking for us after he got Mum home. And just now, with Barney getting all excited, I'm wondering if he might have caught a sight of him.'

Rosie suddenly grabbed hold of him. 'Hey! Did you hear that?'

Harry listened and then he heard it and was so relieved that he danced on the spot. 'It's Dad!' He knew his father's voice and he'd heard his own name.

Now Barney was beside him, chasing his tail and barking for all he was worth, and Harry thought that if he'd been a dog, he'd have been doing exactly the same. 'Oh, Dad, you kept your promise. Thank you, thank you! I knew he'd find us. Look, Rosie, he's there.' Close to tears of relief, he yelled back, 'Dad! Dad, we're up here. Look up . . . we can see you now.'

Like two excited children, they jumped up and down, yelling and shouting, and Harry was whistling.

Patrick yelled up, 'I can see you now . . . but for God's sake get back from the edge!'

While Rosie duly stepped back, Harry gingerly inched down to where Patrick was about to climb up, along some fallen trees. When he was near enough, he grabbed his father's hand and pulled him up.

'Oh, Dad!' He threw his arms about his father's neck. 'Are we glad to see you!'

Barney thought the same as he jumped up and licked Patrick's sweaty face with his long, wet, pink tongue.

'Get off, you dopey mutt!'

Patrick laughed with relief at having found them . . . even Barney, with his bad breath and sloppy drivel.

For the next few minutes, the hill tops echoed with the sound of laughter as they hugged each other, and Rosie gave Patrick a grateful kiss.

'Harry promised me you'd find us. Oh, thank you so much. The thing is, I lost my shoe when I climbed up to here, and Harry said it would be difficult for me to climb back down without it. But he said you'd find us and you did.' By now she was crying in his arms, and Patrick was slightly embarrassed.

'Hey, that's enough o' the bawling!' he told her sternly. 'I'm glad to have found you an' all, but we have to get down before it gets dark.'

Harry showed him where they had been resting. 'I found Rosie here, but I was worried about getting her down, especially with one shoe missing and so many obstacles to mar our descent. So we decided to wait just a little longer and see if you might find us.'

Patrick was also greatly relieved. 'You did right, Son.'

Addressing Rosie, he asked kindly, 'I don't suppose there's any chance we could find your shoe, is there, sweetheart?'

'I don't know,' Rosie replied. 'It came off when I was climbing up here. My foot got caught in a split trunk on the ground and the shoe went tumbling down the hillside, and then I couldn't see where it landed.'

Patrick assured her that they would get her down, ' . . . one way or another, even if we have to take it in turns giving you a piggyback.'

When Harry stared at him in disbelief, Patrick chuckled. 'Don't worry, even I would never attempt such a foolhardy thing. But one way or another, we'll need to make sure that Rosie has both her feet protected as we make our way down.'

'How will we do that, d'you think?' Harry wondered.

'I'm not altogether sure just yet, but let me catch my breath and then we'll need to set off soon to catch the last of the daylight.'

Looking beyond them, he saw the natural shelter, which was obviously made when a huge rock came away and, from what Patrick could deduce, took a couple of trees down with it. 'So you've been waiting in there, have you?'

'Yes, Dad. It seemed the right thing to do, in the circumstances.'

Patrick nodded. 'You did right, Son. At least you're both safe.'

When he handed Rosie the water bottle, it was as though he had given her a fortune. After taking a sip of the cool water, she handed it to Harry, who was immensely thankful, though careful to save most of what little remained for the trek down. 'So, Dad, we're ready when you are. But what do we do about Rosie's shoe?'

Patrick had been thinking about that. 'Well, one thing's for sure, she cannot try climbing down without it.'

He looked at Harry, then he looked at Rosie, and he realised that neither of the ideas he had had would ever work.

'Let me see!' He thought and thought, and then he had another idea.

He stripped off his jacket, then removed his shirt and gave it to Harry, before replacing his jacket over his vest. 'Here, you tear the sleeves off my shirt.' He handed the shirt to Harry. 'I'll not be a minute.'

Harry was puzzled. 'The shirt won't give her foot any protection, Dad.'

Patrick simply waved his hand to acknowledge he'd

heard as he went along the hillside. 'Just do as I ask, there's a good chap,' he called as he went out of sight.

Harry tore the two sleeves off. 'I can't imagine what he has in mind,' he muttered to himself. 'The sharp stones and such will tear this to pieces.'

Within minutes, Patrick was back again, carrying a selection of gathered materials in his arms. 'Come on then, Rosie.' He called her to the shelter, where the two of them sat on the ground opposite each other.

Fascinated to see what was happening, Harry followed.

He watched, curious, as his father unfolded the bulky parcel he'd been carrying. Then Patrick gently stripped the sock from Rosie's sore foot and set about wiping the foot clean with his hands, thereby ensuring that there was nothing sharp or rough to irritate the sole of her foot. Next he began the fiddly operation.

First, he spread out two big leaves that he had snapped from a tree. Then he flattened and shaped two pieces of thick, pliable bark taken from another tree.

He replaced Rosie's sock, making sure it was comfortable all the way round, and then he cleverly wrapped the large leaves gently round and round her foot, shaping the leaves to her foot as well as he could so the makeshift shoe would be as comfortable as possible.

'Keep the leaves tight in place, Rosie,' he instructed, while holding out his hand for Harry to give him back the two sleeves which he'd torn from the shirt. 'We don't want crinkles or pleats.'

Keeping the thick layer of bark and the leaves nice and flat to her foot, Rosie watched as Patrick very carefully slid one sleeve over the entire foot, going back and forth to layer it as much as the length of material would allow.

He then did the same with the other sleeve until the bark, the leaves and the shirtsleeves somehow drew together, looking like a big, well-padded, clumpy foot, secured with some string from his pocket.

'Stand up, Rosie,' he told her, 'but be careful, because it will feel a bit thick and funny at first.'

Harry came to help her, and when she was standing she laughed out loud. 'You're right!' she chuckled. 'It feels ten times bigger than my other foot.'

'Right, see if you can take a step, but be careful. Don't worry, Harry will hold onto you.' Although he had done everything he could, Patrick was still anxious.

Rosie, however, was thrilled. 'Oh, Uncle Patrick,

it's all right. It's nice and tight, and the sole feels really thick and secure. I can walk on it like a proper shoe, only bigger. And I can't feel anything hurting anywhere.'

'That's good!' Patrick felt just a little proud of himself. 'I've no doubt your foot might feel twice its size, but trust me, Rosie, it will work fine. It seems like a hundred years since I was in the Boy Scouts, but they taught us some good stuff, and no mistake!'

'Well, I'm pleased they did.' Rosie was putting all her trust in him.

'Thank you, Rosie. Now, you need to concentrate. Try walking a short distance on your own . . . gently now.'

With Harry hovering close by to catch her if she fell, Rosie took a few, careful steps. 'It's so funny . . . feels like I'm lopsided,' she smiled, 'but my foot is comfortable. There's nothing hurting me.'

The only thing hurting her was the crippling knowledge that her darling father was dead. She would never forget him, or stop loving him, and would forever wish he was still here with her.

Tears threatened, but she choked them back. Now was not the time, nor this the place. And she had something else on her mind: certain things she had seen and heard, that she found hard to understand.

~

Before the three of them set off, Patrick put what remained of his shirt to good use, leaving him with just his jacket and vest for protection in the chilly November afternoon.

He ripped, twisted and knotted the remnants of his shirt until it resembled a crude rope. One end he tied about Rosie's waist, and the other end he kept tight in his fist.

'Right! So now we're as ready as we'll ever be.' Nevertheless, he remained wary. 'We need to go carefully, taking our time, with Harry in front of you and me behind. The two of us will be there if you stumble and we'll have you sandwiched between us. What do you think, Rosie? Are you ready to do it?'

'Yes, Uncle Patrick.' Rosie was eager to be off. 'I'm ready.'

Even Barney shouted his approval before winding his wary way down the slope, instinctively seeking out the flat patches of firm surface. Occasionally wrong-footed, he tripped and slid but slowly continued to go forward. As did the others, carefully following behind.

~

Watching from the patio outside the sun-room, Kathleen grew increasingly anxious. She'd had another telephone call from Molly, still at the police station, and the situation was looking even more bleak. For this past hour and more, Kathleen had been backwards and forwards, in and out of the house, then across the gardens to look towards the foothills, to the spot where Patrick had disappeared from sight some hours before. She was longing to share her new troubled thoughts with him.

Her heartfelt wishes continued to will him home and she prayed that she might see him emerge from the hills at any minute, with Harry and Rosie by his side and Barney bounding along in front.

Time and again, her worried gaze carried across the gardens and on towards the place where she'd last seen him, waving and smiling, looking strong and able.

'Where are you, Patrick? Oh, please God, I hope you have found the children safe and well,' she murmured.

Another hour passed, and when there was still no sign of them she made a decision: I know that if you had stayed safe you would have been home by now, Patrick . . . I just know it! Something's happened, and I can't wait any longer. I'm calling for help!

With one last look towards the place where she had last seen Patrick, she turned away, and as she did so, she heard Barney's familiar, excited bark. In her excitement and hurry to return to the spot where she had watched for them these past hours, she almost fell over. 'Careful, girl!' she cautioned herself. 'You're not as young and agile as you used to be!'

Suddenly, there was Barney, bounding towards the garden, excited and happy, and shouting to her in that familiar, deep bark. 'Barney!' She called him to her. 'Where are they, boy? Are they all right? Where are they?'

She looked up and was greatly relieved to see Patrick, with Rosie and Harry close behind. All three of them looked to be completely and utterly exhausted. The strain of their ordeal was visible in their faces and in the slow, heavy manner in which they walked towards her.

Saying a little prayer of thanks, Kathleen felt a burst of pride and immense relief that they were all safe.

Then she was running, her bruises forgotten, and soon she was flinging her arms about Patrick, before she hugged Harry and Rosie. Nor did she leave out Barney; she ruffled his coat with great affection while he relished the attention.

'I've been so worried,' she said brokenly. 'I was so afraid you were in trouble.'

As they trailed back to the house together, Kathleen heard the story of how Rosie had lost her shoe, and how Patrick had come to her rescue with his old Boy Scout skills. Harry said very little, but gave his step-mother the biggest hug ever.

As for Patrick, he felt too worn out and bone-sore to enter into heavy conversation. Thoroughly exhausted, he could hardly drag one foot behind the other. There would be time enough for him to tell his side of this particular adventure. Meantime, he was simply thankful to be within sight of home, while Harry and Rosie explained their careful descent down to more level ground.

'I'm too old for this kind of malarkey,' Patrick said to Kathleen. 'What I need right now is a strong cuppa tea . . . and my lovely wife right there beside me.'

'And that's what you'll get, my husband,' she answered, 'and maybe another little kiss on the cheek for bringing you all safely back to me.'

'We all did our bit.' Patrick gratefully accepted a helping hand from Kathleen.

'You seem unduly quiet.' He had noticed how she seemed so deep in thought, and her face was serious when she looked away. 'You've no need to worry now,

291

my love.' He gave her hand a gentle squeeze. 'As you can see, although we might be a little battered and weary, at least we're all home safe and well.'

Kathleen smiled. 'No more adventures, then . . . is that agreed?'

Patrick chuckled mischievously. 'Duly noted and agreed, sir!'

Kathleen gave him a playful poke in the arm.

As they continued slowly back to the house, she was all too aware that the news she was keeping to herself for the moment would be as big a shock to the three of them as it had been to her.

During that latest phone call from Molly, Kathleen had taken the opportunity to ask a few niggling questions and, to Kathleen's great surprise, Molly had been only too eager to provide answers, although they had not been exactly what Kathleen was expecting.

Molly was still at the police station answering questions and giving as much information as she could about how John had come to meet his untimely death.

According to what Molly confided in her, Kathleen realised that Molly had become angry under questioning and, feeling threatened, she'd decided to call the family lawyer, who advised her that she should

not answer any further questions; he was on his way
to advise and counsel her.

Her sister's call had troubled Kathleen deeply, but
seeing how weary and thoroughly shaken Patrick and
the youngsters were, she was loath to burden the
family with the shameful news that Molly had
confessed to her. So she kept silent and hoped she
might be able to break the news gently once they
were home and rested.

~

Some time later, while Barney was stretched out
asleep on the patio, panting and groaning, his legs
madly twitching as though he was running in his
slumbers, Kathleen checked on the family inside.

She found them all washed and rested, and after
a few minutes they were enjoying yet another glass
of cool lemonade, which Kathleen had made earlier
with love and attention.

With little appetite for conversation at the moment,
Kathleen discreetly watched her family as they
enjoyed the cold drinks, before appearing to drift
into their own thoughts.

She decided that this was probably the right time
to acquaint them with what Molly had told her about

the train of events that had apparently cost John his life. Discreetly studying Rosie, who remained pale and exhausted, Kathleen felt sorely tempted to leave the news for another, more suitable time, but then she realised that her family had to be told, and there might not be another time when they were all together like this.

After a moment of thought, she again peeped at Rosie, who was deep in thought, staring at the carpet with wide-awake eyes, no doubt reflecting on the painful loss of her beloved father. Kathleen felt somehow guilty that Rosie should have to deal with such a cruel tragedy in her young life and she feared adding to the child's anguish. Kathleen's lately acquired knowledge had to be shared, but maybe not with Rosie just yet.

Kathleen was increasingly nervous about imparting her news. She feared that the true series of events that had led to John being killed would fire huge shame and disgust not only in everyone here, but also in others, who would likely learn of it when the newspapers got hold of the story. Inevitably, their reports would include all the sordid details leading up to the violent death of a well-respected and much-loved family man. But no one would feel such tearing pain for John Tanner as did his devoted daughter, Rosie.

Kathleen's tender gaze again fell on Rosie, still in deepest thought. After a moment, and totally unaware that Kathleen was watching, Rosie bent her head and discreetly wiped away her falling tears.

Having noticed Kathleen watching Rosie with love, Patrick leaned over to take hold of his wife's hand. 'Don't fret, sweetheart,' he assured her in the softest whisper. 'Rosie will be all right. She's not alone . . . she has us.'

His kind words were most reassuring to Kathleen, who thanked her own lucky stars for the love and companionship of this solid, gentle man, whom she loved with every fibre of her being.

Before Kathleen could say anything, Rosie sat up to look straight at her and, as though she had been going through the dark matters in her own mind, she said in a quiet manner, 'I need to go and see Mother. I need to know what really happened.'

'Of course you can see your mother and ask her whatever you need to,' Kathleen assured her gently. 'But for now it's best to leave her to deal with the police. Afterwards, I'm sure it would do no harm for you to ask her any questions that might be bothering you.'

In answer, Rosie gave a little nod of her head. 'So when do you think I can see her?'

'Not for a while, I suspect. Why don't you go and see if Barney's all right? He looked all in.' Kathleen gathered herself to impart news of the recent development while Rosie went off to find her dog.

'Molly rang me again while you were all away,' she told Patrick and Harry. 'She confided in me that the police had been asking her so many questions about the accident and how John met his death that she felt threatened, and decided to call the family lawyer. I'm guessing he's on his way to the police station at this very moment.'

'Why does she feel threatened?' Patrick asked. 'It was an accident, wasn't it? If so, all she has to do is report what happened. There should be no need for endless questions, but then I know little of the law, so I might be wrong.'

'As you know,' Kathleen went on, 'we were led to believe that it was an accident, but I now know, because Molly explained to me, that it was *not* actually an accident. She also told the police, and that's why there were more questions. It's also why she thought to call the lawyer.'

'But if it was not "actually an accident", what the devil was it? I mean, what did happen in that barn, eh? What I can't fathom is why Molly should be frightened or think the police might blame her. Why would they?' Either way, Patrick cared nothing for his sister-in-law, but he was anxious to get to the truth about John.

'Well . . . she seems to think they might put the blame on her somehow.'

'Hmm, I think she might be paranoid. But if it was not an accident, what happened then? How was John killed?'

Kathleen now revealed the truth behind Molly's worries. 'Apparently, Molly did a bad thing. She told me it was because of her that a vicious fight kicked off between her boyfriend and John. John caught them together . . . in the hay barn in a state of undress.'

'What! Good Lord, is there nothing your sister won't get up to, given the chance?'

'It seems not. The thing is, the man she was with is none other than Tom Stevens, an old sweetheart of hers. She was courting him when she met John. For a while they were inseparable but it gradually became clear to me that he doted on her, while she loved the attention, but sometimes treated him terribly – standing him up when she was bored and had a better prospect of a good time with someone else, getting him to take her all over the place on his motorbike, as if he was her unpaid driver, openly flirting with other men just to make Tom jealous and bring him to heel if he showed any sign of objecting to being used. In the end, for material reasons of course, she dumped Tom and married John soon after.'

Patrick laughed. 'We all know why she dumped Tom. It was because he had nothing material to offer, while John had just inherited a farmhouse, with all the land and buildings. We all know your sister is nothing but a gold-digger. She doesn't care who she climbs over or who she gets into bed with to further her own ends.' From the first meeting with Molly, he had neither respect nor liking for her.

'What I still don't know is what caused John's death,' Patrick went on, 'and why Molly is so worried about answering questions from the police. She must know it's the regulation after a fatality.'

Kathleen relayed what Molly had told her. 'Apparently, when John found them together like that, he went crazy. A vicious fight broke out between the two men, and that's when John was fatally hurt. Molly says she thought John was just knocked unconscious when she called the ambulance. She says she tried so hard to revive him, and then realised that Tom had killed him, although he claims he didn't mean to and it truly was an accident.'

Rosie, who had been hovering by the door unseen, came in looking shocked and angry. 'So, it *is* her fault he was killed! She didn't come home from work, and Daddy was worried . . . and all the time she was with another man. She caused his death! I hate her! It's her that should be dead, not my father!'

With a gesture of his head, Patrick indicated for Harry to take Rosie away, but she insisted on staying. 'I need to know what she said to you, Auntie Kathleen . . . please?' Quietly sobbing, she pleaded, 'I have to stay. I have to know the truth!'

And so it was agreed, although she was glad when Harry put a supportive arm about her while she listened to what else Kathleen had been told.

Kathleen began, 'I won't deny that what Molly did was shameful. And I do agree with you, Rosie. If she had not gone into the barn with Tom Stevens, there would never have been a fight, and your father would still be here. But life sometimes takes dark and dangerous turns, and we have no control over what happens.'

She wisely omitted the information that Molly had relayed: that Tom had swung a spade at John's head. It was the fatal blow.

'I'm sorry you had to hear any of this now, Rosie,' Kathleen said.

Feeling cold and empty inside, Rosie asked quietly, 'Who is this Tom Stevens?'

'He was your mother's sweetheart years ago,' Kathleen explained. 'Before she met your father.'

Rosie was curious. 'What does he look like . . . this man?' Her mind went back to the man in the barn . . . the man who had been so very sad.

'Well, I don't know what he looks like now, Rosie dear. But he was never a truly handsome man. Nice enough, I suppose. Ordinary, unassuming. Rather thick-set . . . with fairish hair . . . but that was a long time ago. To be honest, if I saw him now I don't suppose I would even recognise him.'

She felt deeply for Rosie. 'I wish to God you did not have to know all that, but I suppose it could get into the papers, and I wouldn't want you finding out that way.'

'I understand, Auntie Kathleen. And I would rather know the truth from you.' Suddenly Rosie felt as though she had changed . . . grown up somehow. It was odd, but now she could see the danger and ugliness in this world, when before, apart from being the butt of her mother's spiteful nature, she had never felt the world to be cruel.

'Auntie Kathleen?'

'Yes, sweetheart?'

'Will they put her in jail?'

'I'm not sure. I don't see how they would, because even though the fight was about her, she apparently took no part in it. She told me that Tom Stevens confessed it was he who struck the fatal blow. She claims that she tried to stop him but he was beyond her control.'

'Why didn't she help my father?'

'She said she was afraid to get between them . . . that the two of them were in such a wild rage she was forced to keep her distance. Tom Stevens has told the authorities that he and he alone is to blame for what happened, and that Molly has nothing to answer for.'

'Well, he's wrong, because she has a great deal to answer for, and she ought to be locked away alongside him.' Rosie was certain about this. Her mother was the cause of the fight; she had cheated on Rosie's father, and now she had caused his death. Rosie would never forgive her, not for as long as she lived.

Rosie brought her attention back to what Kathleen was saying to answer some question of Harry's.

'All I know is what she told me, Harry. Tom Stevens confessed to what he did. He told the authorities that he was entirely to blame for what happened, but that he never meant to kill John. But whichever way you look at it, he swung out, John was killed, and you may depend on it that with Molly as witness to what he claims, he will surely be made to pay the price.'

'So, what will happen to him?' Harry asked.

'According to Molly, there will be further investigations,' Kathleen explained. 'In the meantime, Tom Stevens will remain safely behind bars.'

Rosie, along with everyone else, was glad of that.

Though Stevens had confessed that he was the one to blame for her father's death, in her deepest heart Rosie continued to believe that her mother was every bit as guilty.

'She should be in prison as well!' she remarked bitterly. 'She's the one who cheated. It was her who caused Daddy to be killed. I hate her. I never want to see her again . . . never!' Scrambling out of the chair, she ran outside, to hide in the garden shed; to be by herself and let it all sink in. She thought of how treacherous her mother was. She recalled how concerned her father had been last night, when he had gone out to look for her mother, and how blindly he loved her although she behaved in this terrible way.

Her daddy was such a gentle man – how could he love such a woman? Why did he not find a warm and lovely soul who would give him the love and devotion he deserved?

Rosie's heart ached for him now. She so needed to see him, to hear his voice and hug him tight. She needed so much to tell him that she would love him for ever and she would never forget him, not for as long as she lived. And she longed to see his bright and lovely smile and hear his laughter just once more. Oh, what she would give for that!

Deep in thought, she was startled to hear Harry's voice outside. 'Can I come in, Rosie?'

'No, Harry. Just now, I'd rather be on my own.'

'I'm worried about you.'

'I'm all right, really I am.' But she wasn't. Maybe she never would be again.

'Please, Rosie, either let me in or come with me to the sun-room, and we'll just sit and talk together. I just want to help you, Rosie.'

Knowing that he also must be devastated by the loss of her father, Rosie opened the door. 'I don't want to go to the sun-room,' she told him. 'I just want to stay here for a while.'

'So, can I come in?'

'Yes, all right. Come in, if you really want to. I'm not good company just now, though.' Having opened the door wider, she returned to where she had been sitting on an old wooden bench.

'Thank you, Rosie.' Harry followed her to the

bench. 'I didn't like the idea of you being here all alone.' He sat down beside her, while gingerly sliding his arm about her shoulders. 'I just want to be with you . . . to hold you, and let you know that I'm here when you need me. I'm always here for you, Rosie, always. We all are.'

Rosie smiled up at him. 'I know, and I appreciate that.' She plucked up the courage to tell him what was haunting her. 'It's just that I have things on my mind . . . to do with Daddy . . . and Mother and . . . certain other things.'

'Do you want to talk about it?'

'Not really, no.'

'It would be just me and you, no one else, I promise,' he gently reassured her. 'Whatever it is that's worrying you, I'm sure it would help if you talked about it rather than fretting and getting upset. Look, Rosie, you must know you can trust me. I won't tell anyone else . . . unless you want me to.'

She felt she could put her trust in him. 'I saw things,' she began. 'I really should tell the police, especially about the man in the barn. Auntie Kathleen told us about the man who was Mother's sweetheart all those years ago, so I was wondering if he was the man I saw in the barn. Before that, I saw him with her. They were outside the barn talking together.'

Harry was taken by surprise. 'What? You mean you were actually there, near the big barn, last night?'

'Yes, me and Barney. We were there, outside the big barn. But we didn't hear a fight going on, or anything like that. We were just looking for Daddy.'

'What do you mean, Rosie . . . why were you looking for him? And why was he out there in the first place?'

'Daddy was worried about Mother. It was really late and she still hadn't come home,' Rosie explained. 'He was so worried that he decided to go and find her. He told me to stay in the house with Barney, and I was not to answer the door or look out of the windows. But he was gone too long, and when I thought I saw him going into the yard, I took Barney with me and we went to find him.'

'And did you – find him, I mean?'

'No, but I saw my mother. She was outside the big barn with a man. They were talking, but I was too far away to hear what they were saying. And now I'm sure that man must have been the one who was with Mother, when Daddy found them together.'

'Good grief, Rosie, so what did you do?'

'We hid and watched, and waited to see if Daddy might turn up. But he didn't. I saw the man, and I saw Mother, but I never saw Daddy.' Rosie thought hard. 'I thought he might be there somewhere, though, so when Mother was not looking, I told Barney to stay put and not make a sound, then I sneaked into the barn. I saw the man inside there, but I was careful not to let him see me. But . . . honestly, Harry, it was really strange.'

Harry was intrigued, but also concerned that Rosie had gone inside the barn on her own. 'What do you mean, "strange"?'

Rosie mentally put herself back in the barn. 'Well, I kept by the wall, and stayed in the shadows as much as I could. Then I saw him – the man. He was standing a short distance away from me in the middle of the floor – just standing there, very still, as though he was in deep thought. And when he stooped down I noticed that right near his feet there was a pile of what looked like old clothes or some-thing . . . but it was shadowy and I couldn't make it out.'

'Oh, Rosie! Why did you put yourself in danger like that? You should never have gone in there. If he had seen you, who knows what he might have done?'

'He didn't see me. He never knew I was there because I was too careful. But I was a little afraid, and I couldn't see Daddy anywhere, so I sneaked out again. But something strange happened just before

I went. The man stooped down to pick something up off the ground. I couldn't tell what it was, but in the hazy light I could see that it was a dark object. He turned it round in his hands, and he stared at it for ages, and suddenly he was crying – really sobbing – like his heart was broken.'

Remembering it now, she felt sad inside. 'I wish I could have seen what the object was, but it was too shadowy. Then I crept outside as softly as I could.'

'Why did you not say this before?' Harry asked. 'When we were back at the house together, why did you not tell my parents about all this?'

'Because I was too afraid!' She instinctively dropped her voice to a whisper. 'I am still afraid, because if Mother knew I was telling you she would harm Barney . . . even kill him. That's what she said.'

'Why would she threaten Barney? When did she say that?'

'When I got back outside I ran into Mother and she warned me to be quiet and go home. I could hear the ambulance coming.'

She would have gone on, but Harry was adamant: 'You have to tell Mum and Dad what you told me; you have to tell them everything.'

'I can't. I won't, and neither must you.'

'What are you saying, Rosie? You have to tell them!

It's possible that what you saw could be crucial information about what happened.'

'I don't see how. I mean, I didn't see anything special . . . except for the man who was crying. And, even if I wanted to, I daren't tell your parents. I should never have told you either because if Mother finds out she'll hurt me, and she'll kill Barney.'

'We will always protect you and Barney. You must know that?'

'You wouldn't be able to protect us. She's wicked. She would find a way to do what she threatened. You weren't there, you didn't hear what she said. And she meant it, she really did. Just before the ambulance arrived, she warned me that if I told anyone that I had seen anything I shouldn't have, or heard anything, then she would hurt Barney really badly. That's what she said, and she meant it, Harry. I know she will.' Her fears were very real. 'Promise me, Harry, you will not tell your parents or anyone else. Please!'

Harry was torn. He could see how frightened Rosie was, and he understood. On the other hand, he realised that Rosie might well have seen and heard things that could maybe help the police get to the truth of what actually happened. Also, Harry was still unable to believe that John Tanner – that big, strong man – could ever lose his life in a fight.

'All right then, think about this. What if the man you saw in the barn really was this Tom Stevens? What if he and your mother had already hurt your father, and he was still there somewhere? He could well have been, because you just told me that the ambulance came, and your mother chased you away. Think about it, Rosie. Why was the ambulance there? And why did she want you out of the way?'

Rosie suddenly collapsed in tears. 'You think they were there to take Daddy, don't you? You think they had already hurt him . . . killed him?' It was all too much for her to think about, and she fell into Harry's arms, her heart made heavy by the thought that her daddy could have been lying only a short distance from where she had been. 'Oh, Harry, he was there, wasn't he? In the barn, with the man who hurt him.'

She fell silent. In her mind she was back in that shadowy barn, watching the man. He was looking down . . . the disturbing memories ran through her mind. 'When he picked something up, Harry,' she recalled, 'I don't know what it was. I couldn't see; it was too gloomy. But he held it ever so gently, and he kept looking at it and he was crying. When he laid the object down again, he did it so very gently.'

'Don't torture yourself, Rosie, but you really should tell my parents everything,' Harry coaxed her gently. 'As for Barney, I give you my word that neither he nor you will be hurt. Trust me, Rosie. Tell my parents. They will know if the police should hear what you know.' As a last resort he said kindly, 'Your father would have wanted you to tell what you saw and heard. You know he would, don't you, Rosie?'

She looked up and said not a word, but her heart was heavy. She knew that her father would have agreed with Harry because he was a good and honest man, afraid of nothing and no one.

Without a word, she slid her hand into Harry's and she felt immensely proud as he walked her back to the house.

'Come on, my lovely Rosie!' Squeezing her hand in his, Harry led her out of that dark shed and into the last of the daylight. 'Barney will be all right,' he told her softly. 'You're doing the right thing. Your father would be so proud of you. I know I am.'

PART THREE

Realisation

One Month Later

CHAPTER TEN

'YOU MUST BE soft in the head!'

The well-muscled prisoner glowered at his timid cell-mate, who was cowering in the corner of the bunk opposite.

'I heard you again, Stevens!' He took a threatening step forward. 'Last night you ruined my beauty sleep – and that's every night since they put you in here. Whimpering like a newborn . . . mumbling and bawling, and chunnering on about how it wasn't you who killed John Tanner, but his cheating wife.'

Folding his thick, muscled arms, he set a menacing stance. 'You're a damned fool, Stevens! Whatever possessed you to take the rap for what she did? Oh, yes, thanks to you talking in your sleep, I know the truth of it, and I reckon you must be out of your tiny mind. Oh, and if I was to let it be known what a soft idiot you are, the real men in this place would eat you for breakfast! As for your fancy piece, well now, she must be on cloud nine. I mean, thanks to you, she's suddenly free as a bird. She can go where she likes, and with who she likes. But you're such an idiot, you fell for it. By now you surely must see her for what she is, because if you don't then all I can say is, you really must be gormless!'

'I'm not gormless. We love each other. We always have.'

'Aw, don't give me that. Just take a minute to think about it. This woman who is supposed to love and want you, according to you and your nightmare rant-ings, she actually bashed her husband's head in with a spade, then she let you take the rap for it. Well, all I can say is, she must have you eating out of her hand. For my money, you're a gullible fool! And you deserve every punishment that comes to you.'

'But it wasn't like that.'

'Oh, really? So, what was it like then?'

Tom shook his head. 'You wouldn't understand. I'm not handsome or tall and strong, and I have no belief in myself. It's a fact that men like me don't find it easy to pick up a woman. But I know Molly will wait for me, however long it takes. She loves me,

I know she does, and I'll do anything to keep it that way.'

'Then you're a bigger fool than I took you for!' Deep down the tough old lag had a sneaking admiration for this little man who was about to lose his freedom because of his blind love for this woman who could twist him round her little finger. 'Tell me something, Stevens.'

'What?'

'OK . . . well, from your moanings and chattering in your sleep, I already know what you've done, and I can see it's haunting you. You're afraid you might lose her, but you're also afraid of what might happen when the case comes up . . . which is any day now. You love her, I can tell, but I'd like you to tell me, matey, where is she, this woman who adores you?'

'What do you mean?'

'Well, I'm thinking what you should be thinking. How many letters have you received from her?'

Angry and embarrassed, Tom gave no reply.

'Right then! So, even though she's allowed to visit, how many times has she applied for a visiting permit? How many times has she sat opposite that screen and talked with you . . . made you feel loved and wanted? How many times has she shown any regret for what happened to her good husband?

Since you've been in here, has she had any communication with you at all? Has she told you she'll wait for you, however long it takes? Or reassured you as to how much she loves you?'

Tom had asked himself those very same questions many times since being locked up, but he was not about to give the other man more ammunition to torment him with so, reluctantly, he defended Molly. 'She has a lot to do at home. Since . . .' he paused, before going on in a quiet voice, '. . . she has a farm to run. There are umpteen things to do, and there are four labourers who depend on the farm for their livelihoods. She also has a grieving daughter who I understand is not yet sixteen. The poor girl must be devastated about her father. Surely you must understand that she needs her mother at a time like this.'

'I do understand, Stevens! I also have a daughter in her early teens. But that doesn't mean to say your woman can't find a moment in her life to think about you, or to take the time to see you, or even to write a short note.'

Tom's cell-mate, an habitual offender, didn't see Tom as a fool or a bad man. Instead, he saw him as being dangerously naïve, and kindly. All that aside, he would not want any man to be caught up in the clutches of such a woman as this Molly Tanner, who was hard-hearted and wicked enough not only to swing that spade and kill her husband outright, but also to allow the man who misguidedly loved her to take the blame for the murder she had committed.

'Tell me, Stevens, since you've been locked up in this place, how many times have you really wondered about her? This woman, Molly Tanner – the woman you foolishly put your life on the line for – appears not to have given you a second thought.'

At that moment, the warning bell rang out for the cell doors to be opened.

As the two men duly walked out onto the landing, the big man leaned forward towards Tom, addressing him in a quiet voice. 'You might be wise to think about this,' he advised. 'If a woman could callously smash her husband's head in, what else would she do in order to live her life the way she wants, with who she wants? And it seems to me that is obviously not you, being as you have foolishly put yourself in a position where you won't see freedom for many years.'

He leaned closer. 'Come on, man! Use your head! For my money, Molly Tanner doesn't give a damn about you. Instead, she's playing you for all you're worth.'

As the day wore on, Tom thought about what his cell-mate had said. He recalled a few sneaking moments of doubt. He had neither heard from Molly nor seen her, and he felt terribly lonely. With all the worry about the court case coming up it had been difficult even to think straight. But now he was made to wonder about Molly's sincerity.

Since confessing that it was he who had swung the fatal blow, he had been made increasingly anxious by Molly's complete silence.

Now, because of what his cell-mate had pointed out, Tom was wondering why Molly had effectively deserted him. But in his deepest heart, he knew the truth, though he was loath to believe what was staring him in the face.

In his dreams, he could still see Molly, with the spade in her fists, and it haunted him.

Asleep or wide awake, in his tortured mind he saw the gleam of raw hatred in her face as she forcefully and deliberately swung the spade at her husband's head.

Of late he had been wondering about that. There had been no real need for her to lash out with such force as she delivered that fatal blow. Haunting his waking and sleeping hours was the thought that a lesser blow to the leg might well have effectively disabled John Tanner, at least long enough for Tom to get out from under her husband's onslaught.

He had reluctantly come to believe that Molly Tanner may actually have intended all along to kill her husband . . . and that the fight presented her with the opportunity.

Whatever her intentions, Tom acknowledged, that good and dedicated family man did not deserve to die in such a brutal manner.

CHAPTER ELEVEN

Fʀᴏᴍ ᴛʜᴇ ᴅᴀʏ Thomas Stevens was arrested, the newspapers had closely followed the explosive story of John Tanner, who, after discovering his wife and her lover together in a compromising situation, had been killed in a fierce and bloody fight between the two men.

Thomas Stevens had confessed straight away that he had accidentally killed John Tanner, while in fear for his own life.

After some weeks of police investigation, however, and with statements from family members and other crucial evidence, both Stevens and Molly Tanner were tried and sentenced. The newsmen were in court to report the finale to the trial.

Barn Murder – The Verdict

Thomas Stevens was yesterday given three years for attempting to pervert the course of justice in consistently claiming that he was single hand-edly responsible for the death of farmer John Tanner.

Under intense cross-examination, he admitted everything: how he had followed the instruc-tions, of Molly Tanner, the victim's wife, to wipe her fingerprints off the murder weapon, a spade, which he did to the best of his ability, using an oily rag he found in the barn.

For this, he was given another five years in custody, bringing his sentence to a total of eight years.

It was discovered under close examination of the murder weapon that there remained a number of Mrs Tanner's fingerprints on the shaft of the spade. This was sufficient evidence to charge Molly Tanner, and following her lawyer's advice she confessed to her part in John Tanner's death.

Yesterday at the Crown Court she, too, was sentenced to twelve years in prison without remand.

She was also charged with attempting to

pervert the course of justice, for which she was given a further sentence of three years' imprisonment.

Mr and Mrs Tanner's daughter, Rosemary, 15, remains in the care of relatives.

Molly might well have been give a harsher sentence, but her lawyer employed all his skills to persuade the jury that at the time of her lashing out with the spade, it was not his client's intention to kill, but to stop the fight. She was convinced that her husband, a stronger, much bigger-built man, was about to kill Thomas Stevens, who at the time was calling out, trapped against the wall and in fear for his life.

When questioned as to her explanation, Thomas Stevens admitted that, yes, he had been afraid at that time, but he could not be certain that John Tanner meant to kill him.

PART FOUR

The Aftermath

One Month Later

CHAPTER TWELVE

'ALL RIGHT, ARE you, Rosie?'

Kathleen had dreaded this day, although while they waited for John to be returned to them, at least that span of time after the court case and the somewhat intrusive follow-up in the newspapers had allowed them time to prepare themselves for the moment when John Tanner would be laid to his rest.

Now, with the winter sun shining down on her tearful face, Kathleen recognised her responsibilities, and she was ready to do what had to be done to close this painful chapter in their lives. John would forever be with them in spirit, she truly believed that.

'I'm all right, Auntie Kathleen,' Rosie assured her shakily. 'Barney won't leave me, though. He lay along-side the bed last night, whimpering and pawing at the sheet, so I let him come up on top of the eider-down, was that all right?'

Kathleen glanced at that beloved family pet as he peered out warily from behind Rosie's legs. 'Yes, of course, Rosie. He must be grieving still . . . like the rest of us. But you must not let him sleep under the bedclothes with you because – as much as we love him – it would not be healthy.'

Rosie nodded.

Just then, Patrick came out, looking decidedly uncomfortable in his grey suit and navy-blue tie. 'This darned thing nigh chokes me!' he grumbled, tugging at the tie. 'I'm not a lover of ties, never have been!'

Harry was right behind him. Not owning a suit, he had opted for a black jacket, a dark-blue tie and white shirt, with dark-blue trousers. 'They don't fit very well, but I've tightened the belt up, so do they look all right, Mum?' He tugged at her shoulder. 'Should I go and find something else to wear?'

Kathleen looked her son up and down, proud that he was such a handsome young man. 'No. You look absolutely fine just as you are, and anyway, you don't have anything else more suitable, do you?'

'No. But I'm sure I could borrow something of Dad's.'

Kathleen smiled at that. 'No, Harry, you look perfectly respectable as you are. So, stop worrying.'

Growing anxious, she glanced back at the door. 'Where's Rosie gone? She was here a minute ago.'

Just then, Patrick informed them, 'The cars are here. Can somebody fetch Rosie?'

Harry found her in the kitchen, sobbing helplessly. 'I don't want to go,' she confessed. 'I can't bear the idea of seeing Daddy being lowered into a deep, black hole.'

'He's at peace now, Rosie. Like Mum said last night, he isn't here any more, he's gone to his Maker.' He felt totally out of his depth. 'And anyway, wouldn't you rather have him in the churchyard where you can visit and remember him?'

Rosie nodded. Peeking up at Harry with red-raw eyes, she told him shakily, 'I just want him here . . . with me . . . to talk with him, and laugh with him, and race across the fields with Barney running ahead.'

Holding her tight, he kissed the top of her head. 'I know that,' he said, 'and who knows, like Dad said last night, how do we know that we won't ever see him again, or run across the field with him, or talk to him? Maybe he can hear us now, and he's feeling sad because you're sad. Oh, Rosie, just think about all the wonderful times you had together. Imagine now that he's standing beside you every step of the way as you live your life. Keep the good memories strong in your mind and heart. They will help you, I promise.'

'Is that what you do, Harry?'

'Yes, because I loved your father as well. He was like a second dad to me, and I will never, ever forget him.' He held her face between his hands. 'And, yes, it does help.'

Harry always seemed to know what to say to make Rosie feel better.

'Come on then,' she slid her hand into his, 'Daddy's waiting for us.'

'You're right, he was always a stickler for being punctual.' Even as he was leading her out, the tears pricked his eyes. 'Oh, Lord,' he murmured under his breath, 'please look after that wonderful man.'

Once outside, Rosie went straight to the hearse, where she saw the wreaths through the windows of the car, carrying his name, her own words written in flowers across the back window – 'Love you, Daddy.'

Growing tearful again, she traced the words with her fingertip, and then Harry was there to hold her hand and help her into the front car.

'Time to go, Rosie,' he said softly.

She held his hand so tightly that he felt as though the blood would drain away. In that very poignant moment he knew in his deepest heart and soul that he could never love anyone else like he loved his darling Rosie. But, as always, in the back of his mind he thought his love was hopeless because Rosie had known him all her life and saw him as a kind of brother.

And knowing that, and carrying the sadness of that day, it was almost too much to bear.

~

The church was filled with flowers, given with love and respect by the many villagers who had always seen John Tanner as a friend; as a pillar of the community; and, for some of them, as an employer. He was always there if ever there was a problem. He was a fine friend, and a much-loved and respected neighbour. Every soul there prayed for him, and many shed a sorry tear for his loss.

After the gathering and prayers came the final commiserations in the churchyard, and then it was time for everyone to depart.

'Thank you so much for being here.' Rosie spoke to each person individually, and they hugged her lovingly, each and every one being too filled with emotion to say much. Rosie was glad of that, for as soon as the mourners had departed, she needed to be alone with her daddy.

'Do you want me to come with you, Rosie?' Harry was loath to leave her side.

Rosie shook her head. 'Later, maybe, but for now I need a minute or two just to be on my own . . . if that's all right?'

Harry understood. 'I'll wait by the gate at the bottom of the path,' he promised. 'I won't be far away.'

'Thank you, Harry.' Rosie reached up and shyly kissed him, being very gentle and hesitant, because she had known him all her life and she was convinced he saw her as a kind of sister.

As she walked away, Harry watched until he could see her no more. He then looked up at the bright skies with a heavy heart. 'Let her be strong, Lord,' he murmured. 'Let her find happiness. And please, help me to accept that she will never love me as I would like.'

That was the saddest thought of all: a life without Rosie to share it with was, to him, no life at all.

~

While Harry waited for Rosie, he strode up and down the pathway.

At one point he noticed a woman standing by a tree, not too far from where he had been waiting. She looked rather lonely, aged probably in her early thirties, or thereabouts. Harry thought her quietly attractive with her long brown hair swooped up in a whirl and tied with a delicate little blue ribbon.

She was dressed in a knee-length light-green coat, and wearing dark ankle boots. Dangling from her wrist was a small, chunky umbrella.

Harry couldn't help but feel that she must be waiting for someone, but as far as he knew everyone had gone except for himself and Rosie.

He continued to pace up and down, and when he looked up again, the woman was nowhere in sight. She must have come to the wrong church, he thought. Poor thing.

When, a moment later, he saw Rosie coming down the path, he ran to meet Rosie. 'Are you all right, my darling?' Reaching out, he took her by the hand and walked her down to the gate. He knew she'd been crying because her eyes were red raw. 'Come on, let's get you to the village hall, eh?'

'We'd best hurry,' Rosie told him. 'By now they'll be wondering where we've got to.' It was hard for her not to think all the time of her darling father, lying up there all alone in the dark earth.

As the two of them walked hand in hand towards the village hall, Harry forgot about the woman who had appeared rather lonely, back there in the churchyard.

The reception was not a morbid affair, although talk was muted and the sadness was highly evident in the hall. People ate and drank and toasted the life of John Tanner, and, with nervous approach, they talked to and hugged Rosie and the family.

When Patrick stood up to give a speech, there was not a dry eye to be seen. Instead, each and every one there was made to reflect on the fact that life was indeed precarious, although in each of them, the memory of John Tanner was bound to live on.

When it was time to leave, they left singly or in small groups: the village shopkeeper; the little widow who owned the flower shop; Fred Pearson, manager of the local garage – all glad to have had the chance to say a proper goodbye to their respected neighbour.

Soon it was time for the family to say a gracious thank-you to both the vicar and the lady who had organised the reception.

As the family made their way out, Rosie said, 'I need to go back to the churchyard, just for a little while.' She was missing her father so much, she could hardly breathe.

'Do you want us to come back with you, sweetheart?' That was Kathleen.

Rosie shook her head. 'No, thank you, Auntie Kathleen, and I really don't want to go home in the official car.' Shuddering at the thought, she turned to her uncle. 'Can we please get a taxi, Uncle Patrick?'

'Of course, Rosie, love, if that's what you want.' He understood. 'I'll use the telephone in the hall to call a taxi to take you and Harry to the churchyard, then he can wait there for you and bring you home whenever you're ready. Will that do?'

'Yes, thank you.'

When the taxi arrived, Patrick and Kathleen hugged Rosie and Harry, then lingered a moment while they climbed inside. Patrick and Kathleen waved the young ones off until the taxi was out of sight, and then they too were heading off, but in the opposite direction.

'Will they be all right?' Patrick asked.

'I'm sure they will,' Kathleen replied, 'but Rosie's positively broken by what's happened. Oh, Patrick, I don't know how she will ever get through this.'

'She's her father's daughter, my love.' He took hold of her hand. 'I know it won't be easy, but Rosie will get through it – with our help and with Harry by her side.'

His remark raised another sorry point. Being aware of the driver up front, Kathleen lowered her voice to a whisper. 'You do know they love each other, don't you, Patrick? I mean, they *really* love each other.'

'Yes, I have realised that,' he replied, 'and I've been thinking of having a serious talk with them. But with things the way they are at the moment, and Rosie having to cope with the loss of her father, it might be kinder if I left it just now. They are so very young yet. What do you think?'

'Yes, I think that would be best.'

For the remainder of the drive home, Patrick was thinking about when he first met Kathleen, and then later when she said yes to his proposal of marriage. Over these past wonderful years, they had been so happy, and so much in love. He considered himself the luckiest man in the world. He only hoped Harry and Rosie would find the same kind of happiness.

PART FIVE

Revelations

CHAPTER THIRTEEN

'ARE YOU SURE you're all right on your own, Rosie?'

'I think so.' Now that they were actually in the churchyard, Rosie was experiencing so many emotions she felt totally lost. 'I just need to be with him . . . just for a minute or two,' she said in a shaky whisper. 'I need to tell him how much I miss him, and how much I wish he was still here, talking and laughing with me, and just to see his smile once again would be so beautiful.'

Harry forced back his tears. 'His smile will always be with us,' he promised, 'because you have it. You have his smile, and you have his goodness, and I will always look after you, Rosie.'

Rosie slid her hand into his, her eyes welling with

tears. 'You are the kindest person I know and I'm so glad I've got you as a cousin,' she said.

Saddened by her innocent remark, Harry nodded. That was how she saw him: as her cousin. 'I'll go inside the church and light a candle for your father. Would you like that, Rosie? After I've lit the candle, I'll wait at the church door for you.'

Rosie smiled on him, and then she turned away and went up the path.

Rosie turned her head to see him enter the church, and then she walked on towards her father's resting place.

When she was within sight of the mound of floral tributes that marked her daddy's grave, she paused, surprised to see someone was there, kneeling down, placing flowers.

Drawing nearer, she saw it was a woman, but she could not get a good look at her because her head was bent, and her light-brown hair was somewhat tousled about her face.

As Rosie came nearer, increasingly curious, she heard the woman softly crying. Her sadness touched Rosie's heart.

For a long, confusing moment, Rosie wondered if she ought to go to the woman and ask her who she was.

Quietly, Rosie approached softly, until she could see the woman more easily. She appeared to be in her thirties, and she was reaching out to lay the prettiest posy of flowers on the grave, the gentlest smile on her sad face.

Curious as to who this woman was, Rosie quickened her steps until she was almost upon her. The woman was seemingly unaware of her presence.

Rosie stepped forward. 'Who are you?' she asked kindly.

The woman looked up and regarded Rosie with tear-filled eyes.

'I'm sorry, but I think you may have the wrong place.' Rosie gestured to the flowers. 'This is my father's grave.'

For what seemed an age, the woman looked at Rosie with such kindness that Rosie's heart seemed to flip over, and then the woman spoke softly to her. 'This is John Tanner's grave, isn't it?'

'Yes.'

'Then I'm not at the wrong place.'

Rosie had a fleeting memory of a distant figure often waiting at the school gates and seemingly watching her.

Tears were now running down the woman's face, and when she slowly rose to stand before Rosie, she looked at her with such compassion that Rosie was taken by surprise.

'You must be Rosie?' the woman asked in the softest tone.

Somewhat confused, Rosie stepped back a pace. 'Yes, I am . . . but I don't know you. At least . . . I don't think I do.'

The woman smiled though her brown eyes remained sad. 'Of course you don't. But I know you, Rosie. I've watched you grow from a toddler. I've stood outside the gates of your school. I've kept you in my heart all these years, and now I share your deep loss. John was a good and beautiful man, and I'm so sorry he's gone.' Her smile deepened. 'But you're here, Rosie, and so am I. And I know he would be happy about that.'

Rosie was now beginning to feel deeply uncomfortable. 'How do you know me? Why did you watch me grow up . . . and who are you?' Her fear turned to anger. 'I want to know. Tell me, who are you?'

The woman hesitated as if she was momentarily sorry for saying the things she had said, but she somehow gathered her courage in order to tell this lovely girl why she was here.

'Forgive me, Rosie,' she hesitated, but then the words just fell softly out, '. . . I'm your mother.'

It was too much for Rosie to take on board, and fearful of this woman and what she was claiming, she fled down the path and across to the church. Then she was in Harry's strong arms, babbling and crying, and trying to repeat what the woman had told her.

'Woa!' Harry walked her to a bench beside the church door and held her tight as he spoke softly. 'Ssh, Rosie, be calm.' A moment later, she was calm.

The woman, who had been standing a short distance away, came to them. 'I'm so sorry,' she said. 'I should never have blurted it out like that. But I need Rosie to know who I am, and why I'm here. She deserves that much.'

Quieter now, Rosie sat on one side of Harry, and the woman sat down on the other side to explain herself.

'John and I met a long time ago. We saw each other off and on for a while and I always thought we would get married, but Molly was a strong personality with an unusual wild beauty, and once he had met her she drew him in and he couldn't resist her. Even after he married Molly, we still had feelings for each other, and although John told me that he had made a mistake in marrying her, it was too late.'

Both Rosie and Harry were dumbfounded.

'Was my daddy really seeing you, even after he married her?' Rosie asked the woman.

'Yes. He loved her but she was so difficult to live with. He tried to leave her, but she always got him back. She was like a crazy woman when she found out about us.'

'So how did she get him away from you? What did she do?' Rosie wanted to know everything.

'During the last time we were together, I got pregnant with you, Rosie. Your father didn't know about you, because I didn't want to put pressure on him, not until after you were born. I made up a story about not wanting him to cheat on his wife any more and I broke up our relationship.' She paused to allow that to sink in. 'Then my mother got taken very ill. She needed round-the-clock nursing, and there was no one to help her but me. My parents were divorced, and my father was travelling all the time with his work anyway. Also, I had two small brothers who needed me. It was so hard, but I couldn't let them down. Eventually I couldn't cope any more. That's when I told your father he had a daughter.'

'What happened?' Rosie asked.

'I took you to my heart, Rosie. I loved you from the first moment I saw you. It was very difficult . . .

you can't understand how hard it was. I was desperate. My family were in dire need of me, and after I had you my life became impossible, especially as my father had decided to stay abroad. When that happened, Mother got worse, and she died within the year. That's when I had to turn to your father.'

She explained, 'In the end, I had to tell John about you. That put him in a very difficult position, although he was thrilled to have you. He couldn't stop cuddling you . . . oh, you should have seen the joy on his face the first time he saw you, Rosie.'

She took a deep breath. 'He was so wonderful, and supportive. He said he would work something out, but that if he managed to persuade Molly to take you on, he would not be able to see me ever again. I agreed. He was married, and I had more than enough to deal with. It was a bad situation.'

Rosie listened while she went on. 'I wanted to keep you, Rosie. But it was just too difficult, and I knew John would take good care of you. I was just seventeen, with so much responsibility that I could hardly breathe, let alone look after a new baby on top of everything else. Molly agreed to take you on as her own, but only if John signed over to her the cottage and five acres at the far end of the farm, the income from these to be paid entirely to her. Your father reluctantly agreed. She wanted more, but your father would not allow it. They kept the secret of your birth and the bargain they'd made.'

She assured Molly, 'Your father adored you. There was no way he was going to let me have you adopted, something I had no choice but to consider if he could or would not help me.'

Reaching out, she touched Rosie gently on the hand, afraid to hold her in case Rosie rejected her altogether. 'It's been the hardest thing, seeing you and not being able to have you. But I knew you were safe with John. And we both loved you so much. We could not have loved you more.'

Rosie was deeply shaken by all this news. 'That land was his father's and his grandfather's before him. How could he let her take it from him?'

'Because he had held you in his arms, and he adored you from that moment, Rosie. Yes, your father was devastated by Molly's demands, but he did not hesitate, not for one moment. You were everything to him, and he so wanted to raise you as his daughter. Molly got what she wanted, but your father thought it a small price to pay for having you in his life.'

For a long time, Rosie was silent; thinking and

realising, and feeling so relieved. 'Now I know why she hated me so much . . . why she liked to hurt me and make me cry.'

In a great surge of joy, she hugged this woman . . . this stranger who was her real mother. 'Thank you . . .' She could hardly talk for the emotions that were shaking her; she could hardly even think straight. 'But I know now . . . why she wanted to hurt me. She said I was no good . . . that I would never be any good, and I believed her.'

Rosie got up and flung her arms about this woman, her real mother, warm and loving, and so sad about what she had had to do. 'Thank you for telling me,' Rosie said. 'Thank you for making me realise that I am not bad, that I don't deserve the worst things in life . . . like *she* always told me.'

Thrilled to his soul at Rosie's news, Harry stood back while this woman held her child.

'You're a beautiful girl, Rosie,' her real mother told her. 'I know how proud your father was to have you with him . . . and he kept my secret for all those years. I only wish I could have done better for you. Please forgive me, Rosie?'

And because she felt this woman's deep regret, Rosie promised her that there was nothing to forgive.

'What's your name?' she asked.

'It's Rossalyn.' She smiled. 'Your daddy gave you a name that was very similiar to mine.'

Rosie thought of the woman who had hated her from as far back as she could remember. She wondered what Molly Tanner would say if she could see her standing here, with her own birth mother.

Shuddering at the thought of Molly Tanner and what that woman had done, Rosie felt heavy of heart. She wondered if, for her own sake and the sake of her loved ones, there might come a day when she felt able to put all behind her, where it surely belonged.

~

The lawyer was adamant. 'I'm sorry, but there is nothing I can do. The terms were lawful . . . written and passed, and they will stand as long as there are Tanners.'

Having taken an instant dislike to this scheming murderer, he now found great satisfaction in revealing that what was cemented in law with regard to the Tanner properties could not be undone, except by a direct descendant of John Tanner. If Molly Tanner thought to contest the lawful deeds, she would get no further than this irrevocable document.

John Tanner had, after some small difficulty, secured the right to give her the small cottage and the parcel of farmland, and so Molly was not altogether penniless. That would be all she inherited. Everything else would go to John Tanner's only child.

CHAPTER FOURTEEN

IN THE WEEKS that followed, Rosie was finding it hard to come to terms with her beloved father's death.

Keeping a close and loving eye on Rosie, Kathleen and Patrick treated her with the utmost kindness. They allowed her the space to grieve when she needed to, but also provided her with good company, and even a measure of laughter to help heal her crippling distress.

'But what is Rosie's new life to be?' Kathleen asked Patrick one evening after Rossalyn had visited and had confided these thoughts to Rosie's loving aunt.

'My darlin', does it matter just yet?' he said. 'That lovely young girl needs time and she needs space.

She can stay here for as long as she likes, as far as I'm concerned.'

Kathleen replied in a quiet voice, 'Thankfully, there's a farmhouse and farm land waiting for her, and yet she hasn't ever mentioned her home or the farm to me since that dreadful business.'

Harry assured them, 'Rosie is still grieving. The last thing she would think about just now is her father's farm. She's still broken by her Daddy's death. And besides, Uncle John's men know their roles – the stable manager is in charge – and have turned up loyally to work every day since his death. There's less to do on the land in winter anyway. She's always loved the farm and she will go to it when she feels good and ready. Also, it would help her to look to the future.'

'Do you think she could cope?' Patrick was a little concerned.

'Well at least she has us. We'll all help her.' Harry assured his father. 'The trouble is, the longer she leaves it, the harder it will be for her.'

'Harry's right,' said Kathleen. 'She needs to go and look. Maybe we should take her over to the house for a couple of hours tomorrow, if she agrees. What d'you say?'

Patrick grinned at his wife. 'I say that, as usual, you are right, Kathleen.'

Somewhat relieved, Kathleen planted a kiss on his rosy cheek. 'Right! So we all agree that we'll wait for Rosie to make the first move?'

Patrick nodded. 'I think that's the best plan, sweetheart, yes. But if she doesn't mention it soon, it may be necessary to encourage her gently.'

~

After a week with Rosie making no mention of the farm, Kathleen gently reminded her that it was now her own, and to Kathleen's relief it seemed that Rosie was feeling able to go there. She did, though, appear to be slightly nervous – it would never be the same without her beloved daddy there.

Harry reassured her. 'We're here with you, Rosie.'

And so, Rosie felt easier. 'You're right,' she told him, and everyone agreed.

On arrival at the farm, Kathleen unlocked the door and opened it for Rosie to go in first.

'It looks different, somehow.' Rosie felt a great rush of emotion, as the tears welled in her sad eyes.

'I hope you don't mind, but I had a little tidy up,' Kathleen revealed. 'I wanted it to be nice for you.'

'Thank you, Auntie Kathleen. I hadn't thought about all the stuff we left – the food and that. I imagine it was all mouldy. I'm sorry . . .'

Rosie could see how neat and tidy Kathleen had left it all, and she choked back the tears. This had been her home, and now it was cold and empty.

Suddenly, Rosie caught sight of one of her father's flat caps on the pegs in the hall. 'I don't know if it will ever feel like home again,' she whispered.

'You could just take a look in your room, see if there's any books you want to bring back,' Kathleen persuaded her. 'Do you think you could manage, while I make us all a hot drink? I brought everything with me.'

Rosie's attention was diverted to Barney at the sound of a whimper, followed by a crash. She went in search of him. 'What is it, boy?' she asked, when she found him by the sideboard where the photograph of Kathleen and Molly was lying broken on the floor. It seemed that Barney had somehow knocked it off.

'It's alright, Barney,' Rosie reassured him. She picked up the picture. In some ways it seemed to her a lifetime since that fateful evening when Barney had sent the very same photograph tumbling to the floor, with the glass all cracked. In that moment, the sight of it brought rushing back to her all the anguish of that long, lonely night. All the anxiety about first her mother, and then her father, and the haunting, eerie sight of that weeping man she now knew as Thomas Stevens. But most horrible of all was the memory of Molly Tanner, confronting her as she hid outside the hay barn.

I am not your mother. What I am is your worst nightmare.

As the sound of those vicious words swept into Rosie's mind she was gripped by a sense of rage. With a cry, she grabbed the photo frame. Then she threw it down on the floor so hard that the glass shattered in every direction. She took up the photo frame again, and tore out the photograph itself, which she ripped in half, parting the smiling sisters. Then she took Molly's image and ripped it into even smaller fragments, until it was littered on the carpet, like discarded confetti. Before anyone else could react, Rosie ran from the room.

The sound of her footsteps echoed as she fled upstairs.

Patrick put his head nervously round the door of the front room and called softly to Kathleen. 'Go after her?'

'No. I'll leave her for the moment; let her think a while.' Kathleen picked up the fragments of the photograph. 'I should have seen that old photo and tidied it away before today.'

A few minutes later, when Kathleen went to Rosie's room, there was no sign of her. After searching, Kathleen found Rosie in her parents' room, and she was shocked at what she saw.

Sobbing bitterly, Rosie was tearing Molly's clothes from the wardrobe and piling them in the middle of the bed.

'I'm throwing the whole lot out,' Rosie announced, although it was already perfectly obvious to Kathleen what she was doing.

'Come on, let's take all it onto the landing,' Kathleen suggested, and Rosie agreed.

'I don't want anything of hers left in this house,' she said. The decision was to empty every wardrobe, cupboard and drawer, until there was no longer the taint of Molly Tanner's person in this homely cottage.

In the bottom drawer, as she threw out some underclothes, Rosie uncovered several diaries and a quick flip through showed them to be in Molly's handwriting, though there were few entries. She was just about to throw them away when she saw a piece of paper stuck between the pages of one of them, like a bookmark. The name 'Ma Battersby' was scribbled on it in pencil. She opened the diary and saw an appointment recorded for the Tuesday of that week, over fifteen years previously: '17 Acament

Street, 2.30'. Underneath, in red ink pressed deeply into the page and underlined twice as if in triumph, the words: 'Your son, John Tanner, done with.'

'What can this mean?' she asked Kathleen, handing her the diary and bookmark.

Kathleen looked at the words, looked at Rosie, looked again at the diary. 'Ma Battersby . . . I've heard that name somewhere . . . ' she murmured. Then her face turned pale as she sank down onto the bed in shock, her hand over her mouth.

'Tell me,' insisted Rosie when the silence had grown unbearable.

'I don't know if I can,' whispered Kathleen. 'Oh, Rosie, it's too awful. Oh, dear God, what can she have been thinking of?' Tears sprang to her eyes and she wiped them away, muttering to herself in her shock and anger. 'The wickedness of it . . . and her with a loving husband who would have doted on his bairn . . . ' Kathleen was rocking back and forward, crying openly now.

'A baby?' Rosie asked softly. 'She was going to have a baby? But what happened?'

'Oh, my innocent sweet angel, you shouldn't have to hear of things like this,' gulped Kathleen.

'Like what? Tell me, Auntie. Are you saying . . . I would have had a brother?'

'I reckon you would, my darling, but Molly didn't want it.'

'So what happened?' But Rosie was already beginning to guess. 'She got rid of it, didn't she? She went to see this Ma Battersby person and she got rid of the baby.'

'That would seem to be so,' said Kathleen quietly, dashing the tears from her eyes.

Rosie sat down on the blanket beside her aunt, her mind racing with the implications of this revelation.

'I can see by what she's written that she was pleased about it. The message to Daddy . . . I'm sure he never knew, but it's like she did it out of spite. Or maybe because she wanted to inherit Daddy's farm. All the time I lived here, with just Daddy and Barney to love me, I was so lonely and the woman I thought was my mother was so unkind. I would dearly have loved to have a brother or sister to play with, an ally. I didn't want my school friends to see how my mother treated me so I hardly ever asked them round. And now I learn I could have had a brother of my very own! I needn't have been alone at all. Oh, Auntie Kathleen, how could she? How could she do that?'

Kathleen took Rosie in her arms as she sobbed pitifully.

Patrick put his head around the door but Kathleen silently shooed him away.

After many minutes, Harry stole a look into the room, his face concerned but a spark of joy in his eyes. Silently, he came over and put an arm about Rosie. Eventually she sat up straight, wiped her swollen eyes and gave Harry a wobbly smile.

'Now then, Rosie, I think I have the very thing to chase away those tears,' said Harry quietly. 'Do you feel up to coming outside and taking a look?'

Rosie nodded, wiped her face again, stood up and let Harry lead her downstairs, out of the door and across the yard to the stables.

'Hush now. No sudden movements,' said Harry, beaming at her.

He led her to the loose box at the far end, where her father's favourite mare resided. Now, long skinny legs folded into the straw, a tiny foal sat at his mother's feet.

'What do you think of that? Born this morning, and what a beauty. What do you reckon, Rosie? Do you think we have a champion there?'

Rosie looked at the new-born foal, his mother nuzzling him gently, and she remembered John's attention to his animals and how he had trained Harry to his standards. She turned to observe the long row of loose boxes, her father's proud horses looking out to greet her, turned back and saw again the glossy coat and perfect head of the new foal, and Harry beside her, looking at her like he really cared about her – like he loved her. Suddenly she knew exactly where she belonged and it was where her father had wanted her to be – here, on this farm, with these horses . . . with this dear young man.

As if he had read her mind, Harry gathered her into his arms, holding her tightly, willing her to feel safe and wanted and loved.

'A new beginning . . .' he whispered into her hair. 'Please, if you felt you could, I'd like you to share it with me.'

'I will,' Rosie whispered back.

She smiled up at him and he bent to kiss her gently on the mouth.

When they emerged from the stables they could see a figure on a bicycle approaching along the lane the other side of the paddock. The figure waved and Rosie waved back.

'Dad told me he'd telephoned Rossalyn and asked her to come over if she could.' Harry laughed.

'That was kind of him.' Rosie smiled. 'Come on, Harry, let's go and tell my mother about the new beginning.'

CHAPTER FIFTEEN

TWO YEARS AFTER that memorable morning, Rosie and Harry walked down the aisle as man and wife. Since they had shared so many mixed emotions on the day of John Tanner's funeral and the appearance of Rossalyn, and then that day of new beginnings, their love for each other had grown ever deeper.

'How do you feel, Mrs Riley?' Harry asked as they got out of the cart outside the village hall where they had celebrated her daddy's life.

'I feel so very lucky,' she told Harry. 'I have you, and I have my real mother, and the family I love are here. I also have my daddy in my heart . . .' her voice broke, '. . . but I just wish he was here . . . so he can see how very happy I am.'

'Oh, he's here, all right,' Harry whispered. 'Look at that.' He pointed to the high window where suddenly the sunshine was pouring in. 'Your daddy will always be here watching over you.'

Rosie looked up and saw Rossalyn smiling on her. And right there beside her mother was the rest of her family, and the sun was shining through the window just as Harry had pointed out.

In that beautiful moment, Rosie felt deeply content. At long last, she felt a true sense of belonging.

~

Rosie and Harry left the wedding reception with the good wishes of their family and friends ringing in their ears, rice and pastel-coloured confetti clinging to Rosie's pretty little veil. Barney followed them out at his own pace. His old legs were tired these days, arthritis troubling him, but he could still rise to the occasion – and what an occasion this had been, featuring his two favourite people. It took him two attempts but, with a little help, he managed to get himself into the back of the waiting cart and settled down for the journey home to Tanner's Farm.

'That's a very modern wedding dress, Mrs Riley,'

said Harry, admiringly, handing his bride into the front seat of the flower-bedecked wagon pulled by their beloved carthorse, who tossed his head proudly, setting his highly polished brasses jingling and the ribbons in his mane fluttering.

'I'm a very modern woman,' said Rosie, primly, smoothing out her elegant bell-shaped skirt and admiring the shine of her new wedding ring as she did so. 'I'm a farmer now, don't forget; a landowner and businesswoman, no less.' She stuck her chin in the air in mock self-importance, then burst out laughing.

'You are indeed! And, best of all, you're mine for ever, my darling,' Harry said, squeezing her hand before he took the reins.

The promise of that earlier sunshine was fulfilled in this beautiful spring afternoon as Harry drove them along the lanes. The hawthorn was full of may blossom with its distinctive pungent smell, baby rabbits nibbled at the grass verges and there was the hint of warm days ahead in the spring air.

'We've had a good number of twin lambs this year,' Rosie said before they had travelled far. 'I'm wondering whether to expand the flock. We've got room if we give over that leek field to pasture. What do you think?'

'I think you look amazing,' said Harry, feasting his eyes on her.

'Even those triplets have thrived,' Rosie went on, smiling, but pretending she hadn't heard him, 'though I shall be glad be finish bottle-feeding them.'

'Well, you might find the practice will come in useful,' Harry grinned.

Rosie laughed and snuggled up close to him on the seat. 'Yes, some human babies are definitely something new to think about for Tanner's Farm,' she said. 'We'll need to do some costings before we expand in that direction. And I hope not triplets.'

'At least we wouldn't have to put them out to pasture,' Harry joked, a twinkle in his eye.

They settled back in their seat in blissful and silent companionship for a few minutes.

'I'm thinking we could maybe start Tanner's Beauty on a career as a show-jumper before long,' Rosie mused. 'He's so intelligent and I don't think I'd ever want to sell him.'

'No, I wouldn't either,' agreed Harry. 'That gorgeous fellow, born the day you returned to the farm, is a symbol of our new beginning to me.'

'And to me,' said Rosie fervently. 'He's got strength and spirit, and if we channel it in the right way I reckon he could be a champion.'

'No point in not aiming high,' Harry said, 'and you have such a way with him. He somehow knows that he's very special to you.'

'Mmm . . .'

They lapsed into silence again, each occasionally glancing at the other in loving admiration as they listened to the jangle of the horse's harness and the clopping of his heavy feet. Soon Harry was turning the cart into the yard in front of the farmhouse.

'Oh, look. How pretty!' gasped Rosie, seeing the door decorated with a wreath of delicate spring flowers and bunting draped between the upper windows. 'Who did that?'

'Mum and Rossalyn, of course,' Harry replied. 'And there are more surprises inside. Come on, let's get Barney out of the back and I'll carry you over the threshold.' He came round and helped her down from the high seat. 'Come on, Barney. Good boy. Out you get.'

Harry opened the tail gate of the cart, and after surveying the drop to the ground, the old dog decided he could make it and jumped inelegantly down. Then Harry produced the door key and let him inside to enjoy the comfort of his basket after a long and exciting day.

'And now . . . I've wanted to do this for so long,'

said Harry, sweeping Rosie off her feet and carrying her into their home, while she squealed with joy and pretended she minded.

Of course, once she was in his arms he couldn't stop kissing her until she gasped between kisses, 'Put me down . . . before . . . you drop me . . .'

Eventually, Harry led her into the front room where the table was laid with a pristine white cloth and Rosie and Harry's new china. 'There are some nice things for supper from the dairy where Rossalyn works,' said Harry, 'and Mum has made your favourite chocolate cake.'

'Delicious! Everyone has been so kind. What's under there?' asked Rosie, indicating a sheet covering a high mound on top of the sideboard, no longer home to Molly's ornaments and photos.

'Presents from Mum and Dad. Have a look.'

Rosie carefully slid the sheet away to reveal, first, a beautiful saddle of the finest leather.

'Oh, it's just lovely.' Rosie stroked the smooth tan hide and admired the tiny even stitches. 'Perfect for Tanner's Beauty when we've got him trained over the jumps.'

'That's what Dad thought.'

'And look what else. A box . . . of writing paper. Oh, look, Harry, it's got my name printed on it.

"Tanner Farm. Proprietor: Rosie Riley. Family Farm for Four Generations."' Suddenly tears sprang to her eyes.

'My darling, don't be sad,' Harry said, holding her tight.

'I'm not really sad, Harry. Only a bit – for Daddy, you know. He'd have been so happy to see us married today.'

'But I told you, he's watching over you, Rosie. He's seen what you've achieved already with the farm he left you, and he'll be minding out for you while you train Tanner's Beauty to be a champion show-jumper. He knows what wonderful, capable hands he left the farm in, and one day he'll be watching the fifth generation of Tanners grow up here.'

Rosie nodded. 'Yes, you're right. And he knows how you have helped and guided me these past months, and the love that Uncle Patrick and Auntie Kathleen have shown me. And about Rossalyn and how I can't imagine not having her in my life now. Most of all, he knows how I feel right now, knowing I have you and I will never be lonely again.'

'And how's that, my sweet Rosie?'

'Happy. Just very, very happy.'

CHAPTER SIXTEEN

MANY YEARS LATER, Molly Tanner was released from prison.

With the money from the sale of her small cottage and land almost used up, she was on the lookout for an easier life.

Still a handsome woman, she dolled herself up and left the grubby little flat she loathed with a passion.

Ever on the lookout for easy prey, she climbed onto a bus that would take her into town. Having paid the fare, she realised she had very little money left, and that it was vital for her somehow to find a measure of security if she were ever to make her life more comfortable than it was now.

Looking for a seat, she noticed a man she decided

might be a good catch. He was grey-haired, and a little older than she, but still looked sprightly and amiable. She could see that the suit he was wearing, though somewhat wrinkled, was not made from cheap cloth.

Putting on her best smile, she sauntered over to him. 'Excuse me . . . but would you mind if I sit here?' she asked.

'Well, no, of course not.'

The smile he gave her as he shifted over sent her pulse racing. But what made it race even more was the gold pocket watch peeping tantalisingly from his waistcoat pocket.

She thought him interesting. Especially when she noticed the bulging leather briefcase on his lap. Oh, yes! She reckoned him to be a well-heeled and likely candidate for what she had in mind.

Even before they alighted at the same stop, she had him eating out of her hand.

Read on to discover
more fantastic reads from

JOSEPHINE
COX

and ways to stay in
touch with all her news

Don't forget to look out for Jo's
new book, coming in early 2016!

Chatterbox

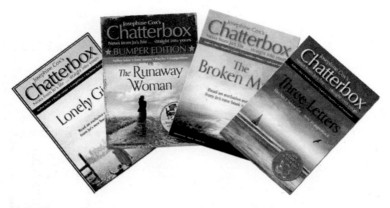

If you'd like to know more about Josephine Cox,
and receive regular updates, then sign up to
Chatterbox, Jo's free newsletter. Simply send a
postcard to the address below, or register online by
emailing chatterbox@harpercollins.co.uk with your
name and full address details.

The newsletter is packed with exciting competitions
and exclusive merchandise and gifts, plus the latest
news and views from other Josephine Cox fans!

And you can now access Chatterbox online.
Simply log on to www.josephinecox.com to
read the latest issue in full.

CHATTERBOX
HarperCollins Publishers, The News Building,
1 London Bridge Street, London SE1 9GF

Keep up to date with Jo

The **JOSEPHINE**

I've been reading her books for years. They just **get better every time**

Carole Keane

There are always characters in Jo's books I feel as if I have already met—and they are not always friends!

Loma Wood

Have read every novel Jo has written. **Once I start I cannot put them down**. She takes you right there with the characters. **Love all the books** and Jo. Keep up the good work, **you are my favourite author of all time** xx

Donna Read

I love your books—it's wonderful you are still doing them. Carry on, **you're great!** Love you loads

Susan Farrell

Every book of Jo's has found a special place in my trove. I've purchased most of them. Great reads and amazing relevance to my life

Sue Alexander

We've bought and read every one. Why? Jo gets you involved in her books. You picture characters and can see them in each story. You can laugh and cry in one chapter, but whatever happens **her stories are always full of love**. Her love for her family is always remembered at the beginning of her book, and she never forgets where she's from. Jo you are **an inspiration to everyone**. Can't wait to read your latest novel.

Deborah Travis

COX effect

I've got loads and loads of her books. **Some make me cry and some make me laugh** but I can't part with any.

Pauline Michael

Love Josephine Cox! My daughter and I have read all her books.

Susan Sands

Love Josephine's books, what I don't like is when I have finished reading it.

Maria Theresa Dormer

So enthralling that I never want to put a Jo Cox book down until I have finished the final page! **Thanks Jo!**

Pam Maslin

I love losing myself in a different time, different town, different life and then when it's all over looking forward to doing it all again!!!

Sindy Stewart

I love Josephine's books. Even when I put the book down I find my mind drifting off thinking about the characters and what will happen next. Not sure my boss is a fan ;)

Chris Green

I **love** Josephine Cox books, once I read them, I have a job putting them down.

Kathleen Gabriel

She captivates her readers from the very first page, and it's so hard to put down. Thank you for each and every novel that you have written, YOU ROCK JOSEPHINE COX

Natacia Kalyan

The Runaway Woman

No-one thought she had the courage...

Those looking in from the outside think Lucy Lovejoy's life is like any other, but at the centre of her family there is a big empty hole where all the love and warmth should be. Over the years, her children have watched while their father chipped away at Lucy's self-confidence. Now the children are following their own paths, and Lucy has never felt more alone.

When tragedy strikes at the heart of the family, it's a wake-up call for Lucy. Everyone has taken a little piece of her, and she isn't sure who she is anymore. So when Lucy faces a betrayal from those she loves deepest, she knows that it's time to make a choice.

Is she brave enough to find herself again?

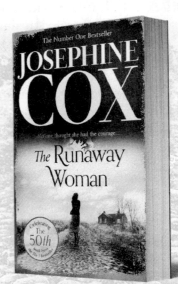

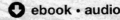

The Broken Man

Sometimes a damaged child becomes a broken man…

It's 1954 and Adam Carter is twelve years old,
an only child with no friends nor any self confidence.
His father Edward is a bully of a man. A successful and
ruthless businessman, he breeds fear into the heart of his
family. Adam's mother Peggy is too cowed to protect
her son, so Adam's only support comes in the shape
of Phil Wallis, the school bus driver.

One particular afternoon, when Adam is his last drop
of the day, Phil decides to accompany him along the
darkening wood land to his house, never suspecting
that as they chat innocently, in the house at the
end of the track a terrible tragedy is unfolding
which will change Adam's life forever.

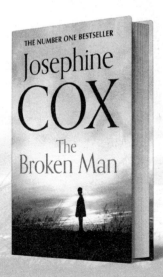

THE NUMBER ONE BESTSELLER

Josephine
COX

The
Broken Man

⬇ ebook • audio

Three Letters

**Eight-year-old Casey's mother Ruth
is a cruel woman, with a weakness
for other women's husbands.**

Casey's father is gentle and hard-working, and has always
turned a blind eye to his wife's misdemeanours to keep
the peace. But then, out of the blue, Tom receives two bits
of devastating news. He realises that from now on their
lives must change, forever.

Tom is made to fight for his son, determined to keep him
safe. But, when fate takes a hand, life can be unbearably
cruel, and Casey is made to remember his father's
prophetic words…

'It's done. The dice is thrown, and nobody wins.'

But, unbeknown to Casey, there are three letters penned
by his father, that may just change his destiny forever.

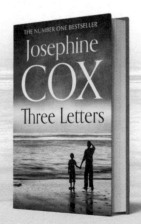

THE NUMBER ONE BESTSELLER

Josephine
COX

Three Letters

Midnight

All Jack's life, the nightmares had haunted him, dragging him back to a place where it was always midnight…

Molly and Jack are deeply in love but their relationship is being torn apart by Jack's nightmares. It is becoming harder for Molly to pull him free from the dark place, and even when daylight comes the haunting visions remain.

Realising that Jack is being driven close to the edge, Molly urges him to seek help, and with their relationship faltering, Jack decides to hunt for answers.

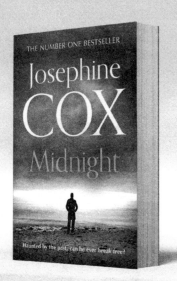

ebook • audio

Born Bad

Harry always knew he would go back one day…

He's somehow carved out a life for himself, but eighteen years ago he left the place he loved and the warm, carefree girl with the laughing eyes.

For Judy Saunders, the pain of her past has left her deeply scarred. Cut off from her family and trapped in a loveless marriage, the distant memories of her first love are her only source of comfort in a dark and dangerous world.

Years later, Harry is heading back. Excited, afraid and racked with guilt, he has little choice. He must confront the past, and seek forgiveness.

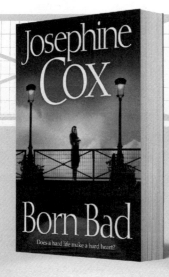

ebook • audio

Songbird

Some secrets can haunt a whole lifetime.

In the riverside town of Bedford, four students can hear
the haunting voice of a woman singing. The beautiful
melody is coming from their neighbour – a reclusive
creature who never opens the door to anyone
or leaves her home in daylight.

They have no way of knowing that the woman next door,
Madeleine Delaney is driven by a dangerous memory
that for over twenty years has controlled her
meagre existence …

Madeleine's angelic voice and striking looks
capture the hearts of many. But she only has
eyes for club owner, Steve Drayton –
a devastatingly handsome but terrifying man.

JOSEPHINE
COX

Songbird

THE NEW BESTSELLER

⬇ ebook • audio

The Loner

**Home is where the heart is –
but it's also where the pain lies…**

Young Davie Adams is all alone. Devastated, he flees
his hometown of Blackburn to escape the memories
of the worst night of his life. With little more than
the shirt on his back he sets off on a lonely,
friendless road, determined to find his father.

Two people are stricken by his departure – Judy,
his childhood friend who is desperate to reveal a secret
she has kept close to her heart for so long, and Joseph,
his grandfather, who is racked with guilt about
that fateful night.

Exhausted and afraid, Davie finds friendship and
a place to stay but when fate deals him another disastrous
blow, he must decide whether to keep running
or return to face his demons…

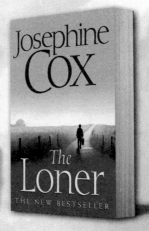

ebook • audio

The Journey

**Three strangers are thrown together by chance.
It's an encounter which is destined to change
all of their lives forever.**

When Ben Morris comes to the aid of Lucy Baker and her
daughter Mary, he is intrigued by the story behind their
frequent visits to the local graveyard. Later, invited into their
home, an old Edwardian place suffused with secrets of the
past, Ben hears Lucy's remarkable tale – one she must tell
before it's too late.

The story of Barney Davidson, his family and the part Lucy
played in his extraordinary life, is one of a deep, abiding love
and an incredible sacrifice.

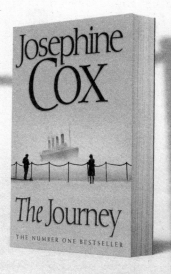

ebook · audio

Journey's End

Like a ghost from the past, she walked along the platform towards them…

It has been over twenty years since Vicky Maitland set foot on English soil. Twenty years since she left Liverpool with her three children, bound for a new life in America, leaving her beloved husband Barney behind.

But this long journey home is the hardest of all. She is here in search of the truth, afraid of what she may find. Why did Barney turn against his family so suddenly, so cruelly? Only her old friend Lucy Baker knows what happened. And Lucy promised Barney she would never tell his secret. Is it time she broke her silence and explained the events of so long ago?

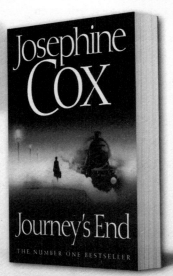

JOSEPHINE COX

JOURNEY'S END

THE NUMBER ONE BESTSELLER

⬇ ebook • audio

Live *the* Dream

**When friendship becomes love, two people must
face their greatest fear – being hurt again…**

Luke Hammond: handsome, rich, charismatic, cursed by private
tragedy. Amy Atkinson: humble and kind with a good –
but wounded – heart. When they meet by chance,
a spark of love takes hold of their hearts.

But neither are sure that they can dare to love again. And what
of Luke's public life, hidden from Amy? The owner of a large
factory, he is a pillar of the community, married – though in
name only. Amy is torn between her head and her heart, but her
sense of honour is paramount – and when she discovers his true
identity, she is thrown into even greater turmoil.

Then disaster strikes and the future looks troubled indeed…

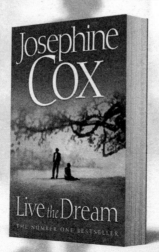

ebook • audio

Win a signed copy of
Lonely Girl

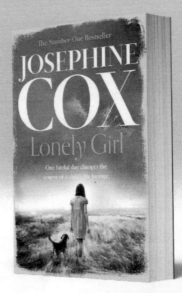

For your chance to win one of 10 signed copies of
Jo's fantastic novel, *Lonely Girl*, tell us in less than
50 words why you love Jo Cox's books.

Email your answers to fictionmarketing@harpercollins.co.uk by
1st January 2016, with the subject line
'Signed *Lonely Girl* competition'

The 10 winners will be contacted via email by 31st January 2016

Full Ts&Cs can be found on Jo's website: www.josephinecox.com